4/21

Novels by Kathleen O'Neal Gear
available from DAW Books:

Cries from the Lost Island

THE REWILDING REPORT

The Ice Lion
The Ice Ghost*

*Coming soon from DAW Books

THE ICE LION

THE REWILDING REPORT #1

KATHLEEN O'NEAL GEAR

DAW BOOKS, INC.
DONALD A. WOLLHEIM FOUNDER
1745 Broadway, New York, NY 10019
ELIZABETH R. WOLLHEIM
SHEILA E. GILBERT
PUBLISHERS
www.dawbooks.com

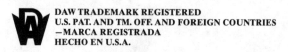

THE
ICE
LION

1

922 SUMMERS AFTER THE ZYME

I lazily blink my eyes open and see a herd of helmeted muskoxen running across a starlit snowfield, beautiful and quiet, as if nothing is wrong. Dark bulky shapes, they have massive horns. Their hooves crack and snap on the ice as their legs part the snow. Halfway through their journey across the field, I begin to hear a low-pitched moaning, part whine, part growl, and the feral musk of lions envelops me.

Puffs of hot meat-scented breath cloud the night air. I want to run, but everything inside me is going slower and slower, freezing up like a winter river in a sudden cold spell. Six shining eyes stare down at me.

I can't move. Can't breathe.

In the distance, I hear a rumble, like a huge herd of bison thundering down the slope, or maybe it's growling . . .

My new wife shrieks, *Oh, dear gods, lions.*

Something rips away our mammoth hides, and my unfeeling body is flipped onto the right side where I can't see her.

Lynx, get up. Where's your spear?

My heart is bursting through my ribs, but I lie still, so still. I—I can't recall my wife's name. Senselessly, I stare out at the muskoxen. A shimmering haze cloaks them as they run faster and faster, their hooves kicking snow high into the air.

Lynx, a lion has got me. He's dragging me. Help me.

Branches crash, and feet suddenly pound away. It can't be my wife running away. She has seen only fifteen summers. How would she get away from lions? But it must be her. Who else could it be? Gasping and screams from ten paces away, then five. Is she trying to get back to me?

Lynx. Run.

I fight to call out to her, to tell her not to run. Just go limp, my wife. Play dead. But when hands grab me and shake me, I am a mindless block of wood.

What's the matter with you? Wake up!

Something falls on me, and warm, wet hair slaps across my face and chest. I smell the tundra wildflowers that decorate her hair. Not the blood. Not the blood. Fingernails rake my leather sleeves like knives. *Get up.* Sounds of dragging, bones cracking, screams.

Finally . . .

I am on my feet, staggering into a brilliant darkness so vast and quiet it swallows my soul. The muskoxen are gone, their trail little more than a black line of shadow stretching across the starlit snow. Where are our wedding camp guards?

"*Rider?*" I shout. "*Dust? Birdboy, where are you? Grasshopper?*"

There is no sound at all. Am I deaf? Even if our guards answered me, I'm not sure I'd hear them.

And her voice is gone.

All of their voices are gone.

Trotting along the game trail, I fight not to weep. They must be dead. All of them. When their relatives arrive, they will find their bones crushed and chewed and strewn across the ground, the air filled with the sweet fragrance of glacial meltwater.

I'm the only one left.

Except I'm not.

Though I hear nothing else, I hear him.

He's behind me.

A walking stick lightly taps the earth, or maybe it's the clicking of claws on rocks.

Tap. Tap. Click, tap, tap.

Coming faster, coming up behind me.

"Stop walking, boy."

I stumble. How is it possible that I can't hear the birds or lions or human screams, but I hear his voice?

I turn.

A pale silver halo arcs over the trees as Sister Moon rises toward the eastern horizon, turning the pines and spruces into dark spikes set against a background of monstrously tall ice mountains. Standing in the middle of the trail is a skinny elder. Wind blows shoulder-length white hair around his strange face. He has a jutting chin and small brow ridge. His translucent blue eyes are too wide and shiny to be human. The legendary Je-men, immortal warriors locked in an eternal battle with the Ice Giants, are supposed to have blue eyes . . .

And suddenly, I'm not alone.

It's so easy now. He's come to help me. Nothing else explains his presence here. I watch him labor up the trail, placing his walking stick with care, back bent beneath his hunting pack. Here he is . . . the sum total of all the dreams I've ever had in my life. All my prayers for courage, for strength so that I could take care of my new wife . . . it's all come down to this.

Death.

That's who he is. I'm sure of it. I've been chasing him my whole life, and now I've caught up with him. My fears drain away. My heartbeat calms as a great certainty possesses me, and I find myself hovering, sailing high above the camp like a fragile dragonfly, climbing toward the Road of Light that leads to the Land of the Dead.

The old man cocks his head. "What are you doing?"

"Wh-what?"

"Why are you just standing there?"

"I'm wondering if I have the courage to face you."

He props his stick and leans on it. "How much courage does it require to face an old man?"

I stagger toward him. "If you're going to take me, just do it. Please."

"Good Lord, boy, don't you want one more day of life? Are you really the coward your enemies believe you are?"

My chest fills as my heart expands. I wanted so much more than this. One more night of sitting around the fires listening to the elders' stories about the beautiful world before the zyme, just another smile from my precious wife. And a son. Dear gods, I wanted sons and daughters. Not now. None of that now.

I choke out the words: "Elder . . . I . . . I'm ready to go. Take me to the Land of the Dead."

The old man looks me up and down. "That would make it easier, wouldn't it? Living is difficult. Believe me, I know."

Suddenly, he cocks his head and seems to be listening to a voice that floats on the air . . . a voice I cannot hear. "Yes. Yes, all right," he quietly answers.

Death gives me a sidelong evaluative look, then he hobbles away on his painful joints, his windblown cloak melting into the forest as though he was never really here. Leaving me.

To live.

2

QUILLER

Lying on my back with my head pillowed on one arm, I stare up at the stars twinkling beyond the smoke hole in the top of our domelike lodge. Mammoth rib bones serve as the lodge frame, then we cover them with mastodon hides and paint the exterior with our sacred clan symbols. The night is so peaceful. My little sister's hair spreads across the bedding hides to my right, and to my left my two younger brothers snuggle next to our parents beneath a warm bison robe. If I wasn't worried sick about Lynx, the night would be perfect. But Lynx and his new bride, Siskin, should have returned from their wedding camp by sunset. They did not.

Wind gently buffets the hide walls and brings me the scent of the sea. Late autumn is a happy time of full bellies and smiling faces. A time of netting birds and bison hunts. And marriages.

Lynx's wedding camp is less than one day away. If I start now and run hard, I'll make it there by noon, providing I'm not hunted by lions, dire wolves, or short-faced bears. Lions are the most frightening. With huge heads and massive front quarters for grabbing and holding prey, the giant animals weigh five times as much as a grown man.

Pushing away my bedding hides, I crawl across the floor to the lodge flap and shrug into my bear coat, then I grab a spear and duck out into the brilliant moonlight. The spear, about as long as I am tall, and tipped with a ground mammoth-bone spear point, makes the perfect walking stick.

To the east, sheathed in the silver gleam, the Ice Giants rise in stunning blue-white peaks. They are never still. Never quiet. Even now they whisper and groan. Our sacred elders say that a thousand summers ago, most of the Jemen sailed to the camp-fires of the dead in ships made of meteorites. We still see them at night traveling along the Road of Light that leads to the af-terlife. We call them the Sky Jemen. A handful of heroes, the Earthbound Jemen, remained behind to carve out a great hol-low in the heart of the glaciers, a place where they hid cages of animals and plants, and vowed to continue their search to find a way to kill the Ice Giants. One day, when they've won the war with the Giants, they will release the animals and plants into a warm and beautiful world.

I don't really believe the tales, but they fill me with such wonder.

Gripping my spear, I walk away from the village and down to the beach, where slithers of zyme sprawl across the sand like luminous green arms. For as far as I can see, the ocean glows green, blanketed with zyme. I've heard people tell of a time when darkness held the world in its arms at night, but I've never seen true darkness. My people, the Sealion People, are a sea people. We live along the shores where the nights are always pale green and shimmering.

Zyme smells pungently fragrant, as though the air is drenched in green grass, but it's an empty-hearted monster.

In the summer, zyme rises and falls upon the water like low verdant hills, but when cold weather arrives, the zyme forests began to die back a little. Which is the only time people dare to be out on the water in boats. Even then, we have to stick close to the edges of the Ice Giants, where the water is coldest. If a boat gets too far from shore and zyme closes in around it, there's no escape. You can't paddle, can't swim. After a time, you can't even float. The slimy tentacles creep over the gunwales, and the weight drags you down to the bottom of the ocean.

Two moons ago, when we first passed beyond the Steppe Lands, one of our boats was struck by a massive wave and shoved far out into the zyme. There was nothing anyone could do. On the third day the boat turned green and sank. The last people dove overboard and tried to drag themselves across the zyme to shore, but the zyme slowly, methodically, pulled them down.

Bad way to die.

Climbing the rocky beach terrace, I search for the closest guard, and finally see a man standing to the north, silhouetted against the glittering campfires of the dead.

When he sees me coming, he calls, "Too worried to sleep?" The scars that cover the lower half of his face shine whitely in the pale light. He escaped from our enemies, the Rust People, several summers ago, but the flayed flesh never properly healed.

"Where are they, Bluejay?"

We both gaze up the mammoth trail that leads to the wedding camp. In the moonlight, it resembles a black serpent.

"Probably just delayed. Newly wedded men and women are so happy enjoying each other, they lose track of time. I'm sure they'll be home by noon today."

"If not, I'm going after them."

"I'll go with you, but I'm sure it won't be necessary."

His words about marriage hurt. Until four moons ago, Lynx was promised to me. Then Lynx's affections shifted to Bluejay's sister, Siskin, and my world changed. At some point, my torn heart will mend, but I keep thinking that the marriage three days ago should have been my marriage to Lynx, not Siskin's.

"Dire wolves have been howling madly. As though they've made a kill."

"Probably brought down a bison," Bluejay says. "Try not to think the worst. We sent four of our best warriors to guard them. They're all right."

But we both know the howls originate from very near the location of the wedding camp.

"Least there's been no sign of Rust People." Bluejay is clearly trying to change the subject.

"They're still behind us. I can feel their footsteps in my heart."

"Hope you're wrong."

"Me, too."

In total, the Sealion People have one hundred and forty-two men, women, and children left. The warlike Rust People, on the other hand, have eight clans, ten villages, and maybe one thousand people or half-people. Once they start hunting you, you have to run and keep running. Like wolves with prey in sight, they never stop. Never slow down. Their rusted-out hulks of ships, powered by zyme oil, are never far behind.

As though tying themselves to the terrible feeling in the pit of my stomach, eerie growls and yips drift down from the wedding camp.

I reach up to rub the medicine bag hanging from a braided leather cord around my throat. My first spirit quest was two summers ago. After four days of fasting and praying, a bull bison trotted across the grasslands carrying Sister Moon between his horns. Before they left, Bull Bison and Sister Moon gave me pieces of themselves, powerful offerings, to remind me of their constant spiritual presence. As I rub the medicine bag, I can feel the silver glow encased in the bison fur that rests inside, and know my spirit helpers are alive and breathing over my heart.

Where is Lynx, Sister Moon? Bull Bison? Is he alive?

Moonlight suddenly blazes from the spruces and pines, and every grain of sand on the beach sparkles. It's my answer. He lives.

"My wife is better, Quiller. Thank you for bringing her soup today. The baby is less fitful tonight. When I left, WayWind was sleeping soundly."

"We've all been worried."

Which is an understatement. Just as many babies are being born dead as alive. Our numbers are dwindling fast. If that doesn't change, in a few summers, our people will vanish from the earth.

"Go check on WayWind, Bluejay. I'll take over your watch. Can't sleep anyway."

"Thanks, but I can't sleep either. Why don't you go talk to Mink? He must be worried about his brother. Tell him that I'm sure everything is fine."

"Where is Mink?"

Bluejay extends an arm. "Standing guard to the south."

"I'll tell him."

Fog hovers over the waves in the distance, and I pray it stays out there. Lion prides and wolf packs use fog as a cover to sneak into the villages on their nightly hunts.

As I walk across the rocky beach terrace, the sweet scent of glacial meltwater carries down from the Ice Giants.

It doesn't take long to spot Mink. A muscular, heavy-boned man, he wears his black hair pulled back and tied with a leather cord, which makes the blocky angles of his handsome face seem sharper. His forehead slopes back severely, and his brow ridge sticks far out over his dark sunken eyes. His nose is wide, his chin blunt. He and Lynx look so much alike it tears at my heart.

"You should be asleep," he says as I approach.

"And you should have assigned me guard duty. I can't sleep."

We stand in companionable silence, both of us staring at the trail to the wedding camp. Out in the darkness, my dog, Crow, sits on her haunches. Crow is the best bear dog in the village.

"Bluejay said to tell you not to worry about Lynx."

"How is he? Worried sick about Siskin?"

"Of course."

For a moment, I study the wavering curtains of purple that flash across the heavens. Sister Sky is dancing furiously tonight, the hem of her dress whirling. She looks happy. I've heard traders say that her colors change the higher you go in the mountains. They are green, blue, and purple, but down here on the shore the vivid luminescent green of the zyme erases everything except the flutters of purple.

"You all right?" Mink gives me a sidelong glance.

"Fine, I just—"

"Not talking about your health, Quiller."

Awkwardly, I reply, "Lynx made his choice, Mink. I've accepted that."

"Personally, I think my brother made the wrong choice. You are worth ten of Siskin."

My throat goes tight. Mink has always been kind to me. "Lynx loved her more than he did me. That's all there is to it. She's small and beautiful. I'm not."

"You are beautiful in your own way, Quiller."

I smile at the lie. I have a flat, freckled nose and red hair, and my green eyes are too large, almost bug-like. Not only that, I'm way too tall and willowy for most Sealion men to find attractive. In fact, I'm a full hand-length taller than Mink . . . almost tall enough to be one of the Dog Soldiers, the strange half-people that travel with the Rust clans.

Mink suddenly steps forward. "See that?"

"What? Where?" My hand tightens around my spear.

"Through the weave of pine trunks, I thought I saw . . ."

The ground shakes. Moments later the Ice Giants rumble. I reach out to grab Mink's shoulder to stay on my feet. The ice quake lasts less than five heartbeats, but the shrieks and moans that carry on the night wind continue for some time. To the north, massive blocks break loose from the ice cliffs and slip beneath the waves with thunderous splashes.

Mink ganders up at the Ice Giants, blinks thoughtfully, and his face shines with moonlight. "Do you believe the old stories, Quiller?"

"Which stories?"

"About the Blessed Jemen breathing upon ten-thousand-summers-old lion bones and seeing them spring to life?"

The story is etched on my soul. I've heard it a thousand times over the long winters. "Not really. Why would anyone want to create such a terrifying predator?"

"According to Elder Hoodwink, setting the lions loose in the world demonstrated the Jemen's magical powers."

"Well, if so, they were fools."

Mink chuckles and points to the brilliant spark of light sailing eastward across the night sky. "I hope they didn't hear you."

I smile and watch the Sky Jemen pass overhead. "I wish she'd sail down here so I could ask her all the questions that have plagued me since childhood. I . . ."

Crow lets out a low growl and scents the wind blowing down off the glaciers. Her hackles are up.

"Think it's just the grumbling Ice Giants, or a bear?" Mink says.

"Don't know." My gaze rivets on the trees, searching for movement.

Only the swaying brightness of moonlit branches catches my attention. The pines appear to be waving their arms at us, warning us.

Then . . .

Against the black wall of trees, waves of purple flash over a staggering figure, and Crow goes wild, leaping and barking. Moments later, every village dog charges out, snarling.

By the time warriors burst from the lodges carrying spears, I'm running up the trail, running hard for the man who reels on his feet. Even in the darkness, the black stains of blood that soak his shredded clothing are visible.

"It's Grasshopper!"

Grasshopper.

One of the wedding camp guards.

3

LYNX

A faint pink gleam lightens the sable sky and drowns the campfires of the dead as serenely as though the world has not changed.

I move each branch aside with a bloody hand before quietly stepping past and continuing along the game trail that circles our camp. My hearing and memory are gone. I keep staring at the drag marks, wondering what caused them. The dark swaths lead from the camp out into the towering pine forest.

Though I can feel my leather boots crunching snow and old pine needles, I can't hear them. The wind-blown trees rock without sound. Up in the branches, birds cock their heads and seem to be watching something back in the deepest shadows. What's back there? All I see are black shapes floating between the trees, as though not quite real. Just odd ghosts going about their morning duties.

Walk. Keep walking.

Deep inside, I know it isn't supposed to be this way. You work hard. Learn everything you can. Prove you can protect a wife and family. Then, as soon as a girl passes her first blood moon, you are granted the right to marry. When you die, it's many summers later, surrounded by children and grandchildren.

Not this reaching. Not this struggling to grasp your heart and stop it from slamming inside your chest.

By the time I circle around again—how many times have I circled?—the light is brighter, the camp clearer. The heap of coals in the fire flash red when the wind gusts. Beside it, mammoth hides lie in shreds and, near them, two packs. Both have been ripped open and the contents strewn around. There's a spear in the grass. Painted yellow diamonds decorate the shaft. It's familiar. Is it . . . my spear? How did it get there? Did I throw it down and run? No, no, not again.

I should go pick it up, but I'm afraid to walk into the open meadow with the yellow eyes watching me.

I don't always see them, but sometimes they gleam, tracking my movements.

Why can't I hear them? Twigs must be snapping as the animals resettle their heavy bodies near the kills.

If only I'd gone blind instead of deaf. I long not to see, but I can't close my eyes. These are my last moments. I must watch them pass. *Need* to. As though somehow the very turning of the seasons depends upon seeing my breath frost the air until the very end.

When I stop and brace my shaking knees, my blood-soaked pants feel stiff. Am I hurt? I feel no pain, only a stunned tingling that makes it impossible to think. How long ago was our camp attacked? Moments? Days? The temperature tells me it might be early autumn.

As Father Sun crests the eastern horizon, the morning warms imperceptibly, and bars and streaks of pale gold puncture the shadows and leave them dying on the forest floor. I seem to be falling through the emptiness at the end of time, and I can see the bottom rising up to meet me.

Nonsensically, I blink at the Ice Giants. Their bodies spread across the horizon for as far as I can see, wrinkling it like a colossal blue-white blanket creased with the shadows of valleys and dotted with trees. There's a . . . a story the elders tell . . . about how the ancient Jemen tried to fight the Ice Giants by casting a necklace studded with gigantic mirrors into the sky to melt them . . .

Where am I?

What is my clan? I can't even remember the name of my village. My only recollections are of rustlings in the grass and the thumps of arms and legs being dragged between tree trunks.

How many lions are out there?

Lightheaded, I walk out into the meadow.

On the way, I pull the spear from the grass and clutch it hard as I head for the campfire.

Where are the guards? There are always guards.

Crouching before the smoldering fire, I tug a branch from the woodpile we gathered at dusk, and place it on top of the coals. Flames lick through the tinder, and the scent of burning pine perfumes the air. I keep adding more and more wood, building up the fire until fantastic flame shadows leap through the dawn trees.

Then I wait for the yellow eyes to come.

What's her name? The woman . . . I remember some things . . . small things . . .

Long before we met, I knew about her. By sight and by notoriety. Though she'd only seen fifteen summers, she was reputed to have had many lovers. I'd watched her dancing with men several times, her slender body and long arms weaving in the firelight at ritual feasts. Her beautiful face—the deep bevel of her nose and those translucent brown eyes—had affected me like a spirit plant rampaging through my veins. Siskin had haunted me until I won her love.

"Siskin!" Leaping to my feet, I whirl around, searching for her. "Siskin, where are you?"

Like a slap, my hearing returns.

When the roar of lions and human whimpers eddy through the trees, my knees fail. I sit down hard and stare at the fire until nothing exists except the fluttering orange glow, no trees, no boulders, no cries for help. It's like living inside flameglow. For a long time, I study the swarms of sparks rising into the air.

Far down the mountainside, waves, thick with zyme, roll toward a distant shore. I must get home. Tell someone. Tell them . . . something.

Rising on shaking legs, I run.

The almost soundless padding of giant paws on dirt seems timed to my heartbeat.

There are no contradictions now. No future. No past. I run suspended between despair and ecstasy. Here in this single instant is the totality of every lesson I've ever learned, every desire I've ever felt. Nothing means anything. All the guilt for the things I've done wrong or never accomplished evaporates with the sound of the panting behind me. But I do wonder why was I ever born? What was the purpose? I've barely lived my life, sixteen short summers. What was it all for?

Clutching my spear in my shaking fist, I pound through the grass.

The beat of paws picks up, loping along.

At the edges of my vision, tan fur appears and disappears amid the dense weave of the forest. A slow lope. There's no need to rush. The lions know I can't outrun them.

4

QUILLER

Cold, cold morning.

On the forested hilltop ahead, where the wedding camp stands, dire wolves trot around yipping and cavorting, chasing each other through the sunlight. This earthen hill is an oasis in the ice. Beyond it, across the distant slopes, fifty-hand-tall cornices frown like pale blue brows and spread for as far I can see.

I charge ahead.

"Quiller?" Mink shouts. "Come back! Nobody runs alone now. Too dangerous!"

Breathing hard, I stop to wait for the other ten warriors to work their way through the mosaic of tree shadows and out into a lingering patch of sunlight where I stand. All around my feet, lion tracks press into the mud. Huge tracks.

Mink crouches and places his hand over the largest paw print, twice as large as his hand. "Think it's Nightbreaker?"

I try to keep my voice even, but strain creeps in, giving it a slightly higher pitch. "I do."

Nightbreaker is a giant lion. The biggest cat anyone has ever seen. The old white-faced lion follows no rules, and he's almost supernaturally intelligent. In fact, some of the elders have begun to speculate that he's not a lion at all, but a witch from the Rust People who takes on lion form to attack the Sealion People. Still others claim the reverse. They say Nightbreaker is one of the Earthbound Jemen who remained behind to carve out the great cavern in the heart of the Ice Giants. Magical beings, the old stories say they had to learn to change into animals to survive the crushing cold that fell over the world just after the zyme.

"I count eight lions," Bluejay calls. "What do you want to do, Mink?"

"They must be out there watching us. Let's form a defensive line." Turning, he gestures. "RabbitEar, you're in charge. Work up the hill slowly. Shout out if you see anything. Bluejay and Quiller are going to go with me to examine the wedding camp."

"Yes, Mink." RabbitEar forms the search party into a semicircle and starts up the slope.

Mink heads straight for the wedding camp.

Walking last in line, I study the pines swaying in the gusts that sweep up from the coast. Lions perch in trees, and wolves love to come at you from the side. They could be hiding anywhere.

"Over here!" RabbitEar points at something.

"What is it?" Mink calls.

RabbitEar lifts a skull and holds it up for everyone to see. Hair clings to the gnawed scalp. "I . . . I think this is Dust."

"*Dust!*" Bluejay cries, and breaks into a run. "Are you sure it's my brother?"

"I think so, Deputy. I'm sorry."

When Bluejay grabs the skull from RabbitEar's hands, his arms shake. "It is. My brother."

Mink exchanges a glance with me. Dust had seen thirty-five summers pass and spent twenty of those summers protecting his people. He will be missed.

"Bluejay? Let's keep moving. We'll return later to take care of your honored brother."

"Yes, I . . . yes." Bluejay reluctantly sets the skull in the grass again, wipes his cheeks with the back of his hand, and returns to Mink's side.

The search party starts up the hill again.

When we reach the edge of the wedding camp, my breathing goes shallow.

The new couple's mammoth hides have been torn apart and dragged around the meadow, probably by wolves, but maybe by lions. Belongings scatter the grass. To my right, a woman's leather boot rests. It's badly chewed. Large chunks of charcoal continue to smolder in the campfire.

"That's a mountain of charcoal," I say, and scan the meadow, praying. "Someone built up a big fire."

Bluejay nods. "Must have been trying to keep the lions away."

"Should have worked. At least, for a while."

Off to my right, a flattened swath of grass heads out into the pines where the wolves hunch, growling and snapping at us. Guarding their breakfast. I try to prepare myself.

"Bluejay?" Mink says. "Give the camp a close gander while Quiller and I follow the drag marks."

Bluejay's eyes narrow as he studies the wolves. Clearly, he wants to be the one to venture out there to see what the wolves brought down, but he softly answers, "I will. Call out if you need me."

"We will."

Walking beside Mink, I squint at the frozen blood that streaks the grass. A lot of blood.

In the trees, a red fragment of hide clings to a pine. I pull it loose from the bark and clutch it in my hand, as though to protect this small part of Lynx.

Bizarre how the human heart works. Was Lynx wearing his red shirt when he left the village? I suddenly can't remember any details of the wedding. Behind my eyes, I'm watching Lynx grow up, seeing him as a laughing boy, finally a timid young man with dancing brown eyes and far too many flaws.

"War Leader?" RabbitEar yells.

The burly warrior waves at them from the northern edge of the meadow. Crow stands beside him with one paw lifted, scenting the wind. Her hackles stick up.

"What did you find?"

"Tracks."

"Take three men and follow them out."

"Yes, Mink."

While RabbitEar gathers his team, I watch Bluejay search the camp. He must be remembering his sister, perhaps with even more agony than I remember Lynx. Small and vulnerable, Siskin had relied on Bluejay her whole life. He'd been her protector. This must be tearing him apart. As it must be tearing Mink apart, though the War Leader shows no emotion at all.

"Keep searching." Mink motions to me, and we return to following the drag marks.

Autumn-dry pine needles crackle beneath my boots as I force my way through a cluster of birch saplings. Where sunlight pierces the trees and falls across the hillside in golden slashes, the forest floor steams. On the other side of the saplings, two dire wolves snarl, half hidden behind a tumbled pile of boulders. The animals hold their ground, their blood-soaked muzzles slathering foam, refusing to run from me. They have a kill close by, and I'm desperately afraid I know what it is. What will I do when I find Lynx's body?

"Mink? Wolves are guarding something over there behind the boulders."

We edge forward together, our spears up, ready to cast at the first wolf that lunges for us. The whole area reeks of wolf and lion urine, and the coppery tang of blood suffuses the air.

When we step past the boulders, the wolves bark furiously.

One of them grabs a bundle and drags it back into the trees. I'm confused for a moment, trying to figure out what it is. Then I see it . . . shreds of red-painted hide tangled with gnawed ribs. The entire clearing is strewn with human bones.

An ache starts deep down inside me.

"Focus, Quiller," Mink says. "Read the sign."

Nodding, I force myself to concentrate on what I'm seeing. Hundreds of claw marks and tracks, some of them human, churn up the dirt around the scattered bones. At the edge of the clearing, a gnawed skull rests canted on its side. Though long black hair still clings to the scalp, most of the face is gone. The skull stares at me through dark, empty eye sockets, as though trying to scream at me to run.

I steel myself before I point to it. "Mink?"

Mink turns, and answers the question eating at me: "Too small to be Lynx's."

"You sure?"

"Yes." Mink bows his head a long moment, then shouts, "Bluejay? Can you come over here?"

As we wait for Siskin's brother to trot up from the meadow, I try to count the bones. Lynx's skull might have been carried off, but the rest of him could be here. How many thigh bones are here? Two or four? How many shoulder blades . . .

When the wolves spy Bluejay coming, the big male growls and gnashes his teeth, upset to have yet another interloper threatening to take his kill away.

Bluejay doesn't say a word as he enters the clearing. Throat working convulsively, he stammers, "Is—is it my sister?"

"I think so, Bluejay."

Bluejay clutches his spear so hard the fingers of his right hand go white. Gods, he has lost both his brother and his sister today. Finally, he strides across the ground, kneels, and picks up the small skull.

Bluejay's shoulders heave, but the cries do not reach his lips. Clutching the skull against his heart, he pets her long black hair, says something soft. Then he slips off his hunting pack and gently places the skull inside. He can't seem to stop frowning at it, as though if he stares hard enough, he will find a tiny clue to tell him it's not Siskin, but someone else. Finally, he rises to his feet, slings his pack over this shoulder, and asks, "Any sign of your brother?"

Mink shakes his head. "No."

"He must be close," I say. "If he was alive when she was dragged away, Lynx would have run after her, trying to kill the lions."

Bluejay wipes his nose on his sleeve. "You sure about that?"

I hesitate. Lynx has run twice in battle. The last time, Deputy Hushy beat him bloody for cowardice. But Hushy is a violent man. He's always challenging Mink for the position of War Leader. Their fistfights have become legendary.

"Of course I'm sure," I answer. "He loved her. He would not have—"

Mink says, "I've seen no dead animals or spears that missed their mark. No sign that anyone tried to fight off the lions. Have you, Quiller?"

"Maybe Lynx didn't have time to cast his spear. Pride could have jumped him while he was asleep. Which means Lynx probably died before Siskin."

Bluejay whispers, "Yes, maybe. Let's keep looking."

Among my people, death is better than cowardice.

The three of us fan out, analyzing the tracks and bone scatter. Here and there across the kill site, human footprints mix with gigantic paw prints. Small prints. Not Lynx's feet. I search hard for some sign that Lynx was here fighting the lions, but all I see are Siskin's tracks. She was only wearing one boot. Her bare toes are clearly visible in places, running back and forth, which means the lions played with her for a long time before the kill, chasing her between them. Blessed Jemen, I hurt for Bluejay. He must be watching it play out in his mind, just as I am. He must be wondering, too, where her husband was while she was dying.

"I don't see Lynx's tracks anywhere," Bluejay says. "Maybe, while the lions toyed with my sister, he ran away."

"Lynx wouldn't do that! He loved her!" I defend, and spin around to look at Mink, waiting for him to back me up.

But Mink's gaze has locked with Bluejay's. They have some kind of silent conversation going on—as though they both suspect Lynx threw his new wife to the lions and charged off to save himself. Lynx is afraid of everything. We all know it. He trembles at the sound of mice scurrying through the lodges at night.

"I'm telling you Lynx would not have done that!"

"Keep searching," Mink orders.

As we push deeper into the forest, the dire wolves go utterly silent and slip between the trunks like gray wisps of smoke, staying just beyond casting range.

The only sound now is the groaning of the Ice Giants and Wind Mother soughing through the pines.

A flicker catches my eye, but it takes ten heartbeats before I realize it's the elusive wink of sunlight on a shell pendant. There's a man standing back in the trees behind the wolves. He's almost invisible through a screen of branches.

"Look. See him?" I gesture with my chin.

Bluejay follows my gaze. "No. Who . . . Wait. Yes."

My gaze surveys the wolves. They stand barely five paces from the man, but don't seem to see him. "Why aren't the dire wolves worried? He's close enough to spear them through the hearts."

"Strange." Mink breathes the word.

As though he's invisible, the dire wolves don't cast a single glance in the man's direction.

Then, in the deepest shadows, there comes a prolonged twinkle of sunlight on shell as the man walks toward us. I start to move, but Bluejay's hand touches my arm to stop me.

"Don't move. Just look. Are those Rust People designs on his shirt? Red-painted lions?"

It's hard to make out the designs visible through the gap in the front of the man's lion-hide cloak. "Can't see 'em. But his clothing isn't silver. What makes you think they're Rust People designs?"

The front of the man's cloak waffles in the wind, revealing more of the designs.

Bluejay squints hard. He doesn't see well at a distance. "I think that's the symbol for the Red Lion clan. Gods, is that Trogon?"

"Trogon? The Rust People's witch?" Mink asks.

"I don't think that's a red lion." My distance vision is excellent. "It's a blue ball filled with white spots, like the campfires of the dead. The red design inside the ball looks more like a bird's wing to me."

"Elder?" Mink calls. "Step out from behind the trees so we can see you."

The old man just stares at us. He is so still that I begin to wonder if maybe we aren't just imagining a human in the weave of shadows and branches. Besides, he doesn't really look human. His small head is oddly shaped, his skull more rounded, his chin more pointed than a human's chin.

Just above a whisper, Mink says, "He's odd, isn't he? We have to capture him. Even if he's not Trogon, we need to find out who he is and where he comes from. He's not one of us, but I don't think he's one of the Rust People either. And his skin is too pale for him to be one of the Dog Soldiers."

"Agreed," Bluejay says.

As though offering himself to us, the old man steps out of the trees and heads straight for us. Thin white hair hangs to his shoulders, and he resembles a walking skeleton more closely than a living man. Gods, his face is wrinkled and cadaverous. Must be a thousand summers old.

"Think he's an albino?" I whisper.

"Doesn't have pink eyes."

"No, but some of the Dog Soldiers have blue eyes. Saw them in the last battle," I say.

Like me, Dog Soldiers are tall and willowy, very different from the short, muscular Sealion and Rust Peoples. They travel with the Rust clans, but never engage in battle. Instead, they stand in the rear, leaping and cavorting, shouting commands to guide the carnage.

The elder aims his walking stick straight at me. "You don't have much time, darling. You need to get going. Right now. Move your butt."

I don't know the words *darling* and *butt*.

"Me? Are you talking to me?"

Bluejay instinctively lifts his spear, ready to thrust it into this strange elder's heart. "Don't let him get too close, Quiller. Can't know what evil he's up to. Probably put a spell on us to . . ."

From down the slope to the north, along the trail RabbitEar took, human cries erupt, followed by the explosive roaring of lions.

Mink whirls around. "Quiller, go find out what's happening!"

I charge down the hill.

5

QUILLER

RabbitEar and three warriors stand in a grove of scrub pines with their spears held high and aimed at six lions. Two of the lions are lying on the ground, but the big lioness that stands no more than three paces from RabbitEar has her head high, her tail switching. Her muzzle drips blood from her recent breakfast. Head cocked, she studies RabbitEar as though he's a curious annoyance. A black ridge of fur trails from her neck to the middle of her golden back. Growling almost playfully, she reaches out with a giant paw and takes a halfhearted swipe at RabbitEar.

He staggers back, breathing hard, and orders, "Hold."

The warriors around him stand their ground, but they mutter darkly and glance over their shoulders, clearly planning their exit strategy.

Beads of sweat glitter in RabbitEar's red hair and beard, despite the freezing morning air. He has one of those extremely masculine faces, squarish, with a thick brow ridge that protrudes far out over his eyes and a broad sculpted nose.

It doesn't occur to me until I ease up behind RabbitEar that the two lions on the ground are curled around Lynx, as though keeping him warm. They have watched my approach with deadly calm.

Stunned, I hiss, "What is this?"

"Wish I knew." He gives me a panicked glance. "When we first got here . . ."

At the sound of our voices, the lions by Lynx leap to their feet and fall into line with the other four, their muscles rippling, preparing to spring forward. One of the lionesses has bright green eyes.

"Why are they just standing there?" I whisper. "They should run or charge. It's like they're waiting for something."

RabbitEar swallows hard. "Don't move, Quiller. Don't even breathe."

"But if we all cast at once—"

"Don't even think it. We may hit four, but the other two will leap for our throats before we can cast again. One or more of us will die."

I go quiet and still. He's right, of course. I'm just desperate to examine Lynx.

"Is Lynx alive?"

"He hasn't moved. Don't know."

I bravely step forward, and lock my knees.

"What are you doing?" RabbitEar lifts his spear higher, ready to defend me. "I told you not to move!"

"Trying to get a better look at Lynx."

"Stop right there! You're going to get us all killed!"

This is bizarrely unnatural. The lioness on the right growls, watching me with unblinking eyes. Lynx should be torn to pieces, yet he rests on his side, with his face half tilted to the sunlight falling through the branches. His heavy brow ridge casts shadows over his wide nose and sharp cheekbones. Lynx's long black hair—braided with marriage beads the color of the Rainbow Serpent—glistens with his slow breaths. He seems to be at such peace, one hand over his heart, the other stretched out across the forest floor as if reaching for someone, maybe

Siskin. Did he run as far as he could, then simply stop and give himself up to the pursuing lions?

Were it not for his blood-soaked clothing, he might be taking a nap. Why haven't they eaten him? Maybe they're full and saving him for later?

"Quiller?" RabbitEar says in warning.

I glance up just as a giant male stalks out of the trees with his head held high. His pungent scent drenches the air. Blessed Jemen, he's terrifying. A good two hand-lengths taller than I am, he looks down at me with glittering feral eyes.

"It's Nightbreaker," I say.

I've never been this close to him. My skin feels like it's on fire.

As though emboldened by Nightbreaker's presence, a lioness licks her bloody muzzle and pads forward until she stares me in the eyes from less than one pace away. All she has to do is lunge, and she can cut me in half with her claws before I can even scream.

"Don't even blink," RabbitEar orders. "If she charges you, I'll kill her, but that's the last thing we want."

In the grass, Lynx's chest rises and falls.

"Lynx just took a breath," I say.

"I don't care about him right now."

Suddenly, all seven lions simultaneously move toward me, forcing me to stumble backward.

"Hold!" RabbitEar sternly repeats to his warriors.

Most people would bolt from the scene, but if that happens, the lions will break and be in hot pursuit. In less than five heartbeats, we will all be dead. But we are Sealion People; we hold.

The moment seems eternal. Crystalline in its clarity. Totally silent.

I don't even realize Mink is there until he gasps, "Is Lynx alive?"

"Yes. Saw him breathe."

RabbitEar adds, "When we found him, two of the lions were lying snuggled against him as though protecting him."

Mink gives RabbitEar a strange look. "More likely protecting their breakfast from the dire wolves."

"Maybe, but that's not what it looked like, Mink."

Mink exhales the words: "Listen carefully. This must be done slowly. Everyone, start moving forward. If we have to fight, it will be a chaos of claws and fangs, so do not cast unless they attack. We just want to scare them off."

We all draw in fortifying breaths, and the five of us start inching toward the huge lions. The closer we get, the more the air tastes like rotting blood . . . like their clotted coats.

Nightbreaker lifts his regal head to scent us, and it's as though some dread enchantment has broken. He trots away, leading his pride into the cold morning shadows. Within moments, they are gone.

Mink says, "Quiller, find out what's wrong with Lynx. Everyone else, stand your ground. They're not gone, just biding their time."

6

QUILLER

Dropping to my knees beside Lynx, I call, "Lynx? Can you hear me? Answer me!"

There's even more blood than I saw at first. Swaths paint his right sleeve and stripe his chest and face. The dead grass around him is drenched with it, but it may not be Lynx's blood. It may have drained from the coats of the lionesses.

"What's the matter with him?" RabbitEar asks. "Why isn't he waking up?"

"Blow to the head, maybe? Can't tell."

"Any other wounds?"

"None I can see."

Mink backs out of the semicircle of warriors and crouches beside me. "Tear off his clothes. We have to know where he's hurt. He could be bleeding to death."

Tugging off Lynx's shirt, I toss it on the grass, then turn Lynx's limp body onto his opposite side to look at his back. His perfect skin gleams in the sunlight.

RabbitEar and the two other warriors keep glancing over, whispering and shaking their heads.

"Not a mark on him. That's not possible." I sit back in the grass and stare at Lynx. I have only loved two men in my life, Lynx and RabbitEar, but I know their bodies almost as well as my own.

RabbitEar grimaces. "If he's not hurt, where did all the blood come from?"

"Part of it is probably Siskin's," I say.

"Siskin?" Grief strains RabbitEar's face. "You found—"

"Up at the top of the meadow. Lions killed her, but the wolves have been at her for quite a while."

RabbitEar runs a hand over his face. "Gods, poor Bluejay."

Mink picks up Lynx's shirt and examines it. "You notice the bloody fingerprints on his sleeves?"

I nod. "Yes."

"The red stripes across the chest look like they were made by her long hair. Must have been completely blood-soaked when she grabbed him."

"Trying to wake him? Drag him to his feet?"

Softly, for my ears alone, Mink says, "If Lynx had tried to help her, he'd be torn apart. Which means he didn't try to help her. I pray he didn't play dead while the lions dragged her off."

"You'll never make me believe that!"

Mink seems to be working hard to find another logical reason for his brother's lack of injuries. A reason other than the fact that he had not been in the fight with the lions. "I don't want to think that way, but—"

RabbitEar repeats, "If he's not hurt, why won't he wake up?"

Mink rises to his feet with his spear clutched so tightly in his hand that his knuckles have gone white. "Might have an injury we can't see. Something deep inside. Let's get him home to our healer. Elder Hoodwink will know what to do."

Up at the edge of the wedding camp, the rest of the search party is gathering. They seem to be waiting for Bluejay to trot down the hill and join them. When he does, the warriors create a semicircle and march down the hill in dire-wolf formation.

Mink's dark eyes narrow as he studies the formation. "Where's the old man?"

RabbitEar asks, "Who?"

"The old man I told Bluejay to capture."

RabbitEar scans the hillside. "There was an old man?"

"Yes. Maybe from the Rust People, but I don't think so."

"Rust People?" RabbitEar says in terror. "Gods, if there's even a chance that they are close, we have to get home to warn the village!"

A current—like lightning about to strike—goes through the group. Our families could already be under attack.

"He's right, Mink," I say as I rise. "We have to get home right now."

When Bluejay and the others arrive, they fan out around Lynx, staring at where he lies half naked upon the ground. Mutters pass through the assembly.

"Bluejay, where's the elder?" Mink says.

"Mink, I'm sorry. I . . ." He spreads his arm. "I swear, I only turned to gander at you for five heartbeats, but when I turned back, he was gone. Tried to track him, but lost him."

"Lost him?" Mink says angrily. "He's an old man! How could you lose—"

"I *don't* know!" Bluejay helplessly slaps his arms against his sides. "He just vanished, Mink! When I searched for him, there was no sign that any human had ever stood there. No moccasin prints. Nothing except lion tracks!"

Warriors glance darkly at one another. The anxiety level is rising, filling the air with its distinctive odor of fear-sweat. The ancient Jemen could change into animals, and he was no ordinary old man.

Mink glares at Bluejay, then turns to the big warrior named Kinglet. A faint haze of windblown snow coats his black hair and beard. "Deputy, what did you find?"

"Birdboy. Isn't much left to identify him, but his shell pendant was lying nearby. I'm sure it's him."

Mink suddenly looks bewildered, as though struggling to put all the puzzle pieces together, and coming up blank, because nothing here makes sense.

But I'm sure everyone is thinking the same thing I am: Everyone else is dead or badly injured . . . except for Lynx. Why?

"Since Rust People may be close, we have new concerns," Mink says. "Kinglet, take two men and gather as many of the bones of our relatives as you can. The rest of us will run home to make sure our families are safe. Want you home by nightfall, though."

Kinglet nods, but gestures to Lynx. "First, tell me what's wrong with your brother?"

"Don't know. May have taken a hard blow to the head or . . ."

The entire party gasps when Lynx suddenly jerks to a sitting position and his wide terrified eyes pan the forest around them. Sunlight glitters through his beaded hair and slides across the dark bands of dried blood on his face.

When Lynx recognizes us, he croaks, "Oh, gods," and falls into breathless sobs.

7

LYNX

itting alone before the central fire, I rock back and forth, watching the people of Sky Ice Village bringing in firewood, feeding their children, whispering behind their hands. No one has spoken to me. It's as though I don't exist. People I've known all my life walk past me without a word. When they do glance down at me, I see confusion and pity on their faces. A few people gaze at me curiously. By now, they've all heard the story about the lions that protected me from the dire wolves. Not even I believe it.

They want to know the details of what happened . . . but no stories will be heard until the elders emerge from their lodge and begin the village council meeting.

I peer wide-eyed at the elders' glowing lodge. The mammoth-hide exterior of the domelike structure is painted with waving green trees, blue dolphins, and swimming salmon. These are our sacred clan symbols. We have origin stories about each one. First Woman came from my clan, the WindBorn clan. Long ago, she lived in the sky world, but one day she accidentally stepped through a hole in the sky and fell toward earth. When Blue Dolphin saw her tumbling through the air high above, she went to the Salmon People and begged them to help her save the woman. Together, they dove down to the bottom of the ocean and brought up dirt, piling it higher and higher, until they'd made a soft place for First Woman to land. On the exact spot where she touched down, a magnificent green willow tree grew. All of that happened long before the Jemen walked the earth like giants.

Shadows move across the fire-lit walls of the council lodge. Quiller must be about to leave. They called Mink in to speak first, then RabbitEar and Bluejay. Finally, Quiller and Grasshopper.

But not me.

My tale will not be heard in private. It's a strange, unbelievable tale that must be heard by the entire village.

When weeping rises and falls on the wind, I turn toward the ocean. The families of the dead move along the beach, erecting burial scaffolds. The four upright posts of the scaffolds are made of mammoth rib bones, bound together with sinew and wrapped with colorful strips of painted hides, red, blue, and yellow. Siskin's family is covering her scaffold with bison hides. Against the luminous green background of zyme, they appear black and sticklike.

I lower my face into my hands and long for death. Was it my fault? Somewhere deep inside, I'm sure it is. I heard my wife's cries for help, but did nothing. I let my wife die.

Voices rise when Quiller steps out of the council lodge and heads toward me. Thank the gods. Her father is a council member. Right now, he's pondering what will happen to me. Has he told his daughter which way he's leaning?

"Listen." Quiller crouches beside me and narrows her buglike eyes. Her large freckles look black in the firelight. I'm always a little intimidated by her height. She's taller than any man in the village. "We need to talk."

"They going to kill me?"

When she shifts uncomfortably, the blue dolphins painted

on her white sleeves ripple as though swimming. "Council won't decide that until after they hear your story, but . . ."

"Go on."

"You'd better remember what happened, Lynx."

"But I can't! My memory is patchy at best!"

She is so different from Siskin. Siskin was beautiful and sentimental, always laughing and touching me when I least expected it. Quiller is the exact opposite, strong and serious. There isn't a shred of sentimentality in her soul. No matter what happens, she stands her ground and faces it head-on. She's the bravest person I know.

"Do they think I played dead while the lions killed my wife?"

"Most people are just heartbroken. Desperate to know every detail of what happened to their loved ones. Just tell them the truth."

"Gods, Quiller, if I tell them the small things I actually recall, they'll call me a coward. Then they'll either execute me or make me an Outcast."

Quiller gives me a hard-eyed stare. "Are you a coward?"

"I . . . I don't . . . I'm not sure what happened to me."

Execution would be the easiest death. Probably a swift club to the head. On the other hand, if they declare me an Outcast, I'll be carried out to sea and dumped in the zyme, or maybe they'll take me high up into the Ice Giant Mountains and abandon me. Either means a slow and painful death.

"Lynx, if you are Outcast, I'll go into exile with you. You won't be alone, so stop worrying about that. You and I will survive."

"You really think I'd let you throw your life away for me? No. I would never let you go with me into exile."

Quiller looks away. Once she's made a decision, it's almost impossible to talk her out of it. She's too stubborn and headstrong for her own good, and part of me is glad. I don't want to die alone.

Quiller turns back to me, and I see the pain in her eyes. She loves me. I've known that since we were children. Last summer, we had a strange triangle going on. RabbitEar tried hard to take her away from me, but she still picked me. Oddly, after the announcement of my betrothal to Siskin, RabbitEar did not instantly step in to ask Quiller to marry him, even though I know he loves her. He was probably still heart-numb after losing her, maybe giving himself time to heal, but it was a huge mistake. Besides that, if he'd married Quiller it would have relieved some of my guilt for begging my clan to let me marry Siskin instead of Quiller.

Now . . . none of that matters.

In the monstrous flame shadows, the trees around the village appear to waver in and out of existence. One heartbeat the pines flash into this world, the next they disappear in an erratic dance of pale green darkness.

"Tell me everything you remember, Lynx."

"Just . . . moments."

"Which moments?"

Helplessly, I shrug my shoulders. "Muskoxen running. Shouts. Then the world went bizarrely silent—as though all the sound had been sucked away into some black nothingness. Thought I'd gone deaf."

She studies my face. "They're going to ask you to explain why you are completely unhurt."

I slam my fists into the ground. "I don't know why!"

From up on the rocky terrace where the guards stand, Mink and Bluejay appear out of the night and walk down the trail to the elders' council lodge. Gods, what is Grasshopper telling the council? He probably saw the whole thing.

"Lynx, listen to me," Quiller orders in that voice that allows no disagreement. "No matter what happens, don't panic. When it's all over, we'll sort everything out, all right? Stay calm and tell the story."

I pause to breathe. "You're my best friend. Always have been."

"And you are mine."

Faint nausea torments my belly. "You know, don't you, that I would have died a hundred times over to save Sis- . . ."

I swallow her name. It is forbidden to speak the name of the dead aloud lest you accidentally call an angry soul back to this world where it might take vengeance upon the living.

"'Course I know. Now, tell me everything you remember."

Closing my eyes, I fight to block out everything in this world, and force myself to remember what happened. "When we first got to camp, I begged the Blessed Jemen for the courage and strength to care for my new wife. Begged for healthy children who would never go hungry, and a safe place for our people to grow old in peace far from the Rust People. That's when it started."

"What started?"

"I felt . . . I don't know . . . strange. Otherworldly. As though the bottom of the world had just cracked open and I could see true darkness for the first time in my life. I kept feeling a . . . a woman's presence. As though one of the Jemen had . . . I don't know . . . come down from the sky or crawled out the legendary cave where they took the animals." I rub my eyes and open them.

"You mean like in a vision?"

"Maybe. I don't know, I've never had a vision."

Her green eyes flash like polished emeralds. "You walk back to camp after that?"

"No, I stood there gandering up at the sky, trying to hear the Jemen's voice in my heart. I told her I would give up everything

I had, and everything I ever would have, if she would grant me those things. That's why it happened."

"What do you mean?"

"Everything started going badly right after that. I swear it was my prayer."

Quiller's brows draw down over her flat nose. "You think one of the Jemen answered your prayer by taking everything you love?"

"She did, didn't she? Everything's gone."

"Lynx . . ." She leans close to stare hard into my eyes. "Night-breaker's pride attacked your wedding camp. That had nothing to do with your prayer. It was a good prayer, and I'm sure the Jemen . . ." Her voice fades as she glances over my shoulder at the council lodge. "Mink just opened the elders' lodge flap. Meeting is about to start."

We both rise. I have to spread my feet to brace my shaking knees.

Mink announces, "The elders come!"

In single file, the three old men and three old women emerge from the lodge and walk toward the mats arranged in a circle on the other side of the bonfire. As they sit down, each gives me a strange speculative look that makes my nausea worse. Have they already decided to kill me?

Chief Dry Cloud remains standing. A medium-sized man who waves his hands a lot, he's seen only twenty-eight summers, but white strands glitter in his black hair. He extends a hand to me. "Step into the middle of the circle, young Lynx."

I step into the circle and lock my knees. The rest of the village—around one hundred people—crowd close to watch. A group of young warriors and older boys stand back, moving at the very edge of the firelight, but I hear them muttering darkly and see them pointing at me. The last time I ran in battle, Deputy War Leader Hushy caught me when I was alone and beat me half to death with his fists, while he screamed *coward* in my face. Gods, I hate him. I suspect he'd love nothing more than to throw me in a thick zyme forest.

Mink and Bluejay take up positions off to the side, awaiting instructions. Fear glints in my brother's eyes. Did he overhear fragments of the private conversations of the elders?

The weave of my life seems to be fraying, the tatters flapping around me like a rotting burial shroud. Friends—people I love—are lifeless bones now. Out on the beach, the scaffolds of the dead stand silhouetted blackly against luminous zyme-capped waves.

Come on! Get this over with.

Dry Cloud prolongs my agony by calling, "Let us offer a prayer to the Jemen for wisdom on this terrible night."

People lift their voices in the sacred song:

> *We ask your permission.*
> *We seek your consent.*
> *To do what is right.*
> *Grant us wisdom this night.*
> *We know that sometimes one life*
> *must give way to another.*
> *Death is just the river stone*
> *rolling on through crystal water.*
> *Show us your sacred purpose, Blessed Jemen.*

To the north and east, the Ice Giants watch with eternal eyes, their presences like boulders upon my soul, crushing the life from it. High up near the icy crests, herds of bison lumber along the trails that crosshatch the broken slopes.

Hoodwink and Grasshopper arrive last.

Thick hide bandages wrap Grasshopper's head, as well as his left arm and upper right leg; all seep blood. I haven't seen him since before the attack, and his injuries shock me. Weaving, he struggles to prop himself up with his walking stick. How did he get home before predators smelled his blood and found him stumbling along?

Grasshopper groans when Hoodwink helps him to sit down in the council circle. Around thirty-eight summers, Hoodwink has silver-streaked black hair. His Spirit Power has saved our people many times. On this night, he wears his best seal-fur shirt and a wealth of shell-bead necklaces.

Dry Cloud lifts both fists to get everyone's attention. "Since my clan lost three people in the wedding camp attack, the council suggested I take charge this evening. Any objections?"

No one objects.

"Very well, then. I call Grasshopper, the last surviving guard of the wedding camp."

Grasshopper tries to stand up to address the council, but Chief Dry Cloud says, "No, warrior, remain seated. Council knows you mean no disrespect."

Grasshopper takes a moment to gander around the gathering as though judging the mood. People cluster in knots, whispering behind their hands. "Wish I didn't have to tell this story. All the way home, kept asking myself what I should and should not say."

Grasshopper gives me a sad shake of his head, before he continues, "I was posted at the base of the hill at the northwest corner of the wedding camp. Had been a beautiful, quiet night, though cold. I was happy, because so often I could hear the young couple talking and laughing. In the middle of the night, muskoxen came to graze at the edge of the meadow. I was watching them when I heard a soft *whoof* erupt from the southeastern corner of the camp where Bluejay's brother, Dust, was posted. Everything after that is a blur. Happened so fast. Lion leaped at me from the darkness. Didn't even know she was there before she was upon me. Bit my arm and dragged me down. Claws ripped my skull and tore through my thigh, and then, I-I . . . I couldn't . . ." Grasshopper stops to close his eyes for a moment, as though trying not to see what happened next.

"Take your time, warrior," Dry Cloud says.

The gathering has gone utterly silent. My throat is so tight I can barely get air into my lungs.

"I managed to spear the lion in the hip twice. Not killing blows, but she ran away to lick her wounds. Shouting and roaring was coming from everywhere. Would have gone to help in the fight if I could have, but I was bleeding badly. Could barely walk."

Grasshopper pauses to take a deep breath. "As I stumbled off, trying to get away, I heard the young bride screaming for Lynx to get up. She kept begging him to help her."

Out in the darkness, Bluejay breaks down in sobs.

Chief Dry Cloud's face tenses. "Continue, Grasshopper."

Grasshopper blinks at the ground and heaves a breath. "Short time later, I saw Lynx running away through the trees."

Conversations erupt everywhere, and people cast hateful glances at me.

"That's all," Grasshopper finishes. "After that, I used my spear as a walking stick and just kept staggering toward home till Mink and Quiller found me."

Hoarsely, I ask, "I ran away?"

Grasshopper gives me a sympathetic look. "Yes, I saw you."

When the conversations among the villagers die down, Dry Cloud presses, "Are you certain Lynx wasn't running from the lions?"

"Could have been. Didn't see any lions behind him. But it was dark."

Cries of outrage spike among the onlookers, and my belly twists.

Dry Cloud shouts above the din: "Wait until you hear Lynx's side of the tale!"

For a heartbeat, my gaze touches Mink's, and I see such fear in my brother's eyes that I long to charge out of the village and run as hard as I can to escape these people I love, these people who are going to kill me.

"Go ahead now, Lynx," Dry Cloud instructs. "Tell us your side of the story."

"Elders . . ." I make an uncertain motion with my hand. "I don't recall most of it. If I ran in the middle of the attack, I don't remember it. Not at all. Wish I—"

"Start at the beginning," Dry Cloud says. "Tell us what you can."

"I . . . remember . . . thunder."

Hoodwink narrows one eye. "Thunder?"

"Like a big herd of buffalo charging at me. It was deafening. Shook the whole world."

Hoodwink steps closer to me. "I suspect the buffalo were trying to warn you, to get you to wake up. What happened next?"

What happened next? Think about it. I push long black hair off my brow and clench my fists.

"The thunder vanished, and I smelled meat-breath, hot breath, panting in my face." I have to stiffen my knees to keep standing.

Oh, dear gods, lions. Lynx, get up. Where's your spear?

Dry Cloud says, "Was it lions?"

"Yes, three of them. Then something ripped away our bedding hides, and I . . . can't explain it, elders. My body turned to wood. I was flipped onto my right side and couldn't move. I—"

"Of course not," Hushy calls. "You froze up because you're a coward!"

Boys laugh, but I barely hear them.

Lynx, a lion has got me. He's dragging me. Help me.

Clenching my fists hard, I struggle to shove away the terrified cries of my wife. "Feet pounded the ground near me, and I heard gasping and screams for help. And shouting from somewhere far away, then I—"

"Was it my sister?" Bluejay calls in a loud agonized voice. "Calling to you for help?"

"Yes."

"Why didn't you get up and defend your new wife?" Hushy demands an explanation.

As murmuring sifts through the crowd, many people nod in agreement, and Mink takes a new grip on his spear.

"My body turned to wood! I don't understand it myself."

Several of the warriors make deep-throated sounds of disgust, and from the rear of the crowd, one of the women yells, "Let Lynx finish his telling!"

As though my soul is once again struggling to fly away, I feel hollow and euphoric.

"Go on, Lynx," Dry Cloud encourages.

"My wife . . . She ran to me. Told me to run. I heard her, but I couldn't do it. Couldn't! Then I felt her grab me and shake me. She cried, *'What's the matter with you? Get up.'* She fell on me. I didn't realize at the time, but now I think a lion must have knocked her down."

For three heartbeats, Bluejay sobs like a man whose life is over, then the big warrior trudges farther out into the darkness to try to get control of himself.

The gazes of the young warriors follow him and when they return to me, I see rage on their faces.

"Continue, Lynx."

"I heard lions dragging her away." I have to swallow several times to fight back the tide of emotion smothering me. "I tried to . . . get up, but . . ."

My lips are moving, still telling the story, but I can no longer hear my own voice. Frantically, my gaze darts around, but it's so dark all I see now are the faces of the dogs watching me with shining eyes. Every human face has vanished in a zyme glare suddenly too brilliant to endure. The lodges and rolling luminescent waves of zyme have twisted into mockeries of themselves, misshapen and evil, warping beyond the firelight.

Stop walking, boy.

"Lynx!" Quiller shouts, and leaps into the circle, trying to break my fall, but I hit the ground like an elk speared through the heart.

"Lynx, you all right? Talk to me!"

The edges of my vision gray out . . .

8

LYNX

Far back in my head, a wrenching moan rings across the night. It takes a moment to realize it's not coming from Sky Ice Village. The cries of dire wolves high up in the Ice Giant Mountains are echoing down the glacial valleys, sounding eerie and haunted. I blink open my eyes and see a ring of elderly faces hovering above me. Beyond them, the pale green darkness flickers with the campfires of the dead. I'm so tired, I just want to sleep.

After ten heartbeats, Dry Cloud leans over, grips me by the shoulders, and forces me to sit up. "Quiller? Outside the circle. Now."

Dazed, not quite here in my body, I wobble before I brace a hand on the ground to steady myself. All around me, lodges glow like seashell lanterns.

"But what if he falls again? He needs—"

"Now!"

She reluctantly backs away, but not before I see her mouth the word *courage*.

As the crowd presses closer, eager to hear the last of the telling, my relatives' faces resemble fire-lit moons with dark holes for eyes. These people are all I have. I grew up with them. They soothed my childhood hurts, taught me lessons as a young man, tried to be my family after my parents were murdered by

Rust People. Though tears streak a few cheeks, tonight most people stare at me with a mixture of despair and confusion. Making any member of the People an Outcast is a wrenching decision, but Hushy makes the throwing-away gesture with his hand. He wants me gone.

"Lynx, finish your tale," the chief orders.

I exhale a halting breath before I say, "First thing I remember clearly is running around the camp trail, but that was much later than when Grasshopper saw me. And then—" I pause, seeing it all again, "—an old man appeared. Out of nowhere."

Dry Cloud gives me a curious look. "What old man?"

"He found me on the trail, spoke to me. I think he was real. Not positive."

Dry Cloud exchanges a curious glance with Hoodwink, and the shaman says, "What did this man look like? Was he a warrior of the Rust People?"

"Rust People? No, I—I mean, I don't know. He was not wearing the shiny silver clothing of the Rust People. He seemed otherworldly . . . maybe not even human. Why would you think he—"

"Forgive us for not revealing this earlier." Dry Cloud turns to address the villagers. "We needed to hear Lynx's story before we made the announcement. Mink, Quiller, and Bluejay saw an old man in the trees near the place where Siskin was killed. Even though his cloak was made of lion hides, Bluejay thought the designs on his shirt identified him as an elder from the Red Lion clan of the Rust People. Some of the paint seemed made of rust."

I turn around to stare at my brother. Why hadn't Mink told me that? Or Quiller?

Elder Crystal Leaf cries, "*Trogon!* Was it Trogon the witch? He's Red Lion clan."

People turn all the way around to scan the shoreline, afraid

Rust People might be sneaking up on them this instant. A few women run for their lodges where children sleep. Most of the others watch the ocean, expecting to hear the guttural roars and metallic clashings of rusty ships speeding toward the beach.

Trogon? The name strikes terror into my soul. "Must have been! That's why I couldn't move! I'd been witched."

"May not have been the same man," Dry Cloud says. "What did the man who came to you look like?"

"Old, really old, with long white hair and burning blue eyes."

Hoodwink turns to Mink. "Is that the man you saw, War Leader?"

Mink's head dips once in a nod.

Hushy yells, "Lynx is lying! Probably heard the rest of the hunt party talking about the old man. Now he thinks he can blame everything on a Rust People witch. Don't forget that he did nothing to save his wife!"

"I'm not blaming anyone else! But I am not a coward! I would have given anything to be able to save her!" From deep inside me, I hear Siskin crying, and I long to sob.

There's a lull as people discuss the strange old man. At last, Elder Crystal Leaf grunts and wobbles to her feet. She has sparse white hair and hollow cheeks. "I wish to address the council now."

"Please," Dry Cloud says.

Crystal Leaf lifts her chin, and her golden doe-hide cloak sways about her thin body. "I have three things to say. By now you've all heard that when RabbitEar found Lynx, two lions were curled around him as if protecting him from the dire wolves. Why do you think they came to protect him?"

Speculation rises out across the darkness. I catch phrases like, " . . . were just going to eat him," and " . . . lions know Lynx is special. Ever since he had that strange fever when he was four . . ." and " . . . always been odd."

Crystal Leaf holds up one frail hand to get everyone's attention. "Seems perfectly clear to me that the Jemen sent the lions to protect him or he'd be dead. That means Lynx is being watched over by the gods themselves. We must ask why. Why save Lynx and attack everyone else?"

Hushy calls, "Perhaps the gods were punishing Lynx for running in that last battle? Many died because he refused to fight."

My heart shrivels in my chest. Mink told me the same thing, so I'm sure it's true. For moons afterward, I kept trying to figure out who might have died because of me. Possible faces floated through my dreams every night. The faces of the children hurt the most.

"Second," Crystal Leaf goes on, "old Nightbreaker loves the taste of human flesh. He will never stop hunting us. We must find him and kill him and his entire pride. And, last, we have to send scouts northward up the coast to see if the Rust People are close. I'm exhausted from not knowing where they are."

"But most important," a man calls, "we must kill Nightbreaker and his pride before they can drag off more of our people!"

"I would speak." Bunting, Quiller's father, stands up beside Crystal Leaf. He has seen thirty-three summers, but still has jet black hair that drapes in thick blue-black locks around his face. "I say we load our boats and head south. In a few days, we will be far beyond Nightbreaker and his pride, and farther away from any Rust People who might be following us. I know this seems like a rich and wonderful place, but we should not have decided to stay here for the winter. Let's head south and see how far we get."

From far back in the gathering, a woman cries, "But what if there's nothing south but ice? It's almost winter. We can't risk getting stranded on a barren ice shelf if a sudden storm blows in. At least here we know we have an abundance of food!"

"May I speak?" Elder Stone Bowl rises to his feet. The oldest man among the People, he's seen forty-seven summers. Thin gray wisps cling to his age-spotted scalp.

Dry Cloud nods. "Of course, elder."

"My People, we are only talking about one old man. He was not dressed as one of the Rust People. I think it more likely that he comes from an unknown people that inhabits this new land. If—"

Bluejay interrupts, "But he spoke our language, elder. He had a strange accent and used some strange words I'd never heard before, but it was definitely our language. What if it was Trogon?"

Gently, Stone Bowl says, "I do not believe it was. Trogon is not a fool. He wouldn't walk away from the safety of his village just to torment one of our wedding camps. He's never done such a thing. Always stays close to his village. Though I certainly agree with Crystal Leaf, we must be prudent and send scouts northward to see if Rust People are behind us."

Stone Bowl and Bunting help Elder Crystal Leaf to sit down again.

Dry Cloud waits to see if more elders wish to comment. When they do not, he says, "Hoodwink? Would you address the council?"

Hoodwink's thick black brows draw into a single line over his bulbous nose. Finally, he steps into the circle and gazes down at me where I huddle like a broken child, my head cradled in my hands. Placing cold fingers on my shoulder, he says, "You all right, Lynx?"

"No, elder."

"Well, take hold," he softly says. "Your people love you. No one wants you dead."

I look up at him, but Hoodwink is no longer gazing at me.

He's focused on the crowd milling out in the firelight. From the hateful expression on Hushy's face, I suspect Hoodwink is wrong.

Hushy calls, "Let's throw the coward away. Outcast him!"

A sad expression creases Hoodwink's face. He sighs and turns to address the elders. "I don't think bravery is something a man is born with, do you? I think he learns it from others. I do not believe Lynx is a coward, and I know you do not either, but even if he is a little fainthearted, it's our fault, not his. After his parents were murdered three summers ago, his older brother did the best he could to raise Lynx well, but we should have helped more. That's clear now. I would ask the council's kindness in this matter. At the age of sixteen summers, he still has much to offer our people. We have entered a new and dangerous land. We need every person."

Elder Stone Bowl gives me a curious look before he says, "I agree with Hoodwink. We all know that Lynx has a holy man's heart. We must not throw that away."

Bluejay stalks forward into the firelight with his jaw clenched, and tears streaking the pink scars that cover his face. "Elders, my little sister was torn apart because Lynx refused to help her fight off the lions. My brother died, as well, but I don't blame Lynx for that. I examined the wedding camp. My brother was the first to die, then my sister fought desperately to save herself. From the sign, I . . . I'm sure the lions toyed with her for quite some time before they killed her." He shakes a fist at me. "He deserves no kindness from us! Outcast him, then let's get in our boats and move on down the coast, as Bunting suggests."

Quiller looks shocked. She keeps casting pleading glances at her father, but Bunting refuses to meet her eyes, choosing instead to lean sideways and whisper to Elder Crystal Leaf.

Just when I'm sure my own brother has given me up for dead, Mink slowly walks into the firelight and stands before the council with his spear propped in front of him. "May I speak?"

"Please, War Leader. I'm glad you came forward."

Mink's gaze drifts around the circle of elders, staring each in the eyes. "I believe everything Bluejay told you. I examined all the tracks. His sister fought valiantly while my brother did nothing to help her."

People tilt their heads curiously, wondering at this admission from Mink. It as much as condemns me to being declared Outcast, or worse. If the council decides the deaths actually resulted from my cowardice, the families of the dead have the right to claim my life. It's called the Rule of Retribution. A fist for a fist. A life for a life.

"However," Mink says, "I also think that when the lions came, my brother's soul flew from his body. Imagine yourself waking to the feel of hot lion breath on your face, then opening your eyes to see three standing above you. As Elder Hoodwink can tell you, fear often causes a soul to fly, and a body without a soul cannot move. If I'm right, Lynx could not have saved anyone, including himself. He must have—"

"You don't know his soul flew from his body," Hushy challenges angrily. "You weren't there."

"No, I wasn't. But I know my brother. He wouldn't have left his new wife to die if he could have saved her."

Tears blur my eyes. *Thank you, Mink.*

Dry Cloud gestures for me to stand up, and I manage to stagger to my feet. "What do you say to that, Lynx? Did you ever feel yourself hovering over the event?"

"Yes, my Chief. Almost the entire time, I was floating through the air above our wedding camp."

Several of the warriors, including Hushy, come forward to stand shoulder to shoulder beside Bluejay.

Bluejay says, "Changes nothing. Even if true, only a coward's soul flies away when someone he loves needs him."

Hushy calls, "That's right! Does a man like that help the People?"

A low hum of voices fills the night. All around me, the world is melting, the colors flowing together, reshaping themselves into the glistening night sky and towering ice mountains . . . and Siskin is weeping my name.

Faintly, I hear Elder Hoodwink say, "Lynx? Can you hear me? I've been calling you for . . ."

I drop my throbbing head to my hands. "Yes."

"This will be over soon. Take heart."

All I can do is nod.

Dry Cloud says, "Council will adjourn to consider this matter."

The elders walk a short distance away to discuss the evening's revelations with Hoodwink. Sensing that it might take a while, the crowd begins to disperse. Women drag children off to their lodges, while men gather off to the side to mutter in dark tones. The youths my age move in closer to call taunts at me.

"Filthy coward," Hushy growls in a low voice. "Killed his wife!"

Quiller strides up and shouts, "Get away from him!" When they back away, she turns and whispers to me, "I'm going to do something. No matter what the council says, agree with me, understand?"

"What are you going to do?"

As she thinks, her jaw moves with grinding teeth. "I'll figure that out on my way over to Hoodwink."

Quiller boldly walks to the elders, pulls Hoodwink aside, and speaks to him in low serious tones. Every now and then, Hoodwink tries to walk away, but she grabs his shirtsleeve to stop him and keeps talking. Even from this distance, I see the fire in her eyes.

What's she telling him? Does it matter? Things can't get any worse.

Finally, Quiller steps back, and Hoodwink rejoins the council members.

She remains standing off to the side, as though waiting in case someone wishes to ask her a question. Several times, the elders call her into the circle to speak with her, then she backs out again. She knows me better than anyone, and they all know it. They watched us grow up together.

Finally, the council breaks and the elders walk back to sit on their mats. No one meets my eyes.

They're going to dump me into a zyme forest. They've decided.

Dry Cloud at last lifts his hands to call the villagers back to hear the decision. "Council has discussed the issue. Please gather round. Elder Hoodwink would speak."

People duck out of the lodges and hurry back to hear my fate.

I stiffen my knees in preparation.

Hoodwink begins, "We all think we know what happened . . ."

He falls silent when shrill cries and booms quiver the air. This happens when we are close to the Ice Giants. They are never quiet for long. As though before any decisions are made, the Giants wish to comment on my fate.

Hoodwink nods as he listens to them, then continues, "We all think we know what happened at the wedding camp, but I wish you to consider another possibility."

"What possibility?" Hushy asks. "Lynx clearly has the heart of a worm."

"Perhaps not, Deputy. It's possible that Lynx spent the night of his wedding journeying from this world to the other side of the campfires of the dead. That would explain the old man who came to him on the trail, and the fact that Nightbreaker's pride protected him from the other animals. The old man was not of the Rust People, but Nightbreaker in human disguise. A spirit helper sent to guide him."

"Nightbreaker?" Bluejay calls in disbelief. "A spirit helper? He's a wild, evil animal!"

"I don't think so. I have long believed that Nightbreaker is one of the Jemen, a magical being born long before the zyme."

Bluejay jerks as though shocked at the very idea. "I don't believe it. The old man was an albino from the Rust People."

Hushy calls, "Tell me, what has Lynx ever done to be worthy of a spirit helper?"

"Only the spirit helper can answer that, Deputy. If Lynx—"

Bluejay cuts him off: "I tell you, the old man was Trogon!"

A din of conversation spreads across the village, forcing Dry Cloud to lift his hands to gain quiet. "Let Hoodwink finish!"

When the uproar dies down, Hoodwink slowly lets out a breath. "If the unknown man was a transformed Nightbreaker, we must not ignore the possibility that Lynx is alive because an old, spirit-filled lion saw something inside him that none of us do. Something powerful. Something important. Maybe something critical to the survival of the Sealion People." Hoodwink pauses and lets his gaze drift over the faces flickering in the firelight before he adds, "Survival is our only purpose now. You all know the truth. The once-great Sealion People stand upon the precipice of the abyss. More babies are being born dead than alive. I think Lynx may be our last hope."

Hushy roars like a lion, flails his fists in the air, and stamps away.

Hoodwink's brows lower as he watches Hushy disappear into the darkness, then he turns back to the assembled elders. "As Quiller pointed out to me, the simple fact is that either

Nightbreaker decided not to kill him, or he could not kill him. The council has discussed this, and all believe Lynx has been chosen by the Jemen. We must know why."

Hoodwink blinks down at me, and my head feels like it's going to explode. The holy man's eyes are so bright and serious, I almost can't look at him.

"Which means Lynx must find Nightbreaker and ask him."

From out in the darkness, Hushy bursts out laughing. He shouts, "You expect Lynx to hunt down the most powerful lion in the world? Alone? Good. That's a death sentence."

"It's the only way we will ever understand the will of the Jemen," Hoodwink says.

I feel like a duck hit in the head with a rock: too stunned to do anything but stare at Hoodwink. Blessed gods, Quiller has doomed me.

Dry Cloud claps his hands to get everyone's attention. "Council has concluded that Lynx will be escorted into the wilderness, where he will undertake a spirit quest. If he truly has been chosen by the Jemen, he will not have to find Nightbreaker. Nightbreaker will find him."

The Ice Giants to the east shimmer as my eyes blur. Their cracked and jagged peaks touch the Road of Light that leads to the Land of the Dead. Is that where they'll take me? Into those high barren peaks? I can feel the Giants' primordial patience, awaiting my arrival, and not caring in the slightest whether I live or die.

"While Lynx is gone," Hoodwink says, "the rest of us will make traps to catch Nightbreaker's pride and kill every last animal. But no one, *no one*, may kill Nightbreaker until Lynx returns or we find his dead body."

9

LYNX

Morning sunlight slants through the door flap and creates odd swirling patterns in the smoke rising from the lodge fire where Quiller and Mink crouch, arguing in taut voices. They both love me, and know I am not up to this task.

I focus on filling my pack with the things I will need for my death journey.

Mink's wife Gray Dove and his two young sons watch me from the rear of the lodge. My nephews observe the proceedings with wide eyes. They both believe I'm some kind of holy man off on a sacred mission, which is what Mink has told them to ease their fears.

Stuffing a pair of bison-hide mittens in my pack, I finally reach for my muskoxen coat. It's a beautiful thing. The hair is turned in for warmth, and the suede exterior is painted with the symbol of the WindBorn clan, a green tree waving in the wind. Over the past two summers, the coat has molded to my body. As I slip it on, I dare to glance at Mink and find my brother shaking his head at something Quiller is saying.

"But it makes no sense. I can't understand why you would—"

"Because I know you, Quiller."

She shakes her fists at him. "Gods, I only wanted them to think that Lynx was worth saving. I had no idea they'd send him off on a—"

"Listen to me!" Mink stabs a finger at her. "Don't get any notions about going after Lynx. The elders have decided you will be part of the scouting party that heads northward in search of Rust People. Go home and gather your weapons and pack. You're leaving right after Lynx is taken away."

Red creeps into Quiller's cheeks. "Sending me off on a scouting trip will not stop me from going after Lynx—"

"Disobey orders," Mink warns, "and the Blue Dolphin clan will Outcast you."

"I don't care!"

I feel physically ill. The only comfort I've had all morning is that Quiller keeps vowing to disobey the elders' orders and go with me. She has saved me so many times in my life, I've come to expect it. But I bravely say, "Don't follow me, Quiller. I couldn't bear losing you, too."

"You can't go out there alone, Lynx. You won't last two days!"

"I know that." I try to smile, and turn to Mink. "Will you lead the scouting party north?"

"I will."

"Which means you've been assigned the responsibility for making sure Quiller does not chase after me. Is that it?"

Mink's dark eyes have a strange gleam. "Partly. We also need to know where the Rust People are, little brother."

"Yes, I—I know."

When I tie my weapons belt around my waist, the bone knife, seal-bladder water bag, and deer-bone stiletto rattle. Reaching down to pick up my pack, I stumble. Quiller leaps to her feet and runs to grab my arm to steady me. Our gazes lock. She is near panic, afraid for me. Only Quiller knows how frail I really am.

Mink stands up with his fists clenched at his sides. In a confident voice, my brother says, "I want you to know that I believe

Hoodwink. This is not a death sentence. It's a sacred spirit quest. Go into the wilderness, find Nightbreaker and ask him the Jemen's will, then come home alive. If you do, you'll have proven that you have both courage and a very powerful spirit helper. Hoodwink told me that if you return, he's certain you will rescue the Sealion People from oblivion and become the greatest shaman our people have ever known."

My gaze is still locked with Quiller's when she whispers, "I'll be coming. You know I will."

Closing my eyes, I manage a nod. The terror eases slightly, but my voice still shakes when I ask, "Where are they taking me, Mink?"

"It's being kept secret. Hoodwink revealed the location only to Kinglet, who will lead your party."

Just beyond the open lodge flap, the latest snow squall drifts across the village, and the shimmer of falling flakes is almost too beautiful to be real—like handfuls of crushed seashells cast upon the sunlit wind. The lodges are turning white.

I work up the strength to say, "You've both tried to teach me the things I need to know to survive out there. If I never see you again, I . . ." My voice fades. Finally, I say, "Thank you."

Mink clamps his jaw, and I suddenly realize that the hard lines of my brother's face are a map of every wrong turn I've taken in my life. Mink tried so hard to teach me to be a man, to hunt and fish, to be a warrior. I failed miserably, and he knows it. Now I must pay the price.

"Take another bag of dried fish, Lynx," Mink says. "They may abandon you in the middle of a glacier. Could be days before you find more food."

"No, I have enough. Save it for my nephews. I'll be all right. Don't worry about me."

"But none of it was your fault!" Quiller cries. "It's my fault! If only I had—"

"Doesn't matter any longer." I spread my feet to brace my shaking knees. At dawn, I watched Siskin's family place her remains on her burial scaffold and sing her to the afterworld, along with the others who were killed. By now, my wife's disembodied soul must be moving like a sleepwalker through the deep shadows cast by the trees that line the Road of Light. In a few days, she'll be within sight of the campfires of the dead. I'll join her there. I'll hold her in my arms again. If she'll let me. Won't be long now.

"Lynx, I . . ." Mink stops. He can't seem to find words to say goodbye, so he points a stern finger at me, and orders, "Stay alive. Come home."

Outside, the village has gathered, waiting for me. I hear people talking. "I'll try, Mink."

My spear leans by the door. I pick it up and duck outside into the cold, snow-scented morning air.

Forcing a breath into my lungs, I march toward the four men who will carry out the council's orders. Four is the minimum number necessary to fight off the big predators that will be trotting along our trail, hunting us. The village cannot afford to send more. These men are risking their lives for me. Once the warriors abandon me to my fate, I'll have to fight off lions, wolves, and bears by myself. A grim smile touches my lips. I can't. I'm not strong enough. I've always been a skinny weakling.

As I pass among the people, I hear them whispering, speculating on why I'm not weeping and pleading with the elders to change their minds. They've seen me do it a hundred times in my life.

By the time I stop in front of Kinglet, I'm shaking so hard I can barely stand. "I . . . I'm ready."

"Very well. Turn around."

Quiller boldly strides forward to stand at my side. Her gaze is a promise. On so many occasions, she has been my salvation, and I suspect she would die in my place right now if I asked her to.

Just before Kinglet slips the blindfold over my eyes, I see Mink walk down to the beach and stand with his back to me, staring at the gigantic icebergs that cut through the zyme forests like gleaming blue animals swimming south. But he has his fists clenched, straining against his own impotence.

Kinglet ties the blindfold over my eyes and the sight of the village, and the faces of all the people I have ever loved, disappears.

Faintly, I hear Quiller whisper, *"I'll find you."*

Two men grip my arms and lead me away up the trail that heads north into the glacial wilderness.

10

QUILLER

Four nights later . . .

My watch.

Leaning back upon the flat rock above our beach camp, I must lift my hand to shield my eyes from the zyme glare that reflects from the two-hundred-hand-tall ice wall that rises behind me. Rust warriors could be up there right now, watching us, and with this intense zyme glare, I wouldn't see them. The wall borders the ocean to the north for as far as I can see, winding along like the frozen body of a monstrous green serpent killed by the Jemen in a legendary battle for which we have no story.

Though Mink, RabbitEar, and Basher talk around the campfire on the beach below me, grief has become my only companion. Lynx must be dead by now. My soul has been showing me his end over and over. Surrounded by lions, or wolves, or being torn apart by a short-faced bear, I see him screaming. And I know, even in his last moments, he's searching for me, waiting for me to save him.

Lowering my hand, I turn to squint out at the ocean. There must be a hot spring emptying into the water here, for the zyme forest has grown massive. Tentacles twine over each other, piling higher and higher until they've formed luminous green towers that ride the waves like mythic creatures. Some have branches like trees. Others resemble many-humped camels. A few seem to have walked straight out of our oldest stories, for they are giants with misshapen heads and tentacles for hair that slither as they blow in the sea wind. Hoodwink says that when the Earthbound Jemen knew they had lost the war with the Ice Giants, most of them walked into the sea and turned themselves into zyme as punishment.

"That what you are?" I whisper, watching two of the shining giants soar upward on a wave until they stand five times my height. "Cursed gods?"

A cry, like the shriek of a faraway hawk, rides the wind.

I cock my head to listen. It's very faint. The cry bounces around the ice cliff, rising and falling.

"What is that, Crow?"

Crow, who stands guard a short distance away, growls softly. Her gaze is fixed on the beach trail that leads north, as though she knows exactly what it is, and it scares her.

Does Mink hear it? Glancing back at the campfire, I study the faces of the men. Mink, RabbitEar, and Basher talk in low voices. They're sipping cups of tea and telling stories. Occasionally someone laughs. No one looks northward.

I resettle myself on the rock. Probably nothing. Just another haunted cry echoing across the icy wilderness.

My gaze is drawn to the jagged peaks of the Ice Giants. Their highest tors glisten above the wall. The air up there, near the Road of Light, shimmers this time of season, filled with great billowing clouds of ice crystals that twist and twine around the peaks. Mink has not spoken a word to me about Lynx, but he's been watching me like a hawk, dutifully following the council's orders to keep me from saving his brother. If I try to run off, he'll drag me back, but I must find a moment when he is not looking to slip away. Even if all I discover are Lynx's scattered bones strewn across a glacier, at least I will have kept my promise to find him.

That strange wail shreds the night air again, jarring me back to the beach. I try to focus on the sound. I'm pretty sure that Crow is right; it's coming from the north.

"Maybe it's dire wolves calling to each other?" I look down at Crow.

The hair on her back stands on end, and she whimpers in a low half growl and pads back to sit at my feet, keeping me close.

Or maybe the cries seep straight up from the massive underworld cavern where the last Earthbound Jemen hauled crates filled with magical animals to save them. Am I hearing the otherworldly voices of Peregrine Falcon, Coyote, and Bobcat? The song blends high-pitched shrieks with haunting yips.

Crow growls again, and I reach down to stroke her black head. "Don't know why, but that wail goes all the way through me. You, too, eh?"

The cries diminish and fade into the background of waves washing across the shore.

The Road of Light is bright tonight. Two Jemen cross the shining path, going in opposite directions. Maybe Lynx is alive? I have no idea how far they took him. Kinglet may not have even abandoned him yet. In that case, Lynx is getting more scared every day, because the longer they are on the trail, the longer it will take him to get home. And the longer it will take me to find him.

Crow shifts to watch RabbitEar when he stands up beside the beach fire, grabs his pack and spear, and trudges through the deep sand toward us. He has a burly swagger. The zyme glare shimmers over his ice-crusted red hair and beard, turning them into haloes of flashing emeralds. Mother has always believed that Salmon clan and Blue Dolphin are related far back in time, because so many of us have red hair, but it's a rare trait among the WindBorn. That's one of our problems. Our clans are too closely related. Everyone is a cousin.

When he gets close enough, he calls, "My watch, Quiller. Go get some fish stew. There's plenty left in the bag."

"Sounds good." I start for the fire, but stop. "RabbitEar, you might want to keep an ear bent for the strange wail that's been drifting down from the north."

"A wail?" He turns to squint northward.

"Yes, I've been hearing it off and on for a while. None of you heard it?"

"No, but with the waves and the crackles and snaps of the fire, it's hard to hear anything. What do you think it was?"

He's giving me one of those soft looks that always makes me want to turn away. He's loved me for moons, and I don't know what to do about it.

I shrug. "Magical voices seeping up from the Jemen's cavern? Maybe just wolves. Maybe mammoths trumpeting. Could be human voices. If you hear it again, and think it's human, tell Mink as soon as possible."

"I will. You look tired." He reaches out as though to touch my arm, but draws his hand back and just smiles instead. "Go eat and get some rest. Tomorrow is going to be a long day. Mink says we're going to run all the way to the ice floes before we turn back."

We passed the ice floes as we paddled down the coast. Created by streams of water flowing out of the high glaciers, they resemble fingers of ice that stretch across the shore and far out into the water.

"All right, I'm off for camp." I motion for Crow to lie down. "You stay with RabbitEar, Crow. Stand guard with him."

Crow stretches out on her belly and blinks up at RabbitEar, waiting for his instructions. RabbitEar crouches to gently stroke her side. As I walk away, I hear him say, "Good girl, Crow. You're the best dog I've ever seen."

Mink lifts a hand when he sees me coming, and calls, "You must be freezing. I'll heat up the pine-needle tea and fish stew."

"Thanks, I am."

The hide bags of stew and tea hang suspended from tripods at the edges of the flames. Mink pulls two sticks from the pile of driftwood and uses them to pick up a glowing rock about the size of a fist, then he drops the stone into the stew bag. Steam explodes as it brings the stew to a boil. He does the same thing with the tea bag.

Sitting down cross-legged between Mink and Basher, I shiver in the fire's wonderful warmth. The boiling fish stew smells good.

Mink waits until the bags stop boiling, then dips wooden cups into the bags to fill them. As he sets the stew cup on the ground in front of me, he hands me the cup of tea. "Anything unusual to report?"

I cradle the hot tea cup in my hands. Oddly, the zyme giants that ride the waves suddenly lean toward me, as though curious about what I will say. The sky behind them ripples a deep green. "Heard a wail riding the wind down from the north."

Mink frowns. "Wolves?"

"Maybe. Sounded strange, though, like an eerie melody of yips and shrieks. I thought maybe a crack had opened in the ice to the north and the voices of the magical animals hidden by the Jemen were seeping up. You know, falcons and foxes crying out from the cages where they're locked deep in the earth."

Basher chuckles. He has the hood of his elk-hide coat up, and the sea breeze waffles it around his pockmarked face. "Magical voices? See, Mink? We're all spooked tonight."

"You two are spooked? Why? See something?"

"No." Basher leans toward me to whisper, "Mink told the

story of the old man at the wedding camp. Heard he called you 'darling.' We were conjuring what that might mean. Probably something like 'ugly girl with the bug eyes.'"

I blow on my tea and take a sip, before I answer, "Maybe, but it sounded strangely affectionate, so maybe it was 'ugly girl with the bug eyes that I adore.'"

Basher laughs out loud. "Or maybe, 'ugly girl with the bug eyes that I piss on.'"

We both laugh, and Mink gives us a disgruntled look. "I'm not sure the old man is something to take so lightly. Hoodwink thought he was Nightbreaker in human disguise, and that's the only thing that makes sense of Bluejay's story about the old man vanishing and leaving lion tracks behind."

My smile fades. I finish half my tea, then set it aside and reach for my stew cup. Taking a bite of fish stew, I chew, and say, "I'm not sure about that, Mink. I suspect Bluejay was in a hurry to follow you down the hill, and took his eyes off the old man for too long."

"You think he lied about only finding lion tracks? Doesn't sound like Bluejay."

Basher's gaze is going back and forth between us as he quietly listens to the details of the story. "I agree with Quiller. Bluejay was distraught from grief and missed the subtle signs of boot tracks amid the lion tracks, he just didn't want to admit it."

Mink's bushy black brows draw together over his broad nose. "The night of the council meeting, before we walked down to get the elders, Bluejay told me the old man laughed before he vanished—as though he was making sport of him because he was about to turn into Nightbreaker and trot off."

Basher makes a deep-throated sound of disgust. "Nonsense. You can't actually believe that."

I eat my stew for a time. I don't believe it, either, but a haunted sensation is creeping through me. He was a strange old man.

Mink's eyes seem to be fastened to the flickering campfire. He doesn't speak for a long time. When he does, his voice is sad. "No, I don't believe it, but I've been thinking a lot about this, and it's the only thing that makes sense. If Hoodwink is right that Nightbreaker is one of the Jemen and can transform himself into a human, then it explains how he could disappear before Bluejay's eyes, and it explains why Nightbreaker did not kill my brother at the wedding camp."

Basher says, "It also means the old lion could walk right into our villages, and we'd let him. Then in the middle of the night, he could turn back into a lion and rip out our throats. Why hasn't that happened?"

Using my fingers, I pull out a chunk of fish and eat it while I study the expressions on the men's faces. Both look puzzled.

Around a mouthful of half-chewed fish, I say, "Basher's right. We see Nightbreaker often; he trots along the shore following our boats and roaring at us as though trying to make us stop. But we've never seen the old man before."

Mink goes quiet, and I wonder if his thoughts have turned to Lynx and he's remembering precious times with his little brother. As I am.

When Mink finally looks over at me, I give him a small smile. Between us are so many memories of Lynx's sunny childhood, all the happy moments we three so unthinkingly shared, and beyond those moments, the fear that the young man we both love might even now be lying dead and frozen in the depths of a glacier. As I stare into Mink's hollow eyes, the beauty of the glittering night fades, and I find myself filled with the sad sweetness of things lost and never to be found again.

The monstrous green pillars riding the waves sway and brush against one another, producing clicks and shishes that resemble the almost-human voices that filled the world before the zyme. Our oldest stories tell of a time when the Old Woman of the Mountain killed all human languages and replaced them with pings and clicks. Human voices did not return until she and the Jemen created the Sealion People, and after them the Rust People and the Dog Soldiers.

"Nothing turned out the way we thought it was going to, did it, Quiller?"

"No," I sigh.

"What made you think it would?" Basher asks. "The Jemen have no obligation to give you what you want. You take what you get and are grateful you're still alive to enjoy what little you have left."

"Frozen way of seeing things," I say.

"Life has never given me what I wanted." Since his wife and children were killed by Rust People, Basher has become the village cynic. "How about you, Mink?"

Mink blinks as though coming back from some great distance. "I have a wife and two sons that I love with all my heart. That's more than I ever thought I'd have. I'm thankful. And . . . I think my little brother is alive."

Basher twists his tea cup in his hands. "He may be. Lynx is a curious sort—and I mean no offense," Basher rushes to add. "Just that I can't figure him. One instant he seems like a born shaman and the next he's the biggest coward in the history of the Sealion—"

"Careful," I warn, and reach for the club tied to my belt. "I'm just about to smack you in the head."

"You know it as well as I do, Quiller. Even when he was a child, Lynx preferred to sit at Hoodwink's feet listening to legends about the world before the zyme than go play war with the other boys. The idea of battle scared him senseless." Basher extends a hand to me. "Whereas you were always out stabbing somebody with your toy spear. Still have the scar in my thigh from when you were eight and sneaked up on me—"

"If you hadn't fallen asleep on guard duty, I wouldn't have had the chance to spear you."

Basher chuckles. "Even then, I swear, you moved as silent as a hawk's shadow. A born hunter and warrior, that's what you are. There was never a shred of cowardice in you, Quiller."

Fortunately, Basher does not know me as well as I do.

Mink says, "Lynx was very brave until that bad fever came over him when he was four. I swear the fever stole part of his soul. After that, he—"

"Quiet." Basher stands up and looks toward RabbitEar. "Is he signaling us?"

I twist around to follow his gaze.

In the reflections cast by the ice cliff, RabbitEar resembles a flickering apparition, his arm extended, pointing northward.

Mink walks away from the fire, and Basher and I leap to our feet to follow him out into the green-tinted night beyond the firelight.

Listening, Mink asks, "Hear that?"

"That's the wailing I told you about."

Basher says, "Sounds like wolves to me. I don't—"

"It's not wolves." Mink's voice is low and filled with dread. "It's screams. Human screams."

"If it is, it's Rust People," I say with a pang.

Mink nods. "Pack up camp. Let's go see how many there are."

11

LYNX

On the morning of the fifth day, Kinglet's distinctive steps wake me. I drag myself up from where I've slumped against the tree in the night. Every day at sunset they shove me down by a tree, pull my arms back, and tie my hands together behind the tree trunk. When I wake in the morning, my arms feel like dead meat.

It's the way of our people. Children heading out on their first spirit quests are treated exactly as I am being treated . . . blindfolded, hauled to the middle of nowhere, and abandoned. Very few die. There are always guards, just out of sight, watching over them while they wander in search of their spirit helpers.

But I will have no guards. I will be alone for the first time in my life.

Sunlight penetrates around the edges of my blindfold. At the very bottom, I see the toes of Kinglet's leather boots and the bed of old needles that covers the ground. The air is alive with the sweet tang of pines and the pained bellows of the Ice Giants. Are they fighting some distant war, or mourning the loss of a loved one? Strange that I could think those sound the same.

"I brought food, Lynx."

"Thank you. I'm hungry."

Kinglet crouches beside me. "Open your mouth."

As he feeds me spoonfuls of caribou stew, I hear the other

men moving through camp, kicking snow over flames. A low hum of conversation carries.

"Now, listen," Kinglet says. "It'll take courage for you to survive the next few days, but if you manage to come home, people will know you are the favored of the Jemen. You will become a great man. Hoodwink says so, and I'm convinced of it."

I chew my stew to keep my teeth from chattering.

"When you've finished eating, I'll untie you. It'll take a while before feeling returns to your arms and you can take off your blindfold. By that time, we'll be gone. Don't try to track us. If you do, it will mean you have disobeyed the orders of the council. I'll have to kill you if I see you on my back trail."

"I won't follow you, Kinglet."

"Good, I don't want to have to kill you. Mink is my friend."

The deputy feeds me one final bite and sets the wooden bowl on the ground. "Big predators are right behind us, Lynx. We've been avoiding them for days. You're going to have to make a run for it. Understand? Once you get your blindfold off, don't just stand here. Get on your feet and start running."

"Th-thank you for telling me."

As he rises, Kinglet's feet scuff the pine needles. "If you're smart, you'll head due south. Do you know which way is south?"

"I—I don't know. I get lost all the time. I'm not very good at directions."

"Well, get ready. I'm cutting your bonds."

Kinglet walks behind me and uses his sharpened bone knife to saw through the ropes around my wrists. Thuds sound when my hands hit the ground, but I can't feel them.

"You're on your own. Don't panic, or I guarantee you will die."

I hear leather boots pounding away across the ice. Shouts echo, then slowly vanish, as Kinglet leads his men farther and farther down the slope. In moments, their voices are gone, and only the forlorn whimpers of Wind Mother surround me.

I still can't move my arms, but I can bend forward and use the toe of my boot to shove up the blindfold.

Blessed Jemen . . .

Vast blue ice rolls on forever, ruptured and split as though wrenched apart by the mighty hands of the gods themselves, and from each fissure, cries eddy upward into the cold morning air. The oldest Ice Giants speak in deep-throated roars, but the whimpers of hungry infants thread their conversations. The entire mountain is alive with unearthly voices. Beneath them all, I hear the faint voice of a woman singing. A strange song, like the musical patter of rain on water, mixed with wind soughing through invisible branches. But I know it's a woman, and it occurs to me that perhaps I'm hearing the voice of the Old Woman of the Mountain, who ordered the Jemen to leave this world and sail to the stars in their meteorite ships. Is she speaking to me?

I search the landscape. I see no one, and I don't recognize anything. Are these the Crushing Mountains? I've only seen them from a distance. The black peaks would orient me and tell me which way is home. Here and there boulders and stunted trees grow in dirt-filled hollows, but they are tiny islands in this vast, broken sea of blue ice. Suddenly, the pines sway above me, as though trying to get my attention, to warn me to run.

Fear starts to gobble up my insides. I have to force myself to think or I'm going to die right here.

"That way has got to be south," I whisper aloud, "but the only thing south is ice. Did Kinglet lie to me? Did the elders tell him to? Is it part of my spirit quest?"

Finally, the pain in my arms and hands becomes excruciating. I stumble to my feet and swing my arms, trying to get blood into them faster. My pack and spear rest behind the tree. When I can, I shrug my pack on over my coat and pick up my spear.

Then I study the yawning wasteland.

For the first time in my life, there's no one to tell me what to do, and I desperately wish there was. I can go anywhere I want to, when I want to. It's overwhelming. Despite what the elders ordered, I don't have to find old Nightbreaker if I don't want to. As soon as I think it, the Ice Giants laugh at me. Their amusement quakes through the heart of the world, shaking the ground beneath my feet.

But there's another sound, too . . .

Claws on ice. Clicking and squealing.

The hair on the nape of my neck stands on end. Above the crest of the hill, frozen puffs of breath rise and drift through the sunlit air.

Bears.

More than one.

12

QUILLER

Evening has just fallen and Sister Sky's dance is vivid tonight, blazing across the sky in ripples of green and bright purple.

"Be careful!" Mink calls. "There's a sheen of water on the ice floes!"

Mink leads the way up the filthy ice that extends like a giant finger into the ocean. Full of gravel and boulders, and cross-hatched with dead trees that have been pushed down out of the mountains, the floe is treacherous.

And the ocean is beautiful . . . not even a hint of green.

It's a strange sight. The streams pouring into the ocean from the mountains have driven the zyme far away, leaving an almost-black expanse of water for as far as I can see. This is the darkest night I've seen in a long while.

"Gods, I hate these floes," I say to RabbitEar, who climbs up to stand beside me.

"We all do, but there's no way around them. Either we climb these frozen hills of debris, or we stop to build a boat and paddle around them."

All last night and all today, we've been scrambling over these fingers of ice. They're not so bad when they're frozen solid, but at the end of the day the surfaces are smooth and wet. It's hard to find footing.

"Well, Mink is not going to stop."

"No, he's not." RabbitEar puts a hand on my shoulder and gives it a tender squeeze. "So let's go. No use complaining."

I struggle up the slope, grabbing any rock or stick we can find to keep moving. Despite the blinding sheen of meltwater in front of us, it's still freezing. We all wear ghostly masks. Our eyelashes, hair, and cheeks are so sheathed with white crystals that our faces are barely recognizable.

Groaning, I grip a chunk of ice and drag myself onto the crest of the debris with my boots furiously slipping behind me. The view from up here is dazzling. Beyond the ice floes, an imposing wall of blue ice rises three or four hundred hands tall. We'll have to trot along the thin strip of sand at the base, mindful that it could calve at any instant and bury us forever.

"You're almost to the top," I call down to RabbitEar.

"Thank the gods."

When I get to my feet, I see Mink and Basher trudging down the other side to the beach to make camp for the night. Mink waves. I wave back.

"Blessed Jemen," RabbitEar says as he climbs onto the crest and rubs ice from his eyelashes so he can look around. "These ice floes are costing us a lot of time."

His hood has fallen back, revealing his frosted hair.

"You look like you've seen about a hundred summers pass," I tease.

"Then I need to knock more ice off my head." Slapping his hair and beard with a mitten, it quickly goes from white to red. "Better?"

"Better."

We smile at each other. The longing in his eyes hits me in the pit of the stomach. I glance away to study the thin strip of sand that runs due north.

"Looks like we'll have a clear path tomorrow morning."

While he surveys the vast open ocean, RabbitEar props his

hands his hips. "I know Mink thought those were human voices we heard, but it's hard to believe screams could carry beyond a dozen small ice floes."

"Might have been wolves. Howls carry much farther than voices."

"Did you think they sounded human?"

"Not really, but from a distance it's hard to distinguish, and you know how voices bounce around ice walls like that one." I extend a hand to the high blue wall. "Screams that hit the wall just right might get funneled for a great distance. But I agree with you. I think it was wolves."

The lines around his eyes crinkle and an awkward silence falls between us.

"Quiller . . ." he says as he bows his head and exhales hard. "I'm sorry that all this happened to you."

"It's nobody's fault, RabbitEar. Council decided he had to go on a spirit quest. None of us could stop it."

He looks up and reflections from Sister Sky's dance bounce off the ocean and cliff and fall irregularly over his face, like diamond-shaped puzzle pieces.

"I know, but I wish you didn't have to go through this. You've been through so much in the past few moons."

"We all have, but thanks. I appreciate that."

When the air rumbles, we both look at the dark ocean, holding our breaths. Is it the low calls of the Ice Giants? Or is there a rusty armada passing by out there just over the horizon? Sounds like . . . motors. Faint voices. Gods, is it . . .

Then in the far distance to the west, where Wind Mother has piled clouds, lightning flashes, and we both exhale in relief.

"Just thunder," I say.

"Must be." But he sounds uncertain.

His lips press tightly together, as though he wants to discuss something else but isn't sure it's the right time, so he clumsily gestures to Mink and Basher. Basher already has a fire going, and Mink is collecting driftwood for our nightly camp.

"Quiller, could we talk? I need to say—"

"They're waiting for us, RabbitEar." I cut him off, afraid to hear what he wants to say, and he blinks and nods.

For a time, he seems to be holding his breath, then he softly answers, "Yes, they are."

Side by side, we start down the slope.

13

LYNX

Splashing through rivulets of water, I continue running up the glacier, hoping I can outdistance the bears strung out like black beads in the darkness behind me.

They are so patient, just following along, sniffing out my tracks. When the warm breath leaves their muzzles, it freezes into moonlit clouds and drifts across their backs, riming their bristly fur with white. They glitter as they lope along. Occasionally, they roar and break into a gallop. That's when panic takes over, and I charge mindlessly ahead. My strength is almost gone.

If I crawl beneath an ice shelf, or down into a crevasse, how long will it be before the hungry bears dig me out, or decide to scramble down into the crevasse after me?

Suddenly, I long for home so badly that I can barely breathe. Where's Quiller? Together we could survive. Tears blur my eyes.

Move. Move!

My leather boots keep slipping off the wet ice and rocks. I fall several times, but drag myself to my feet and keep going.

Ahead, a huge pile of boulders stands with three pines growing out of the center. I run for it. It's not a refuge. It's a trap, and I know it. Bears are expert tree climbers, but it's my only hope.

Just before I get there, I stumble, and almost fall on top of the dead man curled up on the ground in the darkness. He's hunched into a frozen ball . . . and he wears silver clothing.

Oh, my gods, the Rust People are here! Where did he come from?

The body hasn't been chewed up, which means he hasn't been here for long. Was he part of a hunting party? A war party? He looks young, but I don't have time to stand around and ponder.

Stuffing my spear through my belt at my back, I leap for the lowest tree limb, catch it, and swing up into the moonlit pine. Carrying the spear this way is awkward, for it's as long as I am tall. As I climb upward, it catches on the branches and throws me off balance. But I keep climbing to where the limbs are thin and frail, strong enough to hold my weight, but hopefully not the weight of a bear.

While I wait for the giant predators to arrive, I hang my pack on a limb, and pull my spear from my belt.

The vast wasteland of the Ice Giants spreads for as far as I can see in every direction. Their stark blue-white bodies are desolation itself, torn by chasms and striped with dark bands of gravel and boulders. I can feel them laughing at me, shaking my body with invisible hands that will not let go.

"Please, please," I say, "just let me make it through the night."

Soon, whether I want to or not, I'm going to fall asleep. I'm so exhausted I won't be able to stop it. That's when the bears will come after me . . . and Siskin will come, as she does every night, to tell me she hates me.

Weeping, I wipe my nose on my sleeve and reach for my pack. As I pull out a length of braided leather rope, I see the bears lumbering up the ice toward me. The cubs are so happy, roaring playfully and loping ahead of their mother. They've treed me. Now the fun begins. For them.

I use the rope to securely tie myself to the pine. I don't want to fall out when sleep finally overwhelms me. At last, I reach for a bag of dried fish.

While I gobble down handfuls of the flaky meat, I watch the cubs and think about my life, about how I got to this forsaken place.

After our parents were murdered three summers ago, Mink—sixteen at the time—did the best job he could to raise me, to teach me the things our father would have taught me, but Mink's main responsibility had been as a deputy War Leader. It was his duty to take care of his people first, and his family second. And with an infant in her arms, and another one on the way, Gray Dove needed Mink's help far more than I did.

Which left me alone and so sad I was exhausted all the time. It wasn't easy. At the age of thirteen summers, I was struggling with the other boys in the village, trying to win my place in the hierarchy and losing fistfights almost every day. The fights had infuriated Mink—not because I'd gotten into fights, but because I never won. And especially because Quiller had to drive the boys away from me. Mink trained me harder—spear lessons, club lessons, knife lessons, how to throw a punch. Didn't matter. The look in a person's eyes, or an animal's eyes, when I struck him with a club or pierced him with a spear shook me to the bone. I just couldn't do it.

Then two summers ago, the Rust People attacked in the middle of the night, and Mink ordered me to grab my spear and follow him outside to defend Sky Ice Village. The chaos, flying spears, lightning flashes, war cries, and screams of agony stunned my soul. At one point, I was standing in the midst of the battle, getting ready to cast my spear at a Rust warrior, when the man charged straight at me, roaring like an enraged bull bison. I lifted my spear to kill him, and I ran away. I could hear Mink yelling at me to stand and fight, but I kept running.

My people forgave me for that incident. After all, it was my first War Walk. But the second time . . .

Paws grate on gravel, and spouts of frosty breath rise into the moonlight as the bears leisurely follow my trail to the base of the pine, and look up. They could be a trio of frosty white boulders if not for their shining eyes. My only hope is to stay out of their reach. If I can keep them busy long enough for them to get really hungry, they'll leave and go find food elsewhere.

But before they do, one or more of the bears will climb the tree and try to drag me out of the branches.

I have to stay awake.

14

QUILLER

We stand in a line on the crest of the final ice floe, over-looking the decimated Rust People village. Mink and Basher are utterly quiet. RabbitEar's breathing is coming in gasps.

As Sister Moon edges higher into the sky, the waves glimmer from the towering cliff and cast reflections over the dead bodies, shredded silver lodges, and bare lodge poles that stand upon the beach. It has a strange effect, for the poles appear to be alive and walking in an eerie skeletal theater.

"What happened here?" RabbitEar asks.

"Something terrible." I scan the carnage.

The night air smells of sea salt and blood, mixed with the pungency of zyme.

Gripping his spear, Mink says, "Be vigilant. See anything alive?"

"No."

"Not a thing."

"Well, keep your guards up. Could be fifty Rust warriors hiding out there in the darkness."

Mink leads the way down the slope and into the village, barely glances at the dead women and children that line our path, and moves on.

I, however, cannot help but stop to stare at an old woman

who sprawls on her back, staring sightlessly up at the night sky. She made it to the ice floe before she was dragged down and torn apart. The shape of her face fascinates me. Rust People have bigger skulls and much heavier brow ridges than Sealion People do. The woman's belly has been clawed open, the internal organs eaten, but the clan symbols painted on her strange pearlescent clothing are unmistakable.

"Red Lion clan."

"Yes," RabbitEar calls from the beach off to my left. "This boy has the same designs on his shirt. Must be an entire village of Red Lion kin."

"No," I say, and shake my head. "I saw another design. Looked like white waves."

Basher says, "I did, too. So more than one clan camped here."

Six boats float just offshore. Ropes tether them to stakes on the beach. When the tide comes in, the stakes will be pulled loose and the triangular crafts carried out to sea, where they will become a feast for the zyme. Zyme loves iron. Crush a meteorite and toss it into the ocean and the zyme will grow and grow until it covers the world, just as it does in our legends.

I walk toward the boats. Unlike the Sealion People, who build circular, open-topped boats from mammoth hides, the Rust People sail ancient metal boats filled with gaping holes where the iron has rusted through. The motors in the rear run on oil created from zyme. Don't know how they do it, but I've heard that it's difficult to produce enough to keep them running, so usually, during the day, the Rust People hoist big sheets of silver skins and turn them into glittering sails. At night, they rarely camp on shore. Instead, they pull the silver skins over the tops of the boats, effectively turning them into lodges. Small entry holes are left in the front and rear, probably to keep watch.

Mink says, "Let's split up and search for survivors. Quiller, go north. Basher, start on the west side. RabbitEar, take the east."

I trot for the northern edge of the dead village.

Wandering through the lodges is a haunting experience. The lodge covers feel slippery and whine when I run my fingernails down them. I don't know what sort of hide these are made from. An odd fish skin? Dead dogs lie everywhere, as though they bravely fought to the last to protect their human families. Crow seems fascinated by the dogs. She spends several moments at each carcass, smelling them, pawing at them, as though trying to wake them up. The air reeks of lion urine. This was a large village, maybe ninety to one hundred people. They must have had a least a dozen guards posted. How could a pride of lions surprise and defeat a village this size?

RabbitEar walks up behind me. "Looks like the lions did us a favor."

"Yes." I kick at a dropped spear. "Hard to feel sorry for them. If these Rust People had lived, tomorrow or the next day, they would have climbed into their boats and continued south. When they found our village, they would have slaughtered every man, woman, and child."

The lines at the corners of his eyes deepen. He seems to be thinking hard about something. He suddenly turns and looks around the village. "How many dead young men have you counted? I've seen barely a handful."

Dread tightens my chest. "The warriors probably chased the lions out into the darkness. Could still be hunting down the pride. That's why we haven't found more bodies."

"I pray you're right."

"Me, too."

Walking through the village together, we focus on counting the bodies of young men. Some of the young women may have been warriors, but the young men certainly were.

RabbitEar turns to scan the ocean. "There are six boats floating out there. They must have had more than that. Maybe a lot more."

"You think their warriors took a few boats and headed south?"

Nervously, he licks his lips. "I would guess that those six boats could carry fifty people, maybe sixty."

My stomach muscles knot. "Just three boats filled with ten warriors each would be enough to slaughter Sky Ice Village."

RabbitEar shifts to prop his spear over his shoulder. "And where are all the survivors? There are always survivors. I only count around forty-seven bodies."

"Lions probably dragged off some of the dead. A few people might have escaped and fled toward the Ice Giant Mountains."

"Yes, but . . ."

Mink whistles like a kestrel to signal us to gather around him. We trot forward.

When Basher stops beside Mink, he says, "I don't care what the elders say. We can't spend the winter in this country. It's too dangerous. The Rust People are right behind us and these huge predators—"

"This shouldn't have happened," Mink says.

"What do you mean?"

"They must have posted guards. How could they have been surprised by such a large pride?"

A child hiccups, and we all turn, searching for the source of the sound.

"Where'd that come from?" Mink asks in a low voice.

The sound is quickly smothered, as though someone clamped a hand over the child's mouth. My gaze moves to the boats floating out upon the jostling waves.

"Out there. The boat on the far right."

"Sure?"

"Pretty sure."

Propping the butt of my spear on the ground, I lean on it while I squint at the narrow opening in the silver skin that hoods the boat. "Could be ten people inside. There are four of us. What do you want to do, Mink?"

Mink grinds his teeth before saying, "It's riding high on the waves, so high I would have guessed it was empty."

"Must be at least two people in there, the child and the person who smothered its cries."

Mink nods. "I say we grab the tether, pull the boat in, and take care of this quickly."

"I agree." Basher lifts his spear. Hatred already twists his face.

Mink gestures to us, indicating where he wants each of us to go stand, then he says, "I'll pull the boat in while you get into position. Be ready for anything."

Mink jogs over to the stake on the beach, pulls it loose, and grabs the tether, then he waits for us to get into position. RabbitEar and I move to the left, while Basher takes the right. We all have our spears up, ready to cast.

As I examine the boat, I can't believe it floats. The hull is peppered with tiny see-through holes where rust has eaten through the metal, and all along the gunwale, there are holes the size of my fist. Looks like they patch the small holes with boiled pine pitch, but the big holes are just gaping wounds. How do they keep water out? Do they bale constantly?

When Mink starts hauling the triangular boat toward the beach, cries and breathless sobs erupt.

"Three or four children," I say.

"Don't be fooled. Could still be warriors in there." Rabbit-Ear lifts his spear higher.

Hand over hand, Mink drags the boat in until it rolls up on the beach on the next wave, then we rush the bow, ready to spear the first thing that ducks out the entry.

There's movement, a shadow inside. In that strange clipped accent of Rust People, a boy calls, "Please! We are only children. We 'ave no weapons!" His small blond head appears in the entry.

I lift a hand to the rest of the party, asking them to hold their casts so I can get a good look at the boy. "Come out!" I order.

"Please, don't kill us! I've only seen ten summers, and I'm the oldest. We will do anythin' you tell us to!"

When the boy bravely steps out of the entry onto the deck, the heads of three other children, all girls, appear behind him. Tears streak every face. They're terrified and shaking. In the gleam cast by the zyme, their blond hair shimmers with green fire.

"Let's slaughter them," Basher calls. "Mink, why are we holding our casts?"

"Wait." I leap up onto the deck and shove the boy aside so I can pull the girls through the silver skin and out onto the deck, then I throw the skin back and look inside the boat. It's filled with pea-green blankets, which the Rust People weave from the fresh zyme. A lump of rust catches my eye. It's one of the magical iron amulets worn by the Dog Soldiers. Palm-sized and heavy, I stuff it into my pocket to examine later.

"No one else," I yell.

"Good. Get out of my way!" Basher rushes forward to spear the children.

The words that come out of my mouth surprise me: "I claim these children as my property. I found them."

Basher stands for a moment, blinking in disbelief, then shouts, "Get out of my way, Quiller. Rust People killed my wife and children last summer!"

Shoving the boy behind me with the other children, I say,

"As the warrior who found them, it's my right to take these children as my property."

"Move!"

"Basher, wait," RabbitEar says, then turns to me. His red hair is blowing wildly in the wind. "Quiller, think about this. What are you going to do with four children on the run home? They'll never be able to keep up. We'll end up killing them anyway."

"They will be my responsibility alone. None of you will have to do anything."

Mink heaves a disgruntled sigh. "Lower your spears."

"No, Mink!" Basher cries.

"Lower your spears." Mink's voice has a lethal edge, one Basher knows. "It is her warrior's right to take the property of her enemy. She claimed them. They belong to her."

"You can't mean it! If the situation was reversed, and these were Sealion children, the Rust People would drag them over and bash their brains out with rocks! They don't even consider us human!"

"Nonetheless," Mink orders. "Move back. They belong to Quiller now."

Basher growls something incomprehensible, lowers his spear, and stamps a short distance away.

Annoyed, Mink rubs his heavy brow ridge. "But RabbitEar is right, Quiller. We can't run with children. That means it's going to take us an extra day to get home. And what if Rust People come for those children or lions attack us on the way home? One or more of us might die because you're trying to protect a bunch of slaves."

RabbitEar says, "I'll help her carry the children. That way we won't fall too far behind."

I give him a curious look, but he doesn't seem to notice.

"Fools!" Basher snarls the word. "We should kill every last Rust child we can find. That way they won't grow into warriors that want to kill us."

"Listen to me!" I say. "We just lost one woman and three men at the wedding camp. The Sealion People are dwindling to nothing. We need to adopt these children into our families. The new blood will help us survive."

"Rust People blood!" Basher spits on the sand. "It's already polluted our people! That's why we are growing weaker and weaker!"

Jumping off the deck onto the sand, I lift the children down one by one. The three girls look to be between the ages of three and eight. "Do exactly as I say or I'll spear you myself. You understand?"

The boy nods. "Yes, warrior. We will."

Mink aims a finger at me. "As of now, you say when they live or die. Don't make me regret this, Quiller."

"I won't, Mink."

Basher marches over to Mink and gives him a threatening glare. "Let her keep the boy, but every girl we kill is one less female to breed."

Mink leans toward him until they are eye to eye. "If you don't take a step backward, you're going to find my spear in your guts."

"Mink's right, Basher." RabbitEar leaps between them and shoves them apart. "Taking the property of her enemy is her right as a warrior. That has been the way of the Sealion People since before the zyme, and you know it. You've done it plenty of times yourself."

"To work as slaves! Not to adopt them into my clan."

Basher glowers malevolently at RabbitEar, but tramps away.

The little boy watches as though he knows his life depends upon the outcome of this battle of wills.

I put a hand on the boy's shoulder. "What is your name, child?"

"Jawbone." His silver clothing glitters in the reflections cast by the cliff.

"What is your clan?"

"We are of the White Foam clan of Great Horned Owl Village."

"You the children's leader?"

"Yes, I . . . I am. My grandfather left me in charge when he forced us into the boat and shoved it out to sea. I'm the oldest. I didn't want to go into the boat. I wanted to fight, but he wouldn't let me." He weeps the last words.

"Your grandfather was a wise man," I say to the boy. "Only reason you four are alive is because the lions didn't want to swim out into the waves to hunt you."

"Are you positive my family is dead? They could be hidin'. And maybe they got away."

"We found no one alive. Want to hunt for their bodies yourself? I will grant you that right, if you can do it quickly."

"Yes, warrior, thank you."

Jawbone sprints toward a lodge on the eastern side just beneath the ice cliff, probably his home, scrambles through the ruined interior, then ducks out and begins searching the corpses that scatter the ground. Green glimmers and white flashes sheath his young face as he trots from one to the next.

The oldest girl calls, "Jawbone? Please look for our parents and brother?"

"I'm goin' to look for everyone's family. I 'aven't found yours yet, Little Fawn."

The girl tries to hold back tears, while the toddler keeps asking, "Sister, where's Mother? Where's Father?"

"I don't know, Chickadee. We have to wait for Jawbone to search."

In a weak voice, the little girl sobs, "All right."

The other girl, maybe four, keeps hiccuping.

"What's your name, girl?"

"L-Loon."

Jawbone, Little Fawn, Chickadee, and Loon.

The girls huddle closer and closer together. After all, they have only each other now. Unless, of course, survivors escaped into the icy wilderness and will soon return to search for these children. Mink was right to worry about that. I can't help but scan the rim of the ice cliff, expecting to see people with weapons silhouetted against the campfires of the dead.

Out in the village, Jawbone starts crying. "I found our families . . . most of them."

The girls go as quiet as baby rabbits hiding in the brush. Strange behavior for children. I examine their faces, wondering about that. Maybe they are in shock.

I call, "All right, Jawbone, let's go."

He trots back with an agonized expression. "May I tell my friends about their families?"

"Of course."

Jawbone wipes his eyes on his sleeve. "I'm sorry. Our parents are all dead. Lions killed them."

Mink's eyes narrow to slits. "Did you find your grandfather?"

"No."

There's a strange heaviness in the air, as though the weight of the world is about to crash down on us.

Mink orders, "Quiller and RabbitEar, take the lead with the children. I'll cover the rear. We have to get out of here now."

I reach down to pick up the toddler, Chickadee, and prop her on my left hip. I can still carry my spear in my right hand. "Hold on to me, Chickadee."

The girl wraps her tiny arms around my chest in a death hug and quietly sobs.

In her ear, I say, "Shh. Don't cry. You belong to me now. I'm not going to let anyone hurt you."

RabbitEar lifts Loon into his arms. "Move, Quiller. Don't give Basher any excuses."

———

From high up on the colossal ice wall, he props his walking stick and watches, curious about this apparent act of kindness for an enemy's children. It's probably utilitarian, just acquiring property, but perhaps . . . perhaps, it's empathy. That would be a rare and precious development.

Steeling himself, he turns away. He must move on. If he lingers, it will spawn hope, and hope debilitates. Hope kills objectivity. Hope is the death of the earth.

15

LYNX

When the tree shakes, I jerk awake. I've no idea how long I've been asleep. Maybe only moments.

The cub, a young boar, climbs through the branches, pausing often to snuffle at the places my boots touched the moonlit bark. As the cub climbs higher, the pine sways and creaks. His muzzle is bloody, which means he's fed on something.

Far below, I see the sow and other cub ripping apart the corpse in the silver clothing. The sow has her teeth embedded in one shoulder while the cub has a leg. With considerable effort, they tear the frozen corpse apart and start dragging it around, shaking it. Bones crack.

Leaning back against the tree, I try to catch my breath.

I've never seen darkness like this. I had no idea that far inland there was no zyme glow. The Road of Light blazes across a blue-black sky spotted with the campfires of the dead.

Rising and falling through the valleys, the moans of the Ice Giants sound terrifying and beautiful, not quite of this world. Gods, my eyes are heavy. Sleep keeps sneaking up on me, coming at me from behind.

As my eyes fall closed . . .

The rabbit shoots past me, skittering over the ice and down along the shoreline. In a handful of moments, the other village children are way ahead of me in hot pursuit, their short legs pumping after the rabbit, their small spears up and ready to cast. The rabbit speeds over the sand and leaps onto an ice shelf where it runs flat out. I chase after the children, trying to catch up.

My blood sings with the joy of the hunt. It's an instinct so old it knows nothing of villages, or fires, or the petty concerns of humans. I might be a wolf, leaping at the head of the yelping pack, running down warm food with my heart bursting in ecstasy. Every detail is crystalline—the glittering ice, the excited cries of the children, the rabbit flashing forward like some slip of foxfire. Through a quirk of fate, I'm the one who accidentally traps the rabbit beneath an ice shelf. When the moment comes to cast my spear, I peer into the terrified rabbit's eyes and burst into tears.

The other children hound me back to the village, calling me names. Except for Quiller, who has her arm around me, holding me while I cry . . .

The pine wobbles and I gasp awake.

The boar cub has climbed to within three limbs of me. Panic sears my veins. Even at a few moons old, short-faced bears have gigantic heads, twice as wide as mine and three times as long. When the wind blows, moonlight flickers over the cub's frosty back. He sniffs the wind, scenting me, as though trying to identify exactly what sort of creature he's hunting.

I grip my spear hard. "Don't make me hurt you, little bear!"

The cub pants out a white cloud, and I smell his musty breath, like old blood and half-rotted meat.

"Brother, please go feed on that corpse with your mother and sister."

The bear scampers up another branch.

As the limbs progressively get smaller, the cub has a harder and harder time balancing. Nonetheless, he chances taking a swipe at me with his big paw.

Instinctively, I cry out and spear it.

Yipping in pain, the cub shakes his wounded paw, then earnestly takes another swipe. I scramble to pull my feet higher.

"Go eat the corpse, or I'll spear you again!"

He seems to understand. Hunching on the limb, licking his hurt paw, he watches his mother sink her teeth into the corpse's skull and tear it from the neck. As she crushes it, the female cub sneaks in, steals a chunk of brain, and happily trots away with it.

"See what you're missing? Go away!"

Surely by now Quiller has escaped the scouting party and is on her way to find me. Or maybe Mink had a change of heart and is patiently working out my trail. Maybe they are together, coming to find me.

How foolish I am. The truth is right there three limbs below me. I'm not going to make it through this.

16

QUILLER

As I wrap a hide around Jawbone's shoulders, I say, "It's my watch, so I need to go relieve RabbitEar. Call out if you see anything, all right?"

"Yes, Quiller, I will," Jawbone says where he huddles by the small beach fire, surrounded by sleeping girls. His blond hair is golden in the firelight. I stroke his hair, and he leans into my hand, as though desperate for the comfort I offer. I've never touched the hair of a living Rust person. It's fine and silky, like a weasel's coat.

Mink sleeps on the other side of the fire, while Basher crouches out by the surf, maybe thinking about his lost family, maybe remembering old battles. He's spoken to no one, and I hurt for him. After the battle where his family was killed, I helped Basher search for his wife and sons. For weeks after we found their bodies, his eyes had an agonized gleam. Since then, he's filled that empty space in his heart with hatred for Rust People.

I say, "RabbitEar will be back soon."

Jawbone pulls his hide more tightly about his shoulders. "All right."

As I walk away with my spear, I keep glancing back over my shoulder. These children are strange. They're too quiet and bizarrely obedient. I'm sure they are still in shock over what happened to their village, but normal children would be weeping all the time and asking questions about their other relatives. They must have aunts and uncles in another Rust People village, yet they haven't asked me once if they can go live with them. I don't understand this behavior. Sealion children would be pleading to go back to their own people.

RabbitEar sits atop a low pile of boulders overlooking the ocean. He has his hood up, but his red beard is frosted with ice. The cliff at his back stands four hundred hands tall, too tall for anyone with a spear to cast accurately from the rim—though RabbitEar routinely glances up, just in case someone decides to try.

I softly say, "My watch. Go and get some rest."

"Who's guarding the children?"

"Jawbone. Mink is asleep."

His bushy red brows lift. "What if Jawbone steals a spear and drives it through Mink's heart?"

"Don't think we have to worry about that."

"Really? Why not?"

I sit on the rock beside him. "These are peculiar children, RabbitEar. It's as though they've practiced being captives. They are so obedient, it's unnatural. You think the Rust elders teach them how to behave if they are captured?"

"Possibly. Warriors are quick to club any child that slows them down. Obedient children survive. Disobedient children don't."

RabbitEar has a commanding presence. Mostly it's his penetrating gaze, but his deep voice adds to the effect. I've never been quite sure what to make of him, though I've always been attracted to him. For the few short moons that he courted me, I found him to be a gentle lover, and a brutally honest man.

The reflections bouncing off the ice wall give RabbitEar's bearded face a fractured look.

I say, "Maybe we ought to teach our children how to surrender to enemy warriors?"

He shakes his head. "No. When I have sons and daughters, I want them to find every opportunity to escape and run when they have the chance. No matter how old they are."

"Even if it means they are more likely to be killed?"

He takes his spear, which has been resting across his lap, and places it at his side, pointed away from me. It must have bothered him that it was aimed at me. "We are a civilized people, Quiller. The Rust People know there is a good chance we will let their children live. When they capture our children, however, they either work them to death or slit their throats on the spot. I want my children to fight to escape every step of the way."

When I exhale, my breath turns into a white cloud that whips away in the sea breeze. "Tell me the truth. Why didn't you object more when I wanted to keep the children?"

His voice is low. "Because I've heard the elders whispering about the birthing problems. Just as you have. They're frightened that soon none of our women will give birth to live babies. I know you're right. These children may save us. I'm sure you plan to allow different clans to adopt them, don't you?"

I don't answer right away. "Haven't decided. I may adopt them all. I love children. Always wanted a dozen."

"Me, too, but it will be difficult for an unmarried warrior woman to have four little children."

"I know, but I may never marry, and so—"

"Of course you will marry. What a silly thing to say. You are a very desirable and accomplished young woman. Every young man worth the name wants you for his wife."

As the surf rolls up the sand, the zyme hisses. Even the thinnest of filaments has a voice, but tonight their whispers are louder, as though the cursed gods that live in the zyme are trying to make some point that we're too stupid to understand.

"Lynx didn't."

RabbitEar pauses for a few moments. In the zyme glow, his green eyes resemble hard jewels. "Can we talk straightly?"

"'Course. You know I value your opinion."

RabbitEar takes a deep breath, giving himself time to figure out the words. "Don't wait for him, Quiller. I know you still love him, but trust me about this. If he didn't choose you the first time, he won't choose you when he has a second chance. He's not worthy of you."

How can he possibly know I'm praying Lynx will come home and ask me to marry him? Is it so obvious? I feel like a huge hand just squeezed my heart.

"Probably irrelevant, RabbitEar. He won't survive alone among the Ice Giants."

RabbitEar reaches out to gently touch my arm. "Don't give up on him. He's stronger than you think."

"No, he's not. He gets tears in his eyes when he has to a spear a fish for dinner."

"Lynx has a holy person's heart, Quiller. All his life, I think he's been trying to be something he's not. He doesn't have a warrior's strength. Like all shamans, I think he walks with one foot in the Land of the Dead."

Streamers of purple thread the darkness above us, and waver upon the achingly white peaks just visible over the top of the ice wall.

"You're right. Lynx does have a holy person's heart." I've spent my whole life trying to shelter that tenderness. "Both of the times that Lynx ran in battle, you and I were standing just a few paces away. I saw the agony on his face. It wasn't cowardice. It was pain. He didn't want to hurt anyone. You must have seen it, as well."

"I did." RabbitEar toys with his spear. "If I ask you something serious, will you promise to tell me the truth?"

"Certainly."

He's choosing his words carefully. I can see it on his face. His eyes are now nothing but shadows hidden beneath the arches of his heavy brows.

"In order to marry, Lynx had to first become a man. Elders gave him the task of killing a bear. When he came rushing back to the village crying that he'd killed a great frost bear, I knew he was lying." He watches my expression closely. "You killed the bear for him, didn't you?"

I don't answer, but he must see the truth.

"Quiller, why did you do that? If he hadn't killed the bear, he would have still been a boy and unable to marry. Might have given him more time to get over Sisk- . . . the woman he thought he loved."

"He did love her, RabbitEar. Very much. She was frail and vulnerable, all the things I'm not."

"So, you killed the bear for him."

The waves have plucked a clump of zyme and washed it up on the sand, where it glimmers like a small patch of sunlit grass.

Frowning, I say, "He couldn't do it. When he found the den and saw the sow with the cubs sleeping around her, it broke his heart. He needed me to help him."

"He let a woman kill a bear for him so he could pretend to be a man." RabbitEar drops his face in his hands and massages his forehead. "Unbelievable. Perhaps being abandoned in the wilderness is just what he needs to grow up."

Angry, I respond, "Seems to me that being a man is useless if you're dead."

He lifts both hands in a gesture of surrender. "Sorry. Didn't mean that the way it sounded. I'm worried about him, too. Do you know that Mink blames himself for Lynx's cowardice?"

"He's not a coward! He's just tenderhearted. He—"

"Not being mean, Quiller. Just saying that after their parents died, Mink was lost for a time. Apparently, Gray Dove was distraught after the birth of their son. Just trying to make her smile took up half of Mink's life. He told me once that he didn't have the time to teach Lynx how to be a real man. If Lynx doesn't come home, Mink will torture himself."

"He shouldn't. It was my fault."

"But he will. Mink saved my life in battle three times. He's more than a friend. I worship Mink. This will break him."

I inhale a deep breath and hold it in my lungs for a time. "If Lynx dies, *I'm* to blame, not Mink."

As though RabbitEar knows something I do not, he turns to gander northward, where the tors of the Crushing Mountains rise like black sentinels over the rim of the wall. It's a three- or four-day run to reach the Boulder River, depending upon the weather, then another day to scale the slopes to reach the rocky peaks.

"You've been up there," I say. "What's it like?"

His eyes narrow as he looks back at me. "From the top, you can see a vast, unending expanse of ice that rolls on forever to the far eastern horizon. It's barren. Frightening. It's the silence that gets you. You can feel it eating your soul."

"I hate silence."

And being alone. Even at night in my dreams, I am haunted by these fears.

RabbitEar goes on, "Trees exist in a few places, but they're few and far between. Trust me when I tell you that beyond the Crushing Mountains, Death walks. At night, it's black dark. So dark you can't see your feet when you walk." He pauses. "I think that's where they took Lynx."

The bottom falls out of my belly.

"How do you know?"

"Overheard the council members. Only caught a few words, but that's what I thought they meant."

If that's where they took him, he's in even more trouble than I thought. Guilt smothers me.

"Blessed Jemen." I leap to my feet. "I have to go after him."

He gives me a puzzled smile. "You just captured four children. You abandon them to go chase after Lynx, and Basher will kill them."

For a long while, I stare at Jawbone sitting by the fire, guarding the girls. Each time Wind Mother blows the hides off one of the sleeping girls, he pulls them back up to their chins, making sure the girls stay warm. I can already feel these children crawling inside my heart.

"You're right," I say, and know I've just betrayed my promise to Lynx.

RabbitEar glances at the way I've clutched my spear in my fist, then warily looks up at my face, as if trying to read what is now no more than a fluttering pattern of colors. "There will be a time to go, Quiller. After we get the children home safely, perhaps you can slip away. Just not now, all right? You are all they have."

"They have you, too. Don't they? Won't you protect them?"

RabbitEar searches my eyes, looking for something he apparently does not find. He sighs and looks away, down at Jawbone. "If you ask me to protect them, I give you my oath that I will protect them to my dying breath."

17

LYNX

Bears roar, and I wake with terror flooding my veins.

In the distance, the sow and cubs are scattering down the slope, flying over the ice like frost ghosts caught in a haze of dawn-lit snow.

What so scared them that they would . . .

Below me, a shadow moves near the boulders, and my belly muscles clench tight, fearing something worse than bears.

A man appears, wearing a lion-hide cape with the hood pulled up to shield his face from the freezing morning wind. As he wanders around, he seems to be studying the bloody snow and splinters of human bones left by the bear feast. Picking up a splinter, he licks it, makes a face, and tosses it down again. Next, he turns his attention to the swaths of red that stripe the ground where the animals dragged the corpse about, then he cranes his neck and looks up at me with brilliant blue eyes.

"You'd better climb down. They're coming back, you know."

Hoodwink was right. He found me.

Terror numbs my soul. I stammer, "Y-you were at my w-wedding camp."

"Are you deaf? I told you to come down here."

What if this old man really is Nightbreaker in human disguise? He can change form and kill me in a heartbeat, but I have the eerie feeling that all paths forward and back lead to this tiny instant as if it's a puncture in the heart of time.

"If you're not down here in three breaths, I'm leaving you for the bears."

"No, wait!"

I untie the rope binding me to the tree, then roll it up and stuff it in my pack. But I can't convince myself to climb down. The elder moves in an oddly inhuman fashion. When he takes a step, he often stands for a time with one foot lifted, just like an animal. Of course, he obviously has the joint stiffening disease. Maybe it relieves the pain in his knee or hip.

"Okay, I'm leaving."

"No, I'm coming right now!"

Using the limbs like the rungs of a ladder, I climb down and jump to the ground with my pack and spear. "Elder, what are you doing here? Did you follow me?"

"Of course I followed you. You think I'd come out here for no reason?"

A sea eagle sails over the treetops, absolutely silent.

"Why?" I shift the weight of my pack. "If you followed me, you must have had a reason. I am Lynx, of the WindBorn clan from—"

"Yeah, yeah. From Sky Ice Village. I know."

A weightless sensation possesses me, as though I've just stepped over the edge of a chasm and started the long fall down.

"Are you one of the Jemen?"

The man extends his walking stick toward the copse of pines that I ran through last night. "I have a more important question. Are you hungry? I have a snowshoe hare roasting over my fire down in the woods. I'd be happy to share it with you."

Strange that I smell neither fire, nor the rich scent of roasting meat, but Wind Mother could be carrying both away. "Yes, I . . . I'm starving. Thank you. I'd be grateful."

"Good. Come on." Carefully placing his walking stick, he leads the way down the ice toward the trees. His motions are slow and soundless, too graceful to be human.

When we enter the thick trees, sunlight almost disappears and my vision goes tunnel-like. The narrow curving path seems to go on forever through the deepening shadows. It perplexes me, because I don't remember the forest being this big. Here and there, spindly saplings wage a battle of survival with the desolation and darkness, struggling to crowd out their neighbors so they can reach the sunlit sky, but most of the path slithers along through giant black boulders.

"Do you see it?" the man asks without turning around.

"What?"

"My fire."

"No, I . . ." My eyes suddenly clear, and I see fire-lit reflections dancing among the shadowed branches ahead. "Oh, there it is."

"That's my camp. Isn't far."

Then why does it take forever to get there? Maybe it's just my exhaustion. I haven't really slept in days. Where's Quiller? Why isn't she here yet?

"We are all made hollow by waiting, boy. Let the hope go," the man calls over his shoulder.

I squint at the back of his white head. "I'm not waiting for anything, elder. I'm headed home."

"Your hope is so loud it's hard to hear anything else when you're nearby."

"What?"

The elder turns to give me a curious look. "She's not searching for you. Let it go. What's her name?"

"You mean . . . Quiller? How do you know about her?" My heart thunders.

The old man smiles, turns his back to me, and continues on down the path.

As the trail curves around a charred, lightning-struck tree, the camp comes into view. He split the hare—as though expecting a guest—and skewered each half on a stick. The sticks are propped so that the meat leans over the flames to cook. The animal's guts and internal organs rest on a nearby rock. My people do the same thing as an offering to the spirits that haunt the slopes. His lodge, little more than saplings leaned together and covered with brush, is off to the right of the fire.

"You must be thirsty. Why don't you run ahead and sit down on that fallen log. There's tea in the bag that hangs from the tripod by the flames. I'll be there soon."

"Y-yes, elder."

I trot around him on shaking legs and head for the camp. As I slump down on the log in front of the fire and shrug out of my pack, I am aware of being watched by the trees. They lean over me, peering down in curiosity, probably wondering who I am.

Wooden cups are nested beside the tripod. I pick one and dip myself a cup of warm tea from the bag, while I watch the elder make his way down the trail. The tea is strange and sweet. Where have I tasted this before? I have memories of this tea . . . and of being fevered . . . and crying for Mother . . . and lion eyes peering through the lodge flap . . .

"That's better," the old man says as he gingerly lowers himself to sit at the other end of the log. "Now, tell me how long you've been lost. Do you know, or have all the days blended together?"

"I'm not lost. I told you, I'm on my way back to Sky Ice Village. This is the right direction to get home."

The elder picks up a cup that's been sitting by the fire for a long time. Must be stone cold. Why doesn't he dump it out and fill it with hot tea? "You're lost in your soul, boy. This trail won't take you anywhere near the home you need to find."

"What? I didn't understand that."

"'Course not. You're an empty vessel. Listening to your heart is like putting a seashell to the ear."

I take a long drink of tea and frown at him over the rim of my cup. How can he say that? He knows nothing about me. *Old people are crazy sometimes.*

"Forgive me for not asking before. What's your name, elder?"

"Dr. John Arakie."

The words are alien, foreign in a way that creates a primordial echo inside me. "Odd name. Never heard anything like it."

"I'm sure you haven't. You can call me Arakie."

Our gazes hold. Motionless, Arakie's knotted hands are dead white against the dark wood of the cup, like the bloodless claws of an animal.

"Are you an Outcast, elder?"

"Oh," he answers faintly. "I was. Long ago. Not anymore."

The deep wrinkles of his face cast shadows in the firelight. His face appears webbed with darkness. "Is it hard living out here alone?"

"Not as hard as it was at first, when my colleagues made the decision to . . ."

Arakie suddenly cocks his head and seems to be listening to something that I cannot hear—some low voice that calls to him from a great distance. "Did you hear that?"

I listen. "No. What?"

All I hear are the *hoo-hooos* of owls in the trees, and the faint roaring of lions that drifts down the mountainside on the breeze.

"My name is Sick Lynx, because I was sick a lot as a boy. But my people just call me Lynx."

Arakie twists his cup in his hands, as though feeling the

irregular grain of the wood. "So you're named after a squalling cat."

"Well . . . I suppose so."

"Which means you probably have cat blood."

I give him a suspicious look. "Cat blood? How could I have cat blood? That doesn't make any sense."

"Of course it does, boy. Far back in your past your clan was probably humping cats. Figuratively, I mean."

"Humping cats?" I glance sideways at the elder, but he looks perfectly serious.

"Absolutely, boy. An entire species was born of such crisprings. They are ancient now, and almost gone. A tragedy, really. They made the most beautiful sounds."

The elder sounds genuinely heartbroken, but I've never heard this story before, and am not sure I believe it. Humans humping cats? And what's a *crispring*?

As I examine the shadows, I say, "You needn't call me a boy, elder. I killed a great frost bear to become a man."

"Yeah. Sure, you did."

Behind my eyes, Siskin appears. She's crying, and her mouth is moving, probably complaining that she'd unknowingly married a boy, not a man. But I can't hear her words. The harder I try, the more I feel like I'm floating, my body rising high above the camp. I fly higher, so high that the campfires of the dead blaze in my face, and the trees and boulders below turn into tiny black awl-pricks in an endless blanket of white.

Arakie must have risen from the fire and come over to sit beside me. The startling thing is that I didn't see him do it. He's holding me up with icicle-cold hands.

"You okay, Lynx?" His blue eyes have a strange inhuman glitter.

"D-Don't know what happened."

"You toppled over."

"Did I? Guess I'm hungrier than I thought." I brace one hand on the log to prop myself up.

"More of soul than of body, I think."

"What?"

The elder cautiously releases me and slides down the log to give me room. "I just meant that the soul is the place where the heart hungers, where it suffers. You must have been thinking of something wrenching before the dizziness flattened you."

"I—I don't recall, elder."

"Did you just lie to me?"

"No." I can't talk about Siskin's ghost with this curious stranger.

"Hmm." Arakie leans forward to prop his forearms on his knees. He seems to be observing the patches of sunlight that move with the wind-blown branches as he sips his tea. The mosaic of golden light and deep shadow stays in constant motion.

Cradling my cup in both hands, I try to think of something to say. "Will you ever try to go back to your people? You must be lonely."

"Loneliness is a self-inflicted wound. Besides, my people are all around me."

"I don't see anyone. Is your village nearby?"

Arakie waves a hand at the birds in the trees and then at the bison grazing upon a field of grass down the slope. Their constant deep-throated rumbling makes a strangely peaceful backdrop to the roars of the Ice Giants. "The world is filled with life. I'm not alone, and neither are you. You never have been."

Arakie's gaze is like being ensnared by a rope trap laid on a caribou trail. It's hard to escape.

"I was just . . . wondering. Will you ever try to go home?"

He sits back and rests his cup on the damp log beside him. "That worries you, doesn't it? Going home."

"No, I'm not worried. It's just Hoodwink said I have to—"

"Hoodwink is the man who saved you, right?"

Fear prickles my spine. *He must be one of the Jemen.* "What makes you think he saved me? You weren't there. I know that for a fact."

Arakie bends to turn the sticks with the roasting hare, and his wiry white brows pull together. "Knowing everything is such a burden, isn't it? Makes people think you're a stupid prick. Believe me, I know. I used to be as much of a stupid prick as you are."

I have no idea what to say to that. *Prick?*

"Oh, far out, man. Our hare is done. Let's eat." He hands me one of the roasting sticks. "It's hot. Be careful."

"Elder, I don't understand half the words you use."

Arakie takes a bite of hare and grease smears his chin. "Well, don't worry about it. Just listen to the ones you do understand."

The more I examine Arakie, the more I'm convinced he can't be one of the legendary Jemen. Surely the gods are not this annoying.

I blow on the hare and take a bite. "I love hare. It's my second favorite meat, after bison."

The high-pitched calls of wood warblers echo through the forest. Arakie smiles, then he closes his eyes and tilts his head back to sing to them. His deep voice penetrates the air in every direction. Down the slope, the bison pause to listen, enraptured, and the birds stand motionless in the branches, lest they disturb the music with even the sound of their steps. I have the feeling that a day's walk away, warriors in battle just let their weapons fall to the ground.

When he finishes, I say, "That was beautiful, elder. Even the animals stopped to listen."

The old man sits so motionless his blue eyes catch the firelight and hold it like the translucent bodies of the Ice Giants.

I suffer through that weightless sensation again. Very faintly, as though coming from a great distance, the chatter of deer hoof rattles and pot drums shiver the air. I have to prop one hand on the log again to keep from reeling, for I have the feeling that the spirit world just tiptoed into this one to look at me.

"Do you know why?" he asks.

"Why what?"

Arakie's gaze drifts over the forest as though he's looking for something, perhaps seeing something I will never see. In the faint morning light, the snow-laden branches have a soft blue glow. Every time a gust of wind sweeps the forest, the drooping limbs groan and shriek as though endeavoring to create a melody.

"We are all made of music. Bison rumble and birds chirp. Short-faced bears growl and whimper. Put it all together and you have life's most beautiful symphony. Song is the one language we all understand."

Using my sleeve, I wipe the hare fat from my mouth. The paleness of his skin contrasts sharply with the forest shadows, making him appear bloodless and corpselike.

"Are you my spirit helper?"

Arakie's eyes flare as though stunned by the question. "You have no spirit helpers, boy. You haven't earned any."

"I have a spirit helper. Hoodwink said so."

"Well, when you're trying to save a boy's life, one lie is as good as another."

"He didn't lie to save my life."

"Of course he did. You wouldn't be out here alone if your people hadn't abandoned you as punishment. It must have been a question of life or death. What did you do to deserve this little jaunt to the gallows?"

I force a bite of hare down my throat. *Gallows?* "It's a spirit quest. Some people called me a coward, but the council said—"

"Was it just the wedding camp?"

My hand stops midway to bringing the rabbit to my mouth and starts to shake. "You . . . you're not human . . . are you?"

"I'm as human as you are. As far as that goes. Who called you a coward?"

"Deputy War Leader Hushy. I—I suppose I deserved it. I'm not very good with a spear. Don't know why, I just don't like killing."

Arakie smiles as he chews. "Guess you don't want to lead a trivial life."

"What?"

"My friend, weakness is the only useful quality worth cultivating. Without it, forgiveness is impossible. Do you believe you're a coward?"

Embarrassed, I stare down at my half-eaten hare. The truth is I've been afraid my whole life, afraid of hurting and being hurt, afraid of not living up to my clan's expectations, afraid of dying. "I . . . I'm not a brave man, elder."

Arakie's eyes narrow. "Courage isn't the province of the brave, Lynx. It's the virtue of the terrified. It's what happens when you have no options left."

Siskin's screams seep up from the dark chamber inside me where I've locked them. "I know what it's like to have no options left. I—"

"Don't be ridiculous. You could walk away from the wedding camp and did. Men with no options can't walk away." The old man aims the stick with his half-chewed rabbit at me like a stiletto. "When you can't walk away, you'll discover that courage has nothing to do with being a brave man. True courage is a desperate act of faith."

"Faith? I don't understand."

"I mean there's no such thing as a brave man."

I turn to stare at him. "Of course there is. I know many brave men. My brother is our War Leader—"

"Which means he's spent his whole life being scared to death."

"You don't know my brother."

"If he's your War Leader, I know him better than you do. A man like that is frightened all the time that he will fail to protect his family and his people. If he's not good enough, his entire world will die, and he knows it. The burden he carries on his shoulders is unbearable."

That can't be true. After the raid where our parents died and half, *half* of our people were killed, Mink was a pillar of strength, the fearless deputy War Leader pacing around, organizing defenses, checking on the wounded, calming everyone's fears. Is it possible that my brother was really petrified? Maybe even falling apart inside?

Arakie shivers suddenly. "Temperature's dropping. Killer storm coming in today." He gestures to the black wall of clouds pulling over the tops of the trees above us. "The kind that explodes tree sap, and freezes bison so fast you find them the next day standing motionless in the meadow, dead as stones. We'd best finish breakfast and head down the mountain. I know an ice cave where we can hole up and wait it out."

18

QUILLER

Seagulls flap through the morning sky with their wings shining. I glance at them as I trudge along at the base of the towering ice cliff. The children trot at my heels and, up ahead, Crow charges across the beach wagging her tail, flushing the flocks of birds that hunt the shoreline. When they burst into squawking flurries of wings, Crow leaps and barks as though proud of herself.

Basher and RabbitEar walk five paces ahead me, talking quietly, while Mink guards the rear. Every time I turn around, I find Mink's worried eyes upon me. I'm sure he wishes I had not claimed the children. It would have made his life easier. But the children are being unnaturally good. They walk almost silently at my heels in single file, with Jawbone in the lead. Since the little boy found his dead father, he's shed no more tears. I value that. He knows he can't be weak now. The other children depend upon him.

"Jawbone, why don't you walk beside me so we can talk?"

"Yes, Quiller." He runs to my side and looks up expectantly.

The Rust People have such big angular faces, whereas Sealion People have smaller, more narrow faces. Legends say that once, a long time ago, we were the same people. That's why our languages are so similar. It's hard to believe, though, given the hatred we share.

"You're a good leader for the children, Jawbone. Your grandfather chose well."

"I don't think he really chose me. We were all in one tent at the far edge of the village, near the beach. When the lions appeared out of the darkness, he grabbed me in his arms, shouted for the other children to come, and ran for the boat. When he was shovin' us out to sea, he told me to protect the girls. I saw the lions jump on him as our boat floated out into the water. He—he tried to fight them off."

All of the children must have been standing on the deck, calling out to their families as the lions chased them down. The screams of their loved ones must still be ringing in their ears.

"Lions try to swim after you?"

"Yes, a big lioness jumped into the water and paddled hard, but turned back."

"Must have been terrifying."

The boy shrugs, as though that moment was the least terrifying of the night. "What's goin' to happen to us, Quiller?"

"You'll be adopted into families. May adopt one or two of you as my own children."

"Which two?" Hope trembles his voice. He gazes up at me with bright, frightened eyes.

"You want to be my son?"

Jawbone wets his lips. "I was hopin' you might adopt Little Fawn and Chickadee. That way they can stay together. I think it would hurt Chickadee if she and her sister went to live with different families."

"I see. What about you? What kind of family would you like?"

"Doesn't matter about me, but Loon's mother was a baker.

She made the best grass-seed breads in the village. I think Loon might like to 'ave a mother who is a good baker."

"I can probably arrange that."

Jawbone glances up at me with tears in his eyes. "Thank you."

"You've been thinking about this, haven't you?"

"For a while."

A giant condor shrieks, and Jawbone looks up to watch it diving through the cloud-strewn sky. Far to the east, a terrible storm is building. The crests of the Ice Giant Mountains are alive with violet streamers of blowing snow. Like fingers, they reach down the valleys to stroke the glaciers.

If Lynx is still up there, I pray he's found shelter. Very soon, snow will blanket the openings to the deepest crevasses. Accidentally stepping into a crevasse is a death sentence.

I reach down to touch Jawbone's strange silver shirt. The hide is slick. "What kind of skin is this, Jawbone? It looks like fish skin, but it's very fragile."

He looks down at his shirt. It shimmers when he moves.

"It's not skin. It's trayalon. My people found big round rolls of it buried in the ice in the Steppe Lands. Our holy people, the Dog Soldiers, read the sacred books that were with the bolts of cloth. The words said the trayalon would last a thousand summers, but it's been fallin' apart more and more. If you leave it out in the sun too long, it cracks and crumbles. Warm, though. Warmer than your hide clothes."

Crow charges past us, chasing the surf back out to sea, barking at it, but I barely see her. My gaze is riveted to this little boy.

"Tell me about the Dog Soldiers. They always stand so far back during battles that we've never gotten a good look at them. They're very tall."

Jawbone's face lights up. "Yes, when I first saw you, I thought maybe you had Dog Soldier blood. They're amazin'. They belonged to an ancient and fierce military society. They fought bravely to the end to protect their people, but now there are only seven left in the whole world, and Grandfather says they can't 'ave children anymore, so they'll be extinct soon. Just like the Mericans."

"Mericans?"

Excitedly, he says, "They lived here in this land long before the Ice Giants were born. When the Giants grew bigger and bigger, the Mericans threw great clouds of fire at them to kill them, but the Giants ate their fire and destroyed them."

I can tell he loves this story. His elders probably tell it often around their winter fires. "We don't have that story."

"Grandfather says it goes back to just after the Jemen created this world."

Mink runs up beside me and glances speculatively down at Jawbone, before he says, "Basher and I are going to scout ahead. Don't want to accidently run into a party of Rust warriors."

"All right. We'll see you at sunset at Sky Ice Village."

"Unless there's danger. Then you'll see us coming back at a run."

"We'll be ready, just in case."

"Better be."

Mink lopes ahead to meet Basher, and they both sprint south.

Before I realize it, RabbitEar has trotted over to stand in front of me. He waits until Basher and Mink have run out of sight around the curving ice wall, before he says, "I've been thinking about this. Are you still committed to finding Lynx? If so, now is the time to go."

"I thought you didn't want me to. You said—"

"I *don't* want you to. I think it's a very bad idea, but I'll care for the children while you're gone. Do you trust me enough to let me do that?"

His red hair is blowing over his green eyes, which makes him squint, but I suspect he's also squinting in defense. He's afraid of how I'll answer that question. The offer is a strange act of kindness from a man I jilted for another.

"I trust you completely," I say.

He reaches out and grasps my hand with a half-unthinking intimacy, holding it as though he knows I need his support to make such a difficult decision.

"I know you, Quiller. If you don't try to save Lynx, you'll regret it for the rest of your life. At some point, you may even blame the children for the fact that he died. Therefore, I accept the responsibility so that you may do your duty to your own conscience."

It is a gesture of respect, one warrior to another, and I'm grateful for it.

But I hesitate a long time before replying. The longer I hesitate, the more he narrows his eyes, girding himself. So often when he speaks to me his face is tense with struggle, as if he debates within himself what he can safely say.

"RabbitEar, I appreciate that, and I thank you. But I've decided I'll wait until I've gotten the children home to my parents' lodge. They will care for them while I'm away."

He looks disappointed and releases my hand. "Yes, of course. That makes sense."

In the awkward silence that follows, I'm not certain what to say. He turns away to frown at the sea.

"RabbitEar, before I leave, we'll talk, all right?"

He turns back to give me a guarded look. "If you decide you truly want to talk to me, I will expect honesty. Do you understand? No trying to protect my feelings, or—"

"Of course."

He starts to move away, but I reach out and grab his muscular arm, tightening my hold to keep him still. "Truly. I thank you for caring."

"Do you?" he asks with a ghost of a smile. "That's good to hear. Now, let's get moving. I don't like it that it's just two of us here to guard the children. Let's get home quick as we can."

19

LYNX

By noon, the sun dies in a purple sky.

We hike to an ice ridge and get our first clear view of the storm. To the north and west, vast curtains of snow push toward us, blotting out everything in their path. Glaciers, rivers, and rock outcrops vanish beneath the onslaught.

"Come along." Arakie points his walking stick at a ridge dotted with caves that resemble frozen blue eyes. A small grove of pines grows just down the slope from the caves. "We don't have much time to find shelter."

As we strike out, heading south across the frozen expanse, wind blasts us. Within moments I'm forced to squint against the stinging ice crystals. If not for the weight of the pack on my back, the gusts would jerk me off my feet and throw me down the glacier like a hurled rock.

Halfway to the caves we startle a skeletal sabertooth cat hunting mice among the boulders.

Though not as big as a lion, her fangs are gigantic, seven or eight times as long as a lion's fangs, and she has a short, squat face. Her winter coat is thick and tan. At the sight of a vole, the sabertooth skitters away across the ice.

Shouting against the wind, I call, "Legends say the Jemen breathed upon ten-thousand-summers-old bones and brought them back to life. Do you believe it?"

He gives me a vaguely disdainful look. "Well, it's as good as any story we ever came up with. Before my people went extinct on this world, we had many stories of the re-creation. We called them the 'Rewilding Reports.'"

"Re-wilding? What does that mean?"

Pulling up his hood, Arakie hunches inside his cloak and listens to the Ice Giants bleating like a herd of frightened mountain goats. The glaciers have turned an unearthly amethyst as the storm rolls in. "I may tell you before this is all through, but for now, we have to find shelter. Let's make tracks."

I blink solemnly at his back as he walks away. His people are extinct. Why didn't he tell me he was the last of his kind? The very thought is mind-numbing. How did a man survive the loss of everything and everyone he'd ever loved? I would have mourned myself to death and been grateful for the darkness. Perhaps that's why he's so odd. Grief has hollowed out the soul, leaving a husk of a man behind. I barely know him, but I hurt for him.

Arakie reaches the cave first, and slides through a six-hands-wide crack in the ice that serves as a doorway.

When I enter behind him, amazement fills me. "Oh . . . this is stunning."

More of an ice cavern than an ice cave, it stretches fifty hands over my head. Dozens of cubbyholes, places where the ice has melted to form rounded niches, dot the walls. Bags and boxes—made of a material I do not recognize—as well as chunks of frozen meat and fish stuff many of the niches. Some of the boxes appear to be a thousand summers old. Cracked and discolored, they're decorated with the same blue ball design that adorns his shirt. Farther back along the tunnel, massive icicles hang from the roof. Several have melted to the floor to form a shimmering blue-white colonnade that recedes into the darkness. About twenty paces away, a pile of dried mammoth dung rests near a fire pit filled with ashes. Two elk hides have been spread beside the fire. Two. Does someone else join him here? Or does he keep it out to remind him of a friend who is now gone? Perhaps his only friend at the end, before Arakie became the last of his kind?

I glance down at the green tree painted on my coat, then point to the design on the ancient boxes. "Is that your clan symbol? Before your people died? That blue ball with the red slash and white dots?"

He looks over and frowns at it. When he turns back, there is something so sad and profound in his eyes that I can't quite grasp it. It's as though, if he answers the question, it will violate some old pact of sacrifice and remembrance.

Bowing his head, he says, "Yes, 'the meatball' was my clan symbol. Actually, still is. Doesn't matter that they're gone. They're still my people."

"How long have you lived here?"

"Long time. Used to have a log cabin here, before the ice dragged it down and pushed it into the ocean. Now come and help me start a fire, Sick Lynx. It's going to get really cold tonight."

Arakie hobbles to the fire pit, drops his pack, and sinks onto one of the hides, where he lets out a pained sigh. He pats the other hide and says, "You can hope now. But just a little."

I don't know if he's talking to me or himself, or maybe speaking to a spirit that sits cross-legged on the hide, someone who's been waiting a long time for him to return.

20

QUILLER

By late afternoon, the wind has a taste.

Guarding the rear, I frown at RabbitEar, who walks ahead of me with the children. He carries Chickadee on his left hip, and is speaking softly with her. The other children trail along behind him, smiling and laughing. Does he taste it? The metallic tang that claws at the back of my throat?

As adrenaline feathers through my veins, my body goes on high alert, and my eyes are drawn to the ocean, searching. Where are they?

On the sunlit crests of every wave, zyme shimmers greenish-gold, before it plummets down into a trough and shades a darker green. This time of afternoon, the ocean wears stripes like some giant lizard that is expert at camouflage. I don't see boats out there, but they wouldn't be in the midst of the zyme anyway. Not even their metal crafts could cut through the thick forests here.

I shift to scrutinize the narrow strip of water close to shore. It's turned an ugly shade of gray. We tried fishing at noon, but there are no fish here. There are no birds, either. Where zyme grows the thickest, fish, kelp, and crabs die, which means there's nothing for shorebirds to eat. Even the plants that grow upon the rocks have shriveled and turned brown.

I'm trying to shake off the sense of foreboding, but I can taste their ships on the air. Iron-rich, like fresh blood. And I feel their eyes upon me.

"RabbitEar?" I call as I trot forward.

He stops and turns to smile at me, but when he sees my expression, his smile fades. "What's wrong?"

"Let's stop for a moment. I need to speak with the children."

He lowers Chickadee to the ground and says, "Children, gather round."

When we are surrounded by smiling faces, I say, "Jawbone, you may not know the answer to this question, and it's all right if you don't, but how were your people traveling? Since your village was camped alone, I assume the rest of the Rust People were paddling up the shore behind you. How far behind?"

Jawbone frowns in confusion. "They weren't behind us, Quiller. Most of our village got sick about one half-moon ago."

Little Fawn adds, "Lots of people died."

"Yes," Jawbone continues. "When the fever started to spread, Swordfish Village accused our village of causin' the fever by witchcraft. There was a big fight about it. Finally, Chief Three Roads ordered that Great Horned Village be left behind."

"So . . ." RabbitEar's gaze seeks out mine, and he swallows hard. "You were the last in line?"

Jawbone nods.

As understanding begins to dawn on me, I whisper, "That's how the lions could slaughter their village. The Rust People were too sick to get out of their bedding hides to fight them."

RabbitEar glances down at Jawbone, but his question is for me: "Do you remember that night when we were standing on the ice floe, and we thought we heard . . ." He whirls around to look southward again. "Which means they reached Sky Ice Village days ago."

The word "no" has barely escaped my lips, when RabbitEar breaks into a dead run for home.

"RabbitEar, wait! We need to plan—"

Over his shoulder, he shouts, "Find a place to hide! If everything's all right, I'll be back for you!"

21

LYNX

The sound of water makes me open my eyes.

Far back along the beautiful ice colonnade, there's a steady *drip, drip,* as though sunlight has penetrated the tiny cracks in the roof and meltwater is trickling down.

When I sit up, I find the cave dark, the fire burned down to a bed of red coals. Why hasn't Arakie built a breakfast fire? I don't feel very well this morning. I'm hot, as though fevered, and faintly nauseous. The strange, sickly sweet flavor of yesterday's tea coats my mouth. Throwing off my caribou hide, I grab my spear and walk to the mouth of the cave to look outside.

A sparkling world spreads before me. Down the steep slope the pines droop mournfully beneath the weight of new snow, and beyond them the ice falls away into cracked folds that zigzag around granite outcrops and copses of pines. Far away, a thin crescent of blue ocean is visible. Sudden elation fills me. All I have to do is walk straight downhill to the ocean, then follow the shoreline home! I'll make up some story about my spirit quest. Who will know the difference?

"Arakie?"

Last night the old man insisted on sleeping by the fire to keep it going while I slept, but obviously, at some point, he left the cave.

"Elder?" I shout.

If he'd left a short time ago, there would be a shallow trail half filled with snow winding across the ridge, which means he left in the middle of the night. In a blizzard. Why would he do that?

A chill climbs my spine.

"Don't panic. If you're alone, all you have to do is walk downhill."

Quiller once told me that surviving in the wilderness required turning yourself into an animal. She said I had to let go of my human senses and learn to "see" as animals saw, because that's how predators survive.

All of her teachings just came alive inside me.

My nostrils quiver as I sort through the fragrances of pine needles and damp earth that drift on the morning breeze. The faint odor of mammoths, days old, wafts from inside the cave, coming from the dung pile Arakie uses to heat the cave and cook his food.

A snap . . .

My ears don't quite hear it, but I feel the sound in my bones, as though a stalker, maybe a bear, stepped on a twig buried beneath the snow. If I remain quiet long enough, I'll hear ice crunch beneath paws, or a whisper of breathing.

How do I block the entrance to this cave?

Down the slope in the deep shadows cast by the pines, there's movement.

Then I spy Arakie passing between the dark trunks. His pale face is ethereal, glowing, not quite real. Even the trees seem to sense something amiss. The snow-laden branches shake off their white coats with great thumps, and straighten to watch him more closely. The birds in the trees refuse to chirp, but track his movements with their eyes.

How can anyone walk almost soundlessly through fresh snow? When at last Arakie turns to stare at me, I'm afraid to move. It's like being caught in the gaze of a great frost bear—the moment between predator and prey where gazes first meet and time stops.

Arakie lifts a bird, and calls, "Grouse for breakfast!"

Relief rushes through me. Forcing a smile, I call back. "I'm not very hungry this morning, but I'll start a fire, elder."

I trot back for the fire pit and start pulling chunks of dried mammoth dung from the pile and placing them on the warm coals. As I do, I smell the sweet things the mammoth was eating, dry grass and willow twigs, the plants of autumn that line the forested coast. Doesn't take long for tiny flames to lick up around the dung. When blessed warmth touches my cold face, I shiver.

"You're up early," Arakie says as he slips through the cave entry. "I expected you to sleep until mid-morning."

"Sound of dripping water woke me."

"Yes, the roof in here drips constantly until winter sets in. It's like living in the heart of a rain cloud."

Arakie removes his pack, places it beside the fire, and sits down to my left with the grouse.

"Elder, there's plenty of frozen meat stuffed into the holes in the walls in here. Why did you have to go hunting?"

"The food in here is for winter, when I can't go hunting."

"You mean you stay here all winter long?" I ask in surprise.

"I've passed many, many long winters in this cave." His gaze lovingly caresses the ice walls. "After the Ice Giants tore my cabin down, I still came up here. It's been haunting to watch the world change. Especially the ocean. I remember when the water was right down there, not more than two hundred paces away."

"Two hundred?" I say in surprise. "But—"

"Yes, I know. The ocean levels have dropped by five hundred feet. That's why the shore is miles away now."

I frown, trying to understand his measurements. We use hand-lengths. Does he use foot-lengths?

Arakie grunts as he positions the dead bird in his lap. "Could you live here? In an ice cave like this?"

My eyes examine the cavern, trying to see it as he does, following the magnificent fire-lit colonnade of ice pillars as they disappear back into the dimness, and I shudder. Holing up in here for a few days is fine, but the idea of living here alone for moons is too awful to contemplate.

"I don't think I'd like being here in the winter, elder. The Sealion People live outside in the sea breezes, hunting and fishing as we paddle down the shorelines. All of my life, I've awakened to the sounds of waves and wind."

Before he plucks the grouse, Arakie pets the dead bird and reverently says, "I pray that Grouse Above comes to lead your soul along the Road of Light to the afterlife, where it's always warm and there are no hunters, and there are other grouse there to love you." A low growl vibrates deep in his throat, and I wonder if he's imitating the thrumming made by grouse in the springtime? Perhaps he speaks their language? Hoodwink says there are many great shamans who know animal languages.

"You cried a lot in your sleep," Arakie says in a gentle voice.

"Sorry I kept you awake, elder."

"You are not the first boy I've heard cry in his sleep. I raised twelve sons and two daughters."

Arakie pulls out a handful of feathers and lets them fly loose on the air. I didn't notice before, but a faint breeze wafts through the cavern. The feathers drift toward the entry, where they are sucked out through the crack into the sunlight beyond.

"Where are your children now?"

"Oh. Dead. It was a long time ago." Loss fills his voice.

"Shouldn't have asked. Forgive me."

"'Course you should have. If we're going to spend time to-gether, we should know something about each other. Don't you agree?"

"Yes, elder."

But the last thing I want is to speak of my life. My soul feels like a freshly skinned deer, the still-quivering meat exposed to the cold and snow for the first time, the ache so pervasive I can't get away from it, especially when I sleep.

Arakie points to his pack with a feather-covered finger. "In-side my pack there is a red pouch filled with tundra wildflower tea. I don't want to reach in with my dirty hands. Why don't you find it and add some to the boiling bag? It already has water in it. It's frozen, but if you move the tripod closer to the flames, it'll thaw soon."

Pulling open the laces of Arakie's pack, I see a curious array of objects inside. The bottom of the pack is stuffed with old bones, but several small pouches cover them. I grab the red pouch, open it, and add some of the dried contents to the tea bag, then I move the tripod closer to the flames.

"What do you do with the old bones? They look human."

"They are human. Found them melted out of the ice along the Boulder River. I'll analyze them in the near future. Now, Sick Lynx, tell me about you."

"Me? I'm not very interesting, elder. I have a brother. I'm a good rope-maker. That's all."

Arakie strips another batch of feathers from the grouse and lets it go in the cold draft. The tiniest downy feathers stick to his fingers like boiled pine pitch. "Given what you've been through lately, I suspect you're a little more interesting than that."

"No, elder. Truly, I'm not."

"Lynx," he says in a kind voice. "Over the long summers, I've soothed many children who were victims of tragedy. I know the raw looks they get in their eyes. Why don't you tell me what happened?"

I shake my head. "Thank you, but no."

"Well, I can't force you. But you have unfinished business to take care of in your heart. I can help you, if you let me."

"Just need to get home, then I'll be fine."

"Don't think so, Sick Lynx."

My breath has gone fast and shallow. Each breath frosts the air and floats away toward the entry in a shining cloud. "You don't know anything about me, elder. I—"

"I know you need to face your grief. Have you discussed it with your village healer?"

"I don't discuss it with anyone."

He makes that low growl again. "That is a dangerous practice. When a boy is hiding things even from himself, they can sprout dark wings. You must discuss them with someone. If you ever decide you wish to speak of it, I—"

"That what you did among your own people, served as the village healer?"

Arakie finishes plucking the grouse, shoves a stick through the middle, and props the bird over the flames to cook. "Everyone hides things, Lynx. You shouldn't be ashamed of it. Most of the worst things are stuffed down so deep we've forgotten them. The problem is that they have not forgotten us. They watch. They listen. But a person only sees them when he has a chance to float in emptiness for a while."

"I'm not hiding anything."

Arakie wipes his greasy, feather-encrusted fingers on his leather boots. The oils in the grease help to waterproof the leather. "Don't get uptight about it. What I'm trying to tell you is that she's not dead. She's alive inside you. That's why you hear her calling you."

A rush of hot blood surges through me. How could he possibly know that? "Some of my people say you are Trogon, the w-witch from the Rust People. Are you?"

"No, but he's an interesting character. I don't have to be a witch, Lynx, to hear the guilt that runs through your voice like a rampaging bison. It's in your lungs, restricting your air, and in your hands when you start to shake for no reason. You clearly blame yourself for her death. Why? Did you kill her?"

Siskin's face appears behind my eyes, staring up at me from our wedding bed, and I have to squeeze my eyes closed to make it go away.

"Didn't kill her, elder. Didn't save her, either."

"Could you have?"

"I didn't. That's all that matters."

Arakie reaches down to turn the roasting stick to cook the other side of the grouse. Flames crackle as fat drips into the fire pit and the rich scent of roasting meat fills the cold cave air.

"Men are not made of their failures, Lynx, but they are made of their guilt. You must call your wife back from her journey and ask her why she hates you. That's what you're afraid of, isn't it?"

"She doesn't hate me! She—"

"Yelling won't ease your guilt, and it grates on my nerves."

"S-sorry."

Arakie's wiry white brows draw down over his nose. "She wants to speak with you, but she needs your permission. Give her permission."

My hands shake.

Arakie notices and looks away to grimace at the yellow gleam now streaming through the cave entry where feathers lilt in the sunlight. Some have risen to the roof and float there, waiting their turns to go outside.

Is Arakie right? Siskin always sounds lost, like she's trying to come back to me through a thick fog but can't find her way.

"She doesn't hate me."

"You already said that. Trying to convince me or yourself?"

"Not trying to convince anyone of anything!" I shout, suddenly angry with Arakie prying into my personal affairs. "You think I care what a dead woman thinks?"

Arakie bends forward, collects a wooden cup and dips it into the tea bag. As he hands it to me, he says, "Now you're making progress. You've found the question."

The question?

Memories of the dazed moments after the attack flood up, and the intoxicating musk of lions surrounds me. I smell meat-breath, see yellow eyes glinting far back in the forest shadows. Is that her voice? Calling to me for help? My insides are curling up and dying.

Arakie is watching me like an eagle with a vole in sight. "Tell me about the council meeting. You must have been frightened."

I take a sip of tea—that odd sweet tea—before I say, "Yes. I—I thought they were going to kill me, but Elder Hoodwink convinced them that you were my spirit helper."

Arakie's wiry white brows arch. "Smart move. Go on."

"He told the council I'd spent the night of my wedding journeying from this world to the other side of the campfires of the dead, and that you were sent in answer to my prayer."

"Oh," Arakie says in admiration, "he's good."

"Elder Hoodwink also said you were the giant lion, Nightbreaker, in human disguise. He said Nightbreaker was one of the Earthbound Jemen who learned to change shape to survive the crushing cold after the zyme."

He frowns solemnly at the grouse. "One of the Jemen, eh?"

I tilt my head to the side, curious about the way he pronounces the word. "You say Jee-men?"

"That's how my clan pronounced it." As though the hunched-over posture has started to hurt his back, Arakie winces and straightens.

"So your people also believed in the Jemen? Our holy elders say the Sky Jemen still watch over us. And the Earthbound Jemen fight every day to find a way to kill the Ice Giants and turn the world warm again."

He smiles as though I've made a great joke. "You believe that?"

"I want to believe—but I guess I'm not sure they ever really existed."

He lifts his gaze to the ceiling. "The Jemen did exist. Maybe they still do. I'm not sure."

"Did they actually try to kill the Ice Giants?"

Softly, he answers. "Oh, yes."

"I've never understood that. When it was clear the Ice Giants were winning the war, why didn't they just go find a nice safe place to live? If it had been me—"

"Well, I'll tell you why. Because a man who is safe never commits an act of love that seems like madness. He never ventures so far into the emptiness for another's sake that surrendering to the darkness becomes the path of salvation." Lacing his fingers over one knee, he leans back and shakes his head. "And the Ice Giants have not won. Not yet."

"Is there any place on earth that isn't covered by monstrous ice mountains?"

He seems to be looking into some vast distance, and I have the feeling he's watching Jemen walk through a warm, fragrant world. Reverence lines his face. "A few refugia remain, mostly in the Pacific, but . . ."

Arakie breaks off, startled, and whirls to peer at the entry. His head is cocked, listening. I follow his gaze down the glimmering length of the cavern, stopping many times to frown at the boxes and bags that fill the holes in the ice walls, and finally find myself staring at the downy feathers that still lilt through the air in the sunlight.

"Haunting, isn't it?" he asks.

It takes me a few moments to understand. Between the distant moans of Ice Giants, agonized cries rise and fall on the wind.

I whisper, "Sounds like a gut-shot spirit creature."

Arakie grabs his walking stick and shoves to his feet. "Let's find out. Wrap up the grouse. Even half raw, it's better than going hungry. We'll eat it as we walk. And dress warm, warm as you can. Bitter out there this morning, and you're going to be sick for most of the day."

"How do you know I'm sick?" I say as I glance around for something to wrap the grouse in. Any chunk of hide will work.

"You told me you weren't hungry. *Ergo*, you're sick." Arakie uses a crooked finger to point to the tea bag hanging on the tripod. "Dump that out and stuff the grouse inside the bag, then tuck it in your pack."

22

QUILLER

My breathing is coming fast and hard, timed to my pace. Crow lopes along the sand ahead of me. Every hair on her spine stands straight up. She's been growling and yipping plaintively, as though she knows something I do not. Several times she's broken away and tried to gallop home at full speed, but I've called her back.

With Chickadee in my arms, I'm running as fast as I can without losing the other children. By now, I should see smoke rising from Sky Ice Village. In the autumn, fires burn all day to allow people to dry fish and meat for the winter, and to smoke the necessary hides to make new winter clothing and lodge covers. But there's no smoke. More worrisome, we are less than one finger of time away. I should hear people laughing, see boats out on the water, fishing. I do not.

Why aren't the village dogs barking? Wind is at our backs. They should have already smelled us.

"Quiller, where's RabbitEar?" Jawbone calls. "Why hasn't he come back for us?"

"He'll be back. Just stay close to me."

My mind goes on calculating. Handling the worst that life can throw at you comes second nature to Sealion People. We have had to endure so much isolation, starvation, and war that my body is ready for the confrontation waiting just around the curve in the tree-whiskered coastline up there. I am already planning three steps ahead. *Have to set Chickadee down in a hurry, pull a spear from my quiver, pick a target . . .*

When I see tracks dappling the beach, I slow down to scan them. Four sets of prints here. I know each warrior's tread as well as my own. Mink and Basher broke into a desperate run here. RabbitEar stopped briefly to examine their tracks, just as I'm doing, and charged away. Hushy's holey moccasins tell me the most interesting story. His prints run up the beach, then charge back south as though his heart is on fire.

He saw something that made him panic.

Glancing down at the Rust children, I'm pretty sure I know what it was.

"Jawbone? Can you carry Chickadee for a while?"

He runs up and takes the girl from my arms. "Yes."

Pulling a spear from my quiver, I fight to slow my heartbeat so I can concentrate. The children have gathered around my legs like chicks around a mother hen. Fear strains their faces.

"Don't be afraid. We just need to be cautious. I want you to stay behind me, but close, understand?"

The children jerk nods.

I move forward like a hunting predator, one slow step at a time.

23

LYNX

Arakie plunges down the hill through the deep drifts like a man who knows exactly where he's going. Down the hill, always down, always following a narrow stream of meltwater. At times I am so blinded by blowing snow, I lose sight of the old man, and the sound of running water is the only thing that tells me which way is downhill. I've never endured cold like this. The Sealion People spend their lives on the coast, where the ocean warms the shoreline. But up here in this high mountain wasteland, warmth is just a dream. Wind Mother sucks away any heat a man produces and leaves him shivering to death inside his muskoxen coat.

All around me, grotesque black crevasses slit the ice. The Black Serpents, Hoodwink calls them, for that's what they look like from the faraway seashore. A dangerous place where ice lions and dire wolves kill anything that moves.

"Where you going?" I shout against the wind, trying to get Arakie's attention.

He extends an arm to the south. "There's a shelter up here."

"Where?"

"Follow me."

When I round the curve, I see the huge hollow perched on the crest of the ridge. It resembles a bowl set on edge. The sight is stunning. Frozen trees, two hundred hands tall, fill the hollow.

Icicles hang from branches that were long ago bleached gray by dripping water and sunlight. They must be old pines, maybe spruces. Awe fills me. How long ago did this grove die? A hundred summers? Ten thousand? The chalcedony-like treetops paint skeletal images against the translucent roof, which is so thin I can see clouds scudding beyond the ice.

"Come on, Lynx!"

Arakie stands at the far edge of the shelter, staring off to south. His white hair and coat blend so completely with the background, he's almost invisible.

"What is it? What's wrong?"

"Don't you see him? He's right there!" He points.

"Where?"

The slope plunges steeply down the mountainside, dropping away into a windblown haze of snow. I see nothing down there . . . but as the wind shifts a man wavers in and out of existence, dressed in shining silver clothing. He's maybe three hundred hands away.

"Rust People!" Panic fills me. "See any more of them?"

I run to Arakie's side.

"Seems to be alone, but his mouth is moving as though he's talking to someone."

The man clasps his hands together in front of him, and his lips move again. He appears to be speaking to something hidden in the snow in front of him.

"What's he doing?"

"I think he's leaning over a crack in the ice. Talking into it."

Hoodwink says there are openings, mostly in caves and crevasses, that lead all the way down to the feared underworlds, places where a man can hear the voices of long-dead monsters rising up, and if he's lucky, the voices of the legendary Jemen echoing from their sacred cavern. If the opening is big enough, monsters and ghostly Jemen may even climb out and walk in this world.

Arakie's brows pinch together. "He's not moving right. He may have a broken shoulder. Let's find out."

Another wave of blowing snow momentarily erases the man from existence, then he appears again.

Using his walking stick, Arakie plumbs the depths of the drifts before plunging down the slope with me close behind.

Like the colossal waves of a frozen ocean, ice undulates away in every direction, rising in towering white swells that plummet into dark troughs. The voices of the Ice Giants compete with the wind, moaning and growling as though engaged in a primeval torture ritual that never ends.

"Do you see all the cornices, Lynx? This whole slope is on the verge of collapsing into an avalanche. We have to be very smart now."

As we trudge onward, enormous cornices arch high over our heads. It won't take much to bring one down on top of us. An ice quake or even just a powerful gust of wind could do it, and that would trigger the entire mountainside to break loose and come thundering down.

Arakie aims his walking stick at a shallow, snow-filled groove on the slope above the man. "Looks like the place where he lost his footing and slid down."

In the blinding storm, the man probably stepped over the edge and fell before he'd realized it.

When we get closer, the man whimpers and stammers to himself. On occasion, he bends forward and shouts at the ground.

"Are you all right?" Arakie yells.

The youth, maybe sixteen or seventeen, whirls to stare at us with blazing eyes, then he rears backward and lets out a deep-throated howl as he pulls on the rope.

Less than five paces away, I get a better look at the Rust man. His shimmering clothing snaps around him in shreds. "Is that blood?"

"Yes. Lot of it."

The blood creates a perfect circle, about arm's length, in the snow around the youth. Since the blowing snow is continually covering the blood, he must be reaching out with bloody hands to grasp snow to eat.

"We're here to help you!" Arakie shouts. "Lynx, lay down your spear so he knows we mean him no harm."

"Lay down my spear? He's one of the Rust People. They are animals!"

"Some would argue they're less animal than you are, though personally I debate that fact. Now, do as I say. Put down your spear."

I reluctantly stab my spear into the snow and follow him, but my gaze constantly scans the slope for Rust People. This is the perfect place for an ambush. Hundreds of enemy warriors could be hidden behind the drifts or massive black boulders that scatter across the slope.

When we stand beside the man, I see that he kneels before a narrow crack in the ice, perhaps ten hand-lengths across, and he's holding fast to a rope that drops away into the darkness below.

Arakie kneels and examines him. "Bear attack. The claws cut to the bone. But he also struck his head in the fall. See the gore in his hair?"

"Why can't he speak? The head wound?"

"Cold shuts down the brain. He's probably been sitting out here in excruciating pain all night."

The man takes another huge yank on the rope, straining with all his might, then he falls forward and his shoulders heave with wrenching sobs.

"Take the rope from him, Lynx, so I can get a good look at his wounds."

Everything inside me is telling me to run away, that there must be a thousand Rust People coming, but I walk forward and pull the rope from the youth's bloody hands.

As soon as I do, he falls backward into the snow and weeps, "Thank you, thank you."

I'm surprised that the rope is slack, as though there's nothing on the other end. No tug. No weight. But just above the wind, I hear something. I lean over the crack and listen.

"Taiga?"

"Elder, there's a woman down there!"

Arakie turns to the Rust youth. "Is that you? Are you Taiga? What happened?"

Lifting my gaze, I study the shallow groove again, and I can imagine how it might have been . . . Bears were chasing them. They were running through the pitch black with the blizzard raging around them.

"Must have been roped together, elder. Taiga lost his footing, and it took both of them down. Probably didn't see the crevasse until she fell in."

Taiga gazes up at me with enormous, fever-brilliant eyes—eyes with no soul behind them, just mindless fear.

"Taiga?" the faint voice seeps up from the crack again, and the youth valiantly tries to drag himself back to her.

"No," Arakie says. "We'll take care of her. Stay still."

"Taiga? What's the matter with you? Are you still there?"

My fists go tight around the rope as terror grips me. *What's the matter with you?* I know that voice. It's Siskin's voice seeping up from the dark depths of the underworld. She should be in the sky world. What's she doing down there? This can't be real. My wounded heart must be making this up. She is not down there in that crevasse! She's on her way to the Land of the Dead.

"I don't believe it," Arakie says as he pulls apart the bloody, frozen shirt on Taiga's back. "The bear almost severed his shoulder. How could he pull on that rope?"

"Probably why she's still down there. With his injuries, he couldn't haul her out."

I take a new grip on the bloody rope and yank as hard as I can. For a moment I think she's coming up, then I realize I've just taken up the natural stretch in the braided leather rope. "She's not moving."

Arakie gives me a dire stare, as though he understands something I do not. "Taiga's head injury may have left him unconscious for a time after the fall. She probably tried to climb out, but at this time of autumn, the sheer walls of the crevasses have melted smooth. There are no handholds."

"But even if he was unconscious, they were roped together. He was on top and he's a heavy man. She should have been able to grab the rope and pull herself up."

Arakie's gaze roams the blowing snow while he thinks. "Unless they weren't roped together. Maybe he fell, and she walked down to see if he was all right and fell into the crevasse. Maybe when he woke, he threw his rope down to her, but by then it was too late."

"Too late? She's still alive. How could it have been too late?"

Arakie slides over to peer into the crack on his belly, and cups a hand to his mouth. "Hello. Are you all right?"

Nothing.

"Pull again, Lynx."

I heave backward with all my strength, but it's clear I'm just taking up the slack in the rope.

"Did you feel her move this time?"

"No."

Arakie says, "I don't see her. Must be down pretty deep."

"Ask her if she can help us by trying to climb up."

Arakie calls down into the darkness, "We're trying to get you out. Can you climb up at all?"

"No." The word glides up from the abyss. "My legs are . . . are trapped, covered with ice. Is Taiga all right?"

"He's hurt. Need to get him back to your village. How far away is it?"

"Gone . . . dead."

Arakie rises to his feet and walks to where my spear thrusts out of the snow. Powerful gusts assault the slope, peppering us with bits of sand and gravel swept off the faces of the Ice Giants.

I call, "Elder, shall we lower hot food down to her? She must be hungry."

Arakie pulls my spear from the snow and walks back to hand it to me. "That would be cruel."

"Cruel? She probably hasn't eaten since—"

"Jam your spear into the snow and tie the rope to it, so it doesn't fall into the hole. Then come over here and we'll chat."

Taiga lies on his back staring blankly up at the sky as though his strength is completely gone. Blood continues to pump from his wounds.

I drive my spear into the snow, tie the rope to the shaft, and follow Arakie as he walks out of Taiga's hearing range.

"You're not thinking of leaving her, are you?"

Arakie expels a breath. "Listen to me. While Taiga was unconscious, she must have tried to climb out, but after a time, she grew tired and sat down. She may have even fallen asleep waiting for him to wake up and help her. Whatever the reason, it took too long."

"But she's still alive."

Arakie takes a moment to flip up his hood and clutch it

beneath his chin. "While she slept, her body, warm from exertion, melted the ice, and as it cooled it refroze around her like a cocoon. Do you understand? She's part of the ice now. That's why the rope won't budge. You can't pull her out. The kindest thing we can do is put all of our efforts into saving her friend. We have a chance with him. Now, I want you to say goodbye to her, and help me get Taiga to the hollow, and then to the closest village."

I shift my weight to my other foot. I talked to her. She's alive. If it was me down there, I'd want to know that someone was trying to save me. Striding back, I call down, "I'll be right back. We're going to haul Taiga to a safer place where we can tend his injuries."

"Are you really comin' back?"

I wince at the question. "Yes. May take a while. Just don't worry, all right? I'm definitely coming back."

When I rise, I find Arakie looking at me with a speculative expression.

"Elder, I'll help you get Taiga into the hollow, but then I'm going to try to get her out. I have a long rope in my pack. Maybe if I lower my ax down to her, she can chop herself out of the ice."

Arakie nods, as though in understanding. "And when you go down into that hole after her, are you going down to save her? Or to save yourself?"

My mouth opens, but no words come out.

"It's hard, isn't it?" he asks. "We all want to use the dead to redeem ourselves, but trust me that it is the greatest subversion of love."

Icy wind whips his white hair around his face. I watch it until I can find the voice to say, "Elder, she's alive. She's not dead."

"I already told you that."

All I can do is stare at him and wonder if we are discussing two different . . .

It's impossible. How could he know that I heard Siskin's voice down there?

The old, white-haired man lightly pounds my shoulder with his fist. "Let's get Taiga to the cave, then we'll discuss it."

24

QUILLER

Bull boats are gone," I whisper when I see the loose shrouds and ripped clothing of the dead flapping around the burial scaffolds ahead. Clumps of zyme have washed in today and lie like glowing green arms across the beach. "Where is everyone?"

Boats were pulled up on shore when I left, but there's nothing there now, nor are they out in the ocean. And there's no one fishing or playing upon the shore. Which means my people are either dead or gone. There are no other choices.

Thirty paces ahead, Crow charges around the five burial scaffolds, sniffing the air. Sea eagles and ravens flutter above the dead. Even from this distance, I can tell the corpses' faces have been picked clean by hungry sea birds. They've become white skulls with threads of wiry hair. It's the way of the world. Life is meat.

"Jawbone? I'm going to run ahead."

"No!" Little Fawn screams. "Quiller, don't leave us! What if lions come?"

Loon cries, "Quiller, don't go!"

Kneeling down, I take a few precious moments to pat Loon's blond curls and calmly say, "Have you seen any lion tracks?"

"No."

"Then I don't think they can be very close, do you? My village is just up the beach from those burial scaffolds. Even if you walk slowly, you'll be there in a few hundred heartbeats. I just want to scout it first. You'll be all right for a little while, won't you? Jawbone will be here to take care of you."

Her small red face is streaked with tears, but she bravely says, "All right."

Jawbone, carrying Chickadee, says, "Go on, Quiller. We won't be far behind you."

"If you see any danger, run for the trees, and climb as high as you can. Understand?"

"We will."

I sprint toward the burial scaffolds. Crow has vanished. As I careen around the scaffolds, my steps falter. The lodges sit in exactly the same positions, but most of the lodge covers have been stripped off, leaving the rib-bone frames bare.

Crow runs from lodge frame to lodge frame, tucking her nose through the bones to look inside. A few belongings are visible, but many have been blown across the beach. Painted clothing, beaded headbands, and wooden dishes scatter the ground. Mink, Basher, and RabbitEar stand together by the central fire pit.

As I pound across the sand to join them, I gaze around the abandoned village, the trees, and the jagged mountains of ice to the east. A lion trap, made from logs hauled down from the forest, stands to the east at the edge of the trees. Though it is ten hands tall and the same wide, it's forty hands long. The gnawed carcass of a bison rests in the rear of the trap.

"Where is everyone?" I shout.

"Gone," Mink calls.

"No bodies?"

Mink shakes his head. "No. Whatever the threat was, they saw it coming, got in the boats, and left."

"Hushy must have warned them."

"Yes, we figured that out, too."

When I trot up and stand at RabbitEar's side, he gives me a soft look, telling me he's glad to see me. "Where are the children?"

"Out by the burial scaffolds. Coming as fast as they can."

Concern lines his face as he scans the beach, looking for them, worried about them. "I'll go find them . . ."

Jawbone appears, carrying Chickadee, breathing hard, gazing around with wide eyes. Little Fawn and Loon finally catch up with him, and they trot toward me and RabbitEar.

Basher gives them a hateful look. "Well, we know what the threat was. Their relatives."

"Probably, but could have been lions." RabbitEar aims his spear at the mound of bones that rests in the rear of the lion trap, near the bison carcass. "Those are lion bones. Looks like our people trapped two or three lions and ate them, then they tossed the bones back inside, hoping the meat scent would lure more lions into the trap. Lions are smart. May have attacked the village in revenge, but our families made it to the boats and escaped first."

"Maybe," Mink says. "But when did they leave? Last night? Two days ago? Five days ago?"

I reach down to touch the coals in the fire pit. The chunks on top are cold, but as I thrust my hand deeper, I find warm ashes.

"Fire's still warm at the bottom. Two days at most."

Jawbone and the girls have huddled up a short distance away, watching.

Mink glances between me and RabbitEar. "Both of you might want to check your lodges. See what's left. Figure out what you want to take when we go search for our families."

RabbitEar and I trot in opposite directions.

As I near my parents' lodge, my certainty grows. The shredded lodge cover snaps and crackles as wind whips it around the rib-bone frame. Through the rips, I see three extra bedding hides lying rolled in the rear. We only use them on very cold nights. To the right of the hides, my fishing tools are neatly arranged on the ground, just as I left them. Whatever caused them to take the boats and flee happened fast, but not so fast that some people couldn't strip their lodge covers and gather a few of their essential items. Why didn't my parents pack our winter hides? Too heavy to carry in the time they had? Probably food was more important. And they had three little children to herd to the boats.

RabbitEar calls, "Almost nothing is gone. Just weapons, food bags, and dishes." He walks to another lodge and throws back the door flap to look inside. "Same here."

Mink says, "My lodge, too. Gray Dove's pack is gone, along with some of the boys' toys, and all the food. Otherwise, everything is exactly where it was when I left."

"Think they had to run for the boats quickly and didn't have time to grab anything other than necessities?" RabbitEar says.

"If Hushy spotted a Rust People flotilla, our elders would have immediately ordered people to the boats," Basher shouts back. "I'm sure they only grabbed for the things they really needed."

"All right." Mink waves a hand to the village. "Start looking for tracks. Did everyone run for the boats, or did some people run for the trees?"

Finding tracks after two days of gusting sea breezes isn't going to be easy. Sand blows across the beach constantly, filling in every footprint within a few hands of time. Nonetheless, something always remains in sheltered areas around the lees of lodges.

While Mink, RabbitEar, and Basher search for signs, I examine the lion trap. From ten paces away, I smell the feral scent of lions, which means the beasts were caged for a time before being killed, long enough for their musk to seep into the wooden cage. At the back of the trap, three lion skulls are half hidden amid the crisscrossing maze of long bones, but the skull of a dire wolf is also visible. The wolf was probably drawn to the smell of meat, just as the lions were, and once he was captured and eaten, his bones were used as bait to lure more animals into the trap. None of the lion skulls, however, belong to old Nightbreaker. His huge skull is unmistakable. These were lionesses.

As I contemplate what happened, I notice the *outside* of the cage is badly gnawed in the southwest corner. Gnawed halfway through the log. At least one lion spent time lying on the ground and gnawing the wood, trying to free his trapped friend.

RabbitEar calls, "Mink, every track that I can make out was headed for the beach."

"Me, too." Mink trots past the fire pit toward RabbitEar's lodge, where both RabbitEar and Basher stand looking down.

As I walk back toward the men, I hear RabbitEar say, "I think we should kill a mammoth, build a boat from its hide, and head south."

Mink props the butt of his spear on the ground. "I agree."

"You think Lynx made it back before our people left?" I call.

The question seems to bring RabbitEar pain. His lips press into a tight white line and he walks across the empty village to sit down with the children, where his arm goes tight around Jawbone's shoulders, holding the boy reassuringly for a moment before returning to the others.

Mink's gaze drifts eastward to the towering glacial peaks, and he glares for several moments to try to hide his dread. "After this long, if my brother is still up there, he probably isn't coming back. Besides, we have more important things to worry about."

"But what if—"

"Forget about Lynx!" Basher yells. "Think about the rest of us!"

RabbitEar runs back over to the children and kneels before them, telling them everything is all right. Gods, I'd hoped to bring my children home to my parents' lodge, where I knew they would be loved and protected, so I could go search for Lynx. But I don't even know if my family is alive.

Jawbone's timid question rises: "What if we never find your people?"

RabbitEar hesitates, and I walk back to sit down in the children's circle between RabbitEar and Chickadee. I say, "Then I guess we will just keep paddling south until we find a beautiful place to live."

"That's right." In a fatherly manner, RabbitEar strokes Jawbone's hair. "We will be a family no matter where we go."

He obviously said it without thinking. When he turns to give me an apologetic look, there is so much love in his eyes.

25

LYNX

By the time I'm finished chopping down ancient saplings to make a sled to haul Taiga down the mountain, it's late morning, and sunlight streams into the hollow, falling upon Taiga where he lies beside the fire. Once we removed his curious silver clothes, we discovered he was far more badly injured than we thought. Deep gashes slice his belly and back. It's a miracle we didn't find his guts hanging out. How Taiga managed to keep pulling on that rope is a mystery of desperation. He must love the woman in the crevasse very much.

Outside the hollow, ice crystals drift through the air, giving it a shimmer. The wind has died down, and silence reigns again, heavy and ominous, like a monstrous invisible giant crouching in the snow, waiting for us to step beyond the lip of the hollow.

I grip the sled's reins and drag it over to where Arakie sits cross-legged before the fire, sipping a cup of hot tea.

"This is useless, elder. He's dying. He'll be dead long before you get him to a village healer. Leave him here by the fire to stay warm, and come help me rescue the woman."

Arakie sets his cup down hard. "Sit down and dip a cup of tea so we can talk."

"I have to go back to the woman, elder."

"Sit down, Lynx."

Grudgingly, I crouch on the other side of the fire and extend my hands to the warmth. "You're not going to talk me out of it, so you may as well not—"

"Tell me something. When you first heard her voice, you got a terrified expression on your face. Who did you think it was down there?"

I toy with a stick at the edge of the woodpile, then throw it onto the flames. "My dead wife."

He pauses. "How did you feel about that?"

"It's not her, elder. I know that."

"You wanted it to be, though, didn't you? That way you'd have a second chance to save her. I'm asking because even though you know now that it isn't your wife down there, it may still be the reason you want to save her."

"No, no, that has nothing to do—"

"Because saving this woman will ease some of your guilt over not saving your wife."

"That's not it at all! I can't just abandon her, not when she—"

"She can't chop herself out, Lynx, and if you go down after her you will both be lost forever."

"You cannot know that! I'm stronger than I gander."

The crow's-feet at the edges of Arakie's blue eyes deepen. He shifts to pull his knees up so he can brace his elbows atop them. "Let me tell you a story—"

"There's no time," I insist, and brusquely toss another branch on the fire. Sparks explode and gush upward toward the translucent roof. "She's freezing while we're—"

When I start to rise, Arakie orders, "Sit *down*."

I do it, but I'm not happy about it. Every instant I remain here, more and more of her is being gobbled up by the glacier.

Arakie leans toward me and stares hard into my eyes. "I need you to listen carefully, Lynx. A long time ago, I was a mountain climber, a good one. But on a trip up Everest, one of my cousins fell into a crevasse. He fell hard. Broke both legs.

Knocked him senseless. I thought all I had to do was lower my-self into the crack, tie the rope around him, and then climb back up and pull him out." The elder lifts a skeletal finger and aims it at my nose. "I reached the bottom, tied the rope around my cousin's waist, then I tried to climb out. I couldn't. You know why?"

"No."

"The walls of the crevasse had melted smooth and slick. There were no footholds, no handholds. But I was strong. Stron-ger than you will ever be. Just using my feet and hands, I knew I could work my way back up the rope. But halfway to the top, the rope iced up. I couldn't get a grip on it, and every time I tried to brace my feet against the wall to help steady me, my feet slipped off. If our friends hadn't found us when they did, I'd be smothered in ice at the bottom of that crevasse right now." He lowers his finger and clenches it to a fist.

"Did you save your cousin?"

Arakie inhales a deep breath. "No. I'd been hanging there quite a while by the time they found me. I ordered them to lower me all the way down again. When I reached him, only the top of his head was visible above the ice. The glacier had swallowed him."

He must have listened to his cousin's cries for days before the end came.

"Did you cut his dead body out of the ice? Take him home to his family?"

He nods, and gives me a sober look. "Do you know why the rope froze up? Every warm breath you expel inside the crevasse rises and freezes on the rope. If you go down there to try to help her, in a very short while, the rope will be useless."

I blink. That would never have occurred to me.

Arakie finishes his tea and tucks his cup in his pack, which rests near the fire. "Big predators will find my sled trail quickly.

The scent of blood will guide them right to me. With two of us, we can probably fight them off. But I can't do it alone, Lynx. And if something happens to me, no one will be coming back to rescue you and the girl. Get it? No one."

Suddenly, I see Siskin lying beneath me, smiling up with all the love in the world in her eyes . . . then yellow eyes blink at me from her face.

Despair like nothing I've ever known fills me. Is it really futile to try to save her life?

Arakie adds, "I know you saw the ocean this morning. Your village is actually the closest to us. It's probably only a day, maybe a day and a half, to get there. Hoodwink will know how to care for Taiga's wounds. Don't you want to go home?"

The longing for home is suddenly overpowering. If her fate is a foregone conclusion, maybe it is best just to leave her? In two days I could be home sitting in Mink's lodge before the fire, telling stories with my nephews crawling over my lap, asking a thousand questions, laughing at my adventures. And feeling worthless for not trying to save her.

"I have to help the woman first."

Arakie suddenly looks up at the sky and frowns as though upset. For a time, he seems to be listening, then he shakes his head. "That's pure speculation. We don't know that yet."

Glancing around and seeing nothing, I quietly ask, "Who are you talking to?"

Arakie sighs and turns back. "Answer a question for me. Do you understand the principle of the greatest good for the greatest number? I do not believe she's right that you are too primitive to comprehend the greater good. If you are, we may all be lost."

Fear makes my breathing go shallow. "Elder . . . when you suddenly look up at the sky, who are you talking to?"

"What kind of an idiotic question is that? Sister Sky, of

course. She's my spirit helper, and Good Lord, she can be dictatorial."

I glance up at Sister Sky, wondering what she said to him. One of Quiller's spirit helpers is Sister Moon, but Quiller maintains that she's gentle and kind. "Did Sister Sky say I was primitive?"

"Among other colorful adjectives. So, answer my question."

"Trying to help the woman is good."

"Think this through, boy. If four people die because of you, is that truly good? Or was helping her an act of evil?"

Frustrated, I slap my arms against my sides. The truth is that I do not comprehend the issue, so perhaps Sister Sky was right about me. "I'm leaving. I don't wish to argue any longer, elder!"

Without waiting for his response, I turn my back to him and jog down the steep slope toward the crevasse.

26

QUILLER

RabbitEar and I crouch on the beach behind my parents' lodge with the children. We spent all day building bent-willow boat frames, tying each pole in place with strips of fresh sinew. Both circular frames rest on the beach to our right, along with heaping bowls of sinew, stripped from the bison we killed at dawn. The afternoon gleam has turned the slender weaves of poles golden.

"Quiet now," I whisper to the children.

Jawbone taps his lips with his fingers, which must be the Rust People way of telling children to stay silent. The girls clamp their lips together and stare at him, waiting for his signal before they even dare to breathe again.

Up the trail in front of us, hidden on either side of the trail behind blinds made of dead fallen pine, Basher and Mink wait with their spears, watching the mammoth calf that lopes down the trail toward the beach. He's gotten far ahead of his mother, who slowly lumbers down the trail two hundred paces behind the calf. Sunlight shines in the calf's long brown hair. He has his trunk up, playfully switching it around. As he nears Mink and Basher, the calf trumpets to his mother, as though trying to get her to move faster. The cow trumpets back, but doesn't speed up. She seems to be enjoying the stroll in the warm sunlight.

They are so graceful, their massive bodies swaying with their gaits.

When the calf breaks into a gallop and runs between Mink and Basher, both men leap from behind their blinds and stab their spears deeply into the calf's chest, then they charge away, trying to get to the next blinds set up twenty paces down the trail before the cow charges.

The dying calf stands trembling, trying to figure out what happened, then he lifts his trunk and trumpets in panic as he staggers off the trail.

The terrified cow breaks into a charge, thundering down the trail after Basher and Mink, who've just made a mad dive behind their blinds.

"Get ready to run," RabbitEar says.

"She'll never make it this far." But my spear is up, at the ready, just in case I'm wrong.

When the cow gets within range, Basher and Mink jump up, drive their spears into her heart and lungs, then run hard for the trees.

The mammoth cow chases them deeper into the pines, then she walks back to lie down beside her dead calf.

Already blood foams at her nostrils and mouth. But death takes a while. When her huge head finally drops to the ground for the last time, I stand up and step out from behind the lodge. Basher and Mink are moving back through the trees, headed for the kills.

"Quiller?" Jawbone calls. "Can we go up there now and help butcher the mammoths?"

I examine the mammoths. The cow's legs have finally stopped kicking.

"Don't get in Mink or Basher's way. We all have a lot of work to do skinning the animals, drying their meat, and finishing two boats, so we can head south carrying lots of dried meat for our families."

"We won't get in anyone's way."

"Very well, go on. But do exactly as Mink and Basher tell you."

"We will."

Jawbone and the girls run up the trail with wide smiles. The end of a hunt is always a joyous time. Children get to eat the first pieces of sweet meat cut from the carcasses, and have cups of warm blood to wash it down. They'll sleep warm with bulging bellies tonight.

When they reach the calf, the children race around it, playing tag. Basher and Mink already have their bone knives out, ready to begin the hard work of skinning the dead animals. That will take most of the day. When Basher bends over the dead calf, I see him pet it gently, then his mouth moves as he prays the calf's soul to an afterworld filled with mammoths, where it's always springtime.

"Good to see the children playing, isn't it?" RabbitEar asks as he steps up beside me. Sweat mats strands of red hair to his cheeks.

"It is. If we're smart, we'll hurry back to work on our boat frames. While Basher and Mink watch the children, we can get a lot done."

"Yes, we can." He nods and looks out across the village. As Father Sun descends toward the horizon, amber rays of sunlight stream across Sky Ice Village and flicker from the patches of snow that linger in the shadowed places around the lodges.

We walk together to our boat frames. The largest boat spreads forty hands across and eight hands deep. Twenty people could ride comfortably in that boat. It's far too big for the eight of us, but it will come in handy when we find our people.

The smaller boat is only twenty hands across. We will pile it full of dried meat and tow it down the coast behind us.

When I reach the largest boat, I study it with a careful eye. The glossy strips of tendon that bind the poles together are still wet and gleam whitely.

"Hand me another length of tendon, will you?"

RabbitEar reaches into the wooden bowl, pulls out a long strip of tendon, and smiles as he hands it to me.

I wrap it around one of the poles that attaches to the gunwale, pull it tight, and tie it. As the sinew dries, it will shrink and turn rock-hard.

RabbitEar's green eyes light up when he sees Jawbone running after Little Fawn. The girl has a strip of fresh mammoth meat and is squealing in delight.

I say, "I don't understand how the children can sound so joyous. They've lost everything in a matter of days. How can they muster the strength to laugh and play?"

"Children are tougher than adults think. But I know what you mean. It's almost as though they've blocked the destruction of their village from their hearts."

Jawbone snatches the meat from Little Fawn's hand and shrieks in joy as he runs away with it.

Little Fawn bursts out in tears.

Mink calls, "Little Fawn?" and tosses her another strip of meat.

"Thank you, Mink!"

Loon and Chickadee barely notice. They have seated themselves right beside where Basher works, carefully skinning the calf. He's been routinely handing them tidbits.

RabbitEar smiles as he watches them.

"You like Jawbone, don't you?"

A tender smile warms his face. "He's a surprising little boy."

"What do you mean?"

"I mean he takes his duties as protector very seriously. He asked me this morning if I would teach him how to make a spear so he could protect you if we were attacked by lions or bears."

I stop halfway through tying another pole into place on the gunwale, and turn to stare at him. "Protect me?"

"Yes. He's worried about you, and that's a very good thing. I told him I would help him make a spear."

I use my sleeve to shove red hair out of my eyes. That's a strange, fatherly act, and it makes me uncomfortable. "Rabbit-Ear, I'm not sure that's a good idea. Maybe in another three or four moons, when he's settled into the Sealion People, but I don't want him to have a spear just yet. You said it yourself not more than two days ago. What if he drives his spear through Mink's heart while he sleeps, or—"

"It will be a boy's spear, Quiller," RabbitEar sighs, "too little to do any real damage, even if he had the strength to cast it hard, which I doubt."

"Still . . ." I say with reserve.

Patiently, he explains, "Try to see it from his side. He just saw his mother killed before his eyes. Somewhere inside him, he must blame himself because he wasn't there to help protect her. He wanted to fight off the lions. Instead, his grandfather made him get into a boat with the girls and shoved it out to sea. Guilt must be weighing on him. Besides, a boy his age needs a spear."

"He's ten, RabbitEar."

"I had my first spear at the age of six. How about you?"

Strange. I can see that little spear with perfect clarity. I'd painted blue rings around the shaft. My father had made a mammoth-bone spear point, and I remember the day he attached it to the spear and handed it to me. It was one of the proudest days of my life. Receiving a spear meant that he would take me hunting with him. I killed my first partridge the next day.

Grudgingly, I give RabbitEar a nod. "All right. I was eight. But he's not one of our people. Not yet."

"I know that. But he needs to feel like he is. Tell you what, I'll help him make the spear, and you can decide where and when he gets to use it. You can keep it in your quiver the entire time if you want to. He needs a purpose, Quiller, and protecting you and the girls is a good one."

A touch indignant, I reply, "I don't need anyone's protection, RabbitEar."

"Well, if you want him to love you, don't tell him that. We spend all of our lives searching for someone who will let us stand guard over them. Someone who will let us protect them. He's very lonely. It makes him feel needed to have a purpose."

I have to think about that. A boy can't love you unless he feels you need his protection? What a bizarre notion. Though, when I think it through, I know he's right. One of the reasons I loved—love—Lynx so much is that protecting him gives me purpose. Even if he never really loved me, at least he needed me. I could do that for him. Stand guard over him.

"All right. I won't tell him."

RabbitEar reaches out to lightly touch my hand. "You won't regret it. I think he's going to become a great Sealion warrior someday."

I can tell from the wistful expression on his face that he'd like to be the one to teach Jawbone how do that, and it occurs to me that RabbitEar is seventeen. His grandmother has been trying to marry him off for two summers, but he has refused every girl presented to him.

When I look up at him, a stray gust of wind whips his thick tangle of hair around his face. He smiles at me.

There's suddenly a chill in the air. I have the feeling that I'm in way over my head, being swallowed up by feelings I'd rather not feel for him. Down to my bones, I know that my desire for RabbitEar is useless. When I find Lynx, and we find our people, none of this will matter.

Except that it does . . .

I pull away from him and rub my arms briskly to get the blood going.

"Cold today," I say in explanation.

RabbitEar just lowers his eyes and frowns at the sand. "Yes. It is."

27

LYNX

As the afternoon warms, the drifts melt into rounded humps and shine across the mountain like a vast field of gigantic polished pearls. One of the Ice Giants bellows. Another answers with a high-pitched rattle. They must be discussing me, watching me, maybe even gambling on how long I'll last out here.

I'm wondering the same thing.

When I reach the crevasse, I see fresh dire wolf tracks. While I was chopping wood and building a sled, one lone wolf sneaked in and ate almost all the bloody snow. Where is he? His tracks lead down the groove in the snow where Taiga and the woman fell, then he trotted back up it and disappeared over the crest of the hill. He must still be close.

"Don't think about it now," I say out loud. "Think about it later. If you work hard, you'll have her out of the crevasse long before dark."

Leaning over the crack, I call, "I'm here. I'm going to try to get you out . . . Can you hear me? I brought food and water for you."

Finally, a small voice eddies up through the darkness.

"Oh, Lynx, you shouldn't have returned. That was a bad choice."

"You won't think so when you're sitting in front of my warm fire."

Choking on the words, she replies, "The ice has been meltin' in here all day. Water is still runnin' down the walls and freezin' around me. My legs are completely covered with ice. I'm not goin' to make it through the night."

"I'll have you out long before then. I'm lowering food and water to build up your strength. Here it comes. Let me know when you see it."

I pull my rope from my pack and tie the bags of food and water to one end. As I let out the rope, my gaze drifts over the steep slope. Small pools of water have formed in the low spots and shimmer across the face of the glacier for as far as I can see. Ten hands distant, Taiga's rope is still tied to my spear, which thrusts up out of the snow.

"Where's my brother?" Her voice is so faint I can barely hear her.

"My friend, Arakie, is hauling him to the closest village."

"But wasn't your friend an old man? He sounded old."

Dear gods, I swear that's Siskin's voice. My need to save her is overwhelming.

I feed more rope into the hole. I can feel the bags swinging as they descend. "Arakie will be all right."

She weeps the words, "How could you do that? How could you pick me over them? They needed you. I'm a dead woman."

I'm almost out of rope. Gods, how deep is she? "Can you see the bags yet?"

"No, I don't see anythin'."

She doesn't sound that deep, but maybe voices carry differently in the narrow confines of a crevasse. "How long was Taiga's rope?"

"He tied both of our ropes together. I guess . . . I don't know . . . one hundred and fifty feet?"

I'm confused. She measures distances the same way Arakie does? "My people measure in hand-lengths. You use foot-lengths?"

There's a hesitation while she seems to be trying to figure out how to explain it. "One of our feet is about two of your hand-lengths, I think."

My spine goes rigid. That can't be right. She's three hundred hands deep? If it's true, I made so many wrong assumptions. Why didn't I ask her more questions before I decided to try to rescue her?

"Can you tell me about the crevasse? When you fell in, did you fall straight down?"

"No, the crevasse slithers back and forth. I broke through several thin sheets of ice before I stopped."

"How big is the place where you are?"

"Narrow. Really narrow. I'm wedged tight in here."

"All right. Earlier you said there was a larger chamber below you. How do you know?"

"To my right, there's a hole. If I shout into it, it echoes back and forth for a long time. I think maybe I'm sittin' on another of those thin ice sheets, and below me is a huge cavern, or maybe a series of caverns strung together."

A hard swallow goes down my throat. "Was the hole there when you first got wedged?"

"No. My body heat seems to be meltin' it out. It's gettin' bigger."

Which means that at any moment she might melt through the hole and fall into the cavern.

"If I lower you an ax, can you chop your legs free so I can pull you up?"

Laughter or sobbing.

"I can't even feel my legs. The water is freezin' around them, cementin' me in this hole. And it's very dark down here. If I start choppin' with an ax, I'm liable to chop off a foot."

"I want you to try, but first you need to untie the rope from around your waist and let me pull it up. My rope isn't long enough to reach you. I'll tie them both together, then lower you the food and water."

Not a breath eddies up through the darkness.

"Hello?"

That rope is her only link to the world above. She's probably holding on to it with all her strength, afraid to let go.

"I'll lower it right back down to you."

Faintly, she calls, "Will you? Really? I'm one of the Rust People. Our families have been killin' each other for generations."

"Yes, but not today. Not today."

It takes another twenty heartbeats before she calls, "All right . . . I—I'm untyin' it."

While she works at the knots, I pull my rope back up and untie the bags of food and water. By the time I'm done, and can pull on her rope again, it's slack. I pull it up quickly.

"I'm tying our ropes together, then tying the food, water, and my ax to the rope, and lowering it back down. Keep looking for it. Tell me when you see it."

Stretching out on my belly in the snow with my head suspended over the crevasse, I watch the bags and ax swing as I lower them down into the darkness.

She yells, "I hear them bangin' off the ice. . . . Oh, there they are. They slid down the ice and right to me!"

"Good." I heave a sigh of relief. "You might want to eat something first, before you start chopping—"

"No, no, I—I'm choppin' first!"

Sharp cracks arise from the depths.

As I watch Father Sun getting lower in the afternoon sky,

my fears grow. Despite my promises, I won't get her out by nightfall. I know that now. Can she last the night? Can I?

The woman calls up, "Lynx, please talk to me. Tell me about you and Arakie."

A veil of snow whips across the glaciers in the distance, and a small icy tornado spins to life and bobs across the slope.

"I don't know much about Elder Arakie. He lives out here alone. His people are extinct."

"Extinct? He is the last of his kind?"

"Yes. When you see him, you will instantly know he is different. He has an oddly shaped head and face."

Crack. Bang. Crack, crack.

"What about you? Why are you out here?"

I consider what I should tell her. "My . . . my wife was killed. Many people said I was coward. They said I let her die. But our village council did not say that. They just said I needed to go on a spirit quest. That's why I'm here. The council ordered that I be abandoned in the wilderness to search for my spirit helper. He's a . . . a giant lion."

The chopping stops.

After a time, she sobs, "Lynx, more and more water is floodin' down the walls and freezin' over my legs. I can't seem to get ahead of it."

The air temperature has warmed greatly since midday. Rivulets of meltwater cover the slope.

With lightning quickness, I begin scooping snow from around the crevasse, throwing it aside, trying to verify my suspicion. When I'm finished, I stand up, breathing hard, staring down. Trickles of water have been flowing beneath the snow into the crevasse. The sight brings me true terror. The walls of the crevasse must be funneling it right down on top of her. She'll never get ahead of it.

Panic starts to burn through me.

"I know you don't remember your name, but I need something to call you. What should I call you?"

"I—I don't know. Sunbird feels familiar, but it may not be my name, just the name of someone I know."

You promised you wouldn't . . .

"All right, Sunbird, I'm going to pull a log down and lay it across the crevasse, then I'm going throw one end of the rope over the log and tie the other end around my waist to slowly lower myself down to help you. Once I've chopped you out of the ice, I'll use the rope to lift you up to the log, so you can crawl to safety."

"Don't even *think* of comin' down here, or we'll both be lost!"

"Trust me. I know exactly what I'm doing. I'll be right back."

"No, don't leave me! Lynx?"

As I trot away up the trail through the snow, I hear her screaming my name.

When I enter the ice hollow, I go straight to the woodpile and drag out a log around fifteen hands long. For several moments, uncertainty fills me. Is this the right decision? *Think this through.*

The thought of spending the night in the crevasse is paralyzing. It will be utterly black down there.

I set the log down and go to the woodpile, where I stuff my pockets with twigs, then stare at the burning coals. If I place some coals between two layers of rock, and wrap them in a piece of hide, I can fold the hide up around the edges and tie it to my belt. It might catch fire, but if I'm careful, it shouldn't.

Takes a while to find two perfect flat rocks . . .

When I've created my bundle of coals, I walk over and pick up one end of the log.

Most of the trail is slick, which means the log slides pretty easily. At the crevasse, I drag it over the narrowest section of the crack to make a bridge and make sure it's secure. My next step is the tricky one. I'll need to drape the ropes I've tied together over the log, tie one end around my waist, and hold on to the other end while I lower myself down into the darkness.

But the story Arakie told me is starting to weigh on me. With two people down in the hole, twice as much warm breath will be rising, icing the rope up faster. What if I knot the rope at regular intervals? Even if it ices up, I should be able to hold on, shouldn't I? Should I take my pack down? No. The crevasse might get too narrow, and if it does, the pack will only be a hindrance. My pack will have to stay up here.

Another half-hand of time passes before I've finished knotting my rope and I can tie it around my waist.

"Best do it before my guts turn runny."

I shinny out across the log. When I'm in the middle, I swing out over the edge . . . and hand over hand lower myself down into the black maw.

"I'm coming down!"

At first the ice is blue, then it turns dark green, and finally fades to gray. As the light grows dimmer, my teeth start to chatter. I pass through the first broken ice sheet and the crevasse begins to curve, spiraling down into the darkness. I have the vague sense that I'm going down the throat of a whirlpool, being sucked into the underworlds. Above me, I can still see the log, which is a relief, but the ice here is dirty, banded with gravel and sand. There are a few stones protruding where I can brace my feet as I continue downward.

And I reach the end of the rope. I'm now about one hundred and eighty hands deep. I have to untie the rope from my waist, then tie both ends together and leave the rope here. What if the rest of the crevasse is so slick, I'll never be able to make it back up to the rope? I gander up at the log. Now it's just a small black slash against the faint sunlight.

Blessed Jemen, I'm terrified.

"Where are you? Can you hear me?"

"Here. I'm here!"

Her voice reverberates around the crevasse, but she's close. Extending one foot as far as I can, I use my boot to feel for the shape of the ice. As my eyes adjust, I can see the crevasse a little better. It's very narrow here, like a tunnel, and the air smells dank and oddly old, as though I've entered an ancient portal to the legendary underworlds and can smell the breath of sleeping monsters. The cries of the Ice Giants encircle me. The deep belly groans, whistles, and falcon-like shrieks vibrate through the ice until my whole body shakes with their voices.

"I hear you, Lynx!"

"Keep talking."

"You're gettin' closer."

The crack narrows until ice hugs against my shoulders. It's horrifying. Blessed Ancestors, what a feeling this is. I wriggle deeper. Several times I think I'm wedged . . . but I manage to work my way down until the crack widens to about twice my body width. What if the water running down the walls freezes and narrows the crack so that neither of us can wriggle back up through it? I extend my right foot . . . and touch a flat place, a floor.

I cry out when a hand grabs my leg.

"Sorry! I didn't want you to step over the edge. You're standin' right above me. I'm melted down tight in this hole."

"I need light to work. I don't want to accidentally hurt you. Give me a few moments." My voice echoes, sounding deeper and more resonant than it does in the world above.

Untying the bag of coals from my belt, I place it on the floor and unwrap the hide. The rocks inside are warm. Carefully, I lift the top rock to expose the glowing coals that rest on the bottom rock. Awe expands my chest when the faint red gleam flickers from the ice around me.

Sunbird gasps, "Light!"

Digging in my pocket, I place a single twig on the coals and gently blow until a tiny flame springs to life.

I see her staring at me with enormous terror-filled eyes. Tears have frozen on her lashes turning them into ice sculptures. Her long blond hair and strange silver shirt are frosted from her breath.

"Oh, gods, you're real. I—I wasn't sure. I've been s-seein' things down here," she sobs. "Dead people. Strange creatures."

Her angular face and heavy brow are striking, much larger than mine. "We need to work fast. Hand me my ax, and I'll finish chopping you out of the ice."

"Here." She passes it to me with a shaking hand.

I take the ax and arrange the tiny lamp on an ice ledge above the hole. As I arrange my feet on either side of the hole, water soaks my boots. I could be standing in a freezing stream. That's how much water there is, but it must be draining out the hole she talked about, the one that leads into the large cavern, or she'd be dead by now. That's the only possible reason her body isn't already completely buried in ice.

"Please h-hurry. When it gets full dark in here, it's . . . it's unbearable."

"I understand."

"No, gods, you do not! You can't. No one can." She's shivering so violently, it looks like a convulsion.

Ice chips fly as I chop. In the faint firelight they resemble sparks shooting around a deep blue throat.

28

QUILLER

Afternoon sunlight turns the sand into a glimmering expanse of tiny amber jewels.

For a few moments, I watch Mink and Basher where they stand beside the central fire. Between tending the pots of boiling pine pitch, they cut the mammoth hides into rounded shapes for our circular bull boats.

Turning back, I smile at RabbitEar. For some time, we've been sitting out here on the beach teaching the children to make bone tools in the way of the Sealion People. Though I know Rust People pound meteorites into tools, it's strange to me that the children do not know how to fashion tools from bones. Bone tools are far easier to make and more practical. So far the children have completed several choppers and cleavers shaped from mammoth shoulder blades, and bone knives and fleshers made from the leg bones, which are laid out in a line on the sand.

"Jawbone?" I say. "Why don't the Rust People use bones for tools? Bones are everywhere, meteorites are rare."

He licks his lips and thinks about it, before he answers, "We need to learn. It's gettin' harder and harder to find iron. We can't even patch our boats now. I guess it's all at the bottom of the ocean from when the enemies of the Jemen cast meteorites on the zyme."

I stop to stare at him. "The enemies of the Jemen cast meteorites on the zyme?"

His eyes light up. "Don't you know the story of how the Ice Giants were born? It's one of our Beginnin' Time stories."

"I know our story, but I want to hear yours. Please, tell me."

Jawbone gestures to emphasize his words, and I'm sure he's mimicking the Rust elders when they tell this story to their children. Jawbone spreads his arms wide to the ocean. "Nine hundred summers ago, just after the Jemen created the zyme, it grew legs and walked on shore like an army of men to eat the Jemen. When the Jemen realized the zyme had turned itself into a monster, they created magical potions to try to kill it. But the enemies of the Jemen, the Iron People, were watchin'. They didn't want the zyme to die. They wanted it to eat the Jemen." Jawbone flaps his arms like a bird. "So they turned themselves into birds and flew high into the sky. When they got to the middle of the thickest zyme forests, they dropped huge bags of powdered meteorites, great clouds of it, over the forests. The zyme gobbled it up and grew and grew. As it spread over the whole ocean, the world turned colder and colder, and gave birth to the Ice Giants. And that's the story of how the Ice Giants were born." He smiles broadly. The story clearly delights him.

RabbitEar gives the boy a curious look. "The stories of your people are very different from our stories."

Jawbone seems to sense disapproval. He nods, as though in apology, and reaches down to toy with a bone scraper lying on the sand.

I say, "What an excellent story. I wonder if our peoples don't just have different pieces of the Jemen's tale, and if we put them all together—"

"We'd understand what truly happened just after the zyme?"

"Exactly."

RabbitEar must realize he hurt Jawbone's feelings. He

reaches out to stroke the boy's blond hair. "Perhaps, but I'm not sure the gods really want us to understand. How do you stay a god if humans know all your secrets?"

That makes Jawbone laugh. "Grandfather says the Jemen wove magical spells around their secrets and carried them to the campfires of the dead, so no one could ever discover them."

"See?" RabbitEar says with smile. "I knew it."

Jawbone smiles back as though everything that matters can be found in RabbitEar's eyes.

"All right, shall we get back to our lesson? Who wants to know how to make a bone spearhead?" RabbitEar holds up a chunk of bone, about the length of his hand, for the children to look at.

The children leap up and down in excitement, saying "I do, I do," almost simultaneously.

"All right. Watch closely. The first thing we have to do is crack the bone in half."

The children, especially Jawbone, move in for a closer look. RabbitEar places the arm bone on a flat rock, then lifts a heavy river cobble and brings it down hard, splitting the bone in half.

"Little Fawn, you are the keeper of the marrow today," I say. "Where's your marrow bowl?"

"I forgot!" The six-summers-old girl charges for the wooden bowl, grabs it, and brings it back. "I'm ready now."

RabbitEar uses a horn spoon to scoop the marrow from the broken bone into the bowl. "Thank you, Little Fawn. Please carry it over and empty your bowl onto the bark slabs with the rest of the marrow."

Little Fawn, smiling broadly, carries her bowl to the bark slabs beside the fire and dumps it onto the growing marrow pile. Once it is melted, we will pour the fatty marrow onto the mammoth hides to help waterproof our bull boats. Mink ruffles her hair while she's there. Drying racks, made from woven willow poles, cluster near the fire. Covered with strips of dry-ing meat, the racks scent the air with the rich fragrance of warm mammoth steaks.

I glance away to study Basher and Mink. They've cut the mammoth hides to shape, fitted them over the circular boat frames, and just begun to fold the edges over the willow rim of the first boat and whip-stitch it down. They use their mammoth bone punches, long sharp pieces of bone, to poke holes in the hide. The tool makes a distinctive *pock-pock* sound as they punch the bone through the hide and pull it out. After puncturing a hole, they thread lengths of tendon through and wrap it over the rim of the frame. As the day warms, the tendons will shrink tight, binding the hide to the frame, then we will seal the holes with the pine pitch.

Were it not for the absence of Lynx and my family, it would be a perfect day. The smell of meat drying, and the sounds of boat and tool making, make me unbelievably happy. As well, the frequent laughter of children and Crow's delighted barking as she chases the shorebirds fill me with contentment. And then there's RabbitEar, who keeps gazing longingly at me when I least suspect it.

"Now watch me," RabbitEar instructs. "I'm going to show you how to make a platform the way Sealion People do it."

Jawbone is concentrating so hard that lines etch his ten-summers-old brow.

RabbitEar turns the sliver of bone to show Jawbone the different angles, then he picks up his rock and begins to carefully strike the bone, fashioning the perfect flat spot on one end. "Do you see how flat this is?"

"Yes. Now you're goin' to smack it to drive off a flake of bone, aren't you?"

"I am. And that's the difficult part, because you have to strike the platform firmly in the middle to drive off the perfect flake, or you'll crush the platform and have to start over again. Are you watching?"

Jawbone's eyes widen. "Yes."

RabbitEar strikes the freshly made platform and a thin flake of bone shoots off, angling toward Jawbone, who leaps to get out of the way. RabbitEar picks it up and holds it so Jawbone gets a good look at it. "Next, we're going to use our rock to shape the edge."

"To make it sharp?"

"No, at this point, I'm just creating a spearhead shape." RabbitEar grips the flake with one hand and uses his rock to carefully knock off chips all the way around the piece of bone. When he has a basic leaf-like shape, he holds it up. "Do you see how jagged this edge is?"

"Yes."

"We made the perfect spearhead shape, but the edge is too irregular. So, when the bone dries a little more, we will grind the edge on a slab of sandstone until it is sharp, straight, and strong enough to penetrate the ribcage of a mammoth."

RabbitEar hands the rough spearhead to Jawbone. The boy takes it with a fascinated frown and turns it over and over in his hand, examining every detail.

The girls have apparently lost interest, for they've trotted away to play chase on the beach. As they veer around the burial scaffolds, their delighted cries ring out, which spurs Crow to yip and bark at their antics. I smile. The children's voices will please the dead.

RabbitEar stretches out on his side on the sand and props himself on one elbow to gaze up at me. "The boats will be finished in another two or three hands of time, I suspect." His deep voice is filled with happiness.

"I hope Mink doesn't order us to paddle at night. Wouldn't mind so much if it was just the four of us, but with the children along, I think it's risky. If we get hit broadside by a monster wave, we'll capsize. In daylight, we can see the children to save them. If it's dark, they could sink below the waves or drift out into the zyme, and we'd never find them."

RabbitEar nods. "I'm sure he plans to spend the night here. The sinew needs another day to shrink and pull the hides tight over the willow frames, then we still have to cover each hole with pine pitch and pour fat to waterproof the rawhide."

"That's in an ideal world, RabbitEar. I'm afraid Mink is in a hurry. Our families are far south by now. Mink wants to find them before the Rust People do. He knows that if an attack comes, they will need every warrior."

"Yes, they will."

RabbitEar watches Jawbone pull bone chunks from the knapping pile, examine each, then place them in a line on the sand. A smile turns his lips, and it has a strange effect on me. I know he likes all the children, but he truly seems to adore Jawbone. There's a warmth in his eyes when he looks at the boy. I've started to cherish my moments with RabbitEar and the children.

When RabbitEar looks back at me, his gaze caresses the lines of my face and runs down my throat before returning to my eyes.

"Quiller . . ." He starts and awkwardly stops. "I know you love Lynx, but I was hoping you and I could—"

"I—I'm leaving, RabbitEar."

Time seems to stop. Conflicting emotions dance across his face: fear, desperation, and the need to say something to me that he knows I do not want to hear.

When I stand up, he leaps to his feet. We stand looking at each other for far longer than I intended. Fifteen heartbeats, thirty. The longer I look into his eyes, the more loudly blood rushes in my ears.

He says, "You're going after Lynx?"

"Yes. Tomorrow morning."

I can tell that the news has stunned him. He's clenched his fists.

"Will you keep the children safe while I'm gone?"

"You know I will."

Far away, somewhere up amongst the high, jagged peaks of ice, a bull bison lets out a lion-like roar, and the echo carries down the slope, bouncing around like a hide ball. It's late in the season to hear a bull roar, but I often hear that roar in my dreams—usually when my spirit helper is warning me of some impending calamity—so I instinctively turn to look up at the Ice Giants. The highest peaks have shed their snowy cloaks and shine pale turquoise in the sun.

"Once I've found Lynx, I . . . we . . . will follow the shore southward until we locate you."

As though he can't help himself, RabbitEar reaches out, catches a lock of my windblown hair, and gently tucks it behind my ear. Then he places his warm hand against my throat. The tender, lover-like gesture makes me stare at him.

"I don't want you to go," he softly says.

"Have to. You said it yourself. If I don't try, I'll . . ."

He suddenly wraps his arms around me and clutches me hard against his chest. I'm surprised that his muscular arms are shaking. In my ear, he says, "Please, don't do this."

"If he's still alive, he needs me, RabbitEar. I have to try."

It takes a full ten heartbeats before he releases me and steps back to give me a heartrending look. "Be careful. With the fresh snow, anything and anyone will be able to track you."

"Absolutely."

"Have you set a time limit? How long will you search for Lynx before you give up hope?"

The words strike terror in my soul. How long will I search?

I have no idea. "One half-moon, maybe. Guess I'll know when I get up there. Depends on what I find."

"Fourteen days is long time. Lot can happen, and by then we will be far, far south of here."

Apprehensively, I watch the children playing with Crow around the burial scaffolds. "Will you take care of Crow for me, as well? You will need her more than I will. She'll help you guard the childr—"

"I'll take care of her."

"Thank you." Anxious to get away, I add, "Now, I—I should get my things ready."

I walk across the beach with the deep sand dragging at my boots and my heart pounding against my ribs. First, I have to repair my parents' lodge so the children can sleep warmly tonight, then I must prepare my pack. At some point, I have to tell Mink . . . and the children.

There is no doubt in my mind but that I am risking everything. If I find Lynx and bring him home, RabbitEar will drift away, just as he did before when I chose Lynx over him. And the children, who are just starting to love RabbitEar, will be heartbroken.

The most curious thing I must examine is my own heart. When I asked RabbitEar to keep the children safe while I was gone, I knew without a doubt that he would do it. He's an accomplished hunter and warrior. Someday, I expect him to be voted War Leader.

Would I have asked Lynx to keep the children safe?

No. I wouldn't. Because he's a boy who hates hunting and fighting. Lynx is simply incapable of keeping anyone safe.

And I know it.

But I still love him.

29

LYNX

Y ou're free of the ice! I'm going to try to lift you out of the
hole. Ready?"

"Yes, hurry, please!"

Bracing my feet on either side of her, I grab her beneath the
arms and rip her from the ice. When she's loose, her arms go
around my neck in a grip that almost cuts off my air.

"Thank you, Lynx," she says, and falls into suffocating sobs.

"All right, let's get out of here. I'll go first. Can you hold on
to me and walk along behind me?"

"I don't know. My legs are completely numb. Can't move
them."

"Then I'll drag you." I tuck my ax inside my coat and reach
for the lamp where it rests on the ledge.

"Let me hold the lamp? Please? I'll hold it while you drag me
by the collar of my coat."

"All right. Just don't drop it, or you'll catch yourself on fire."
When I hand her the lamp, it flickers over the heavy bones of
her face and dances through her blond hair.

"Ready?"

"Yes."

Taking a good grip on her collar, I start pulling her up the tunnel. The lamp cupped in her hands casts a thousand reflections

upon the walls. Every time I exhale, my breath frosts and hangs in the air like a golden cloud.

"Another five or six paces and it widens up a little. How are your legs? Getting some feeling back?"

"They're tinglin'. Please hurry. I want out of here!"

"I know how you feel."

"N-no, you don't! Until you've spent a night down here, you can't possibly understand the terror."

I tug her up a few more paces.

Finally, I drag her out of the narrow tunnel and see the rope swinging maybe twenty hands away. High above it, I can make out the log spread across the crevasse. "Almost there."

A faint breeze blows down the crevasse and fans the lamp coals to life. Shadows—like gigantic amber wings—flutter around us. As though in response, one of the Ice Giants lets out a long string of bird-like chirps. I'm sure I'm imagining it, but the chirps seemed to be timed to the flutters.

"My legs are still numb. I don't think I can climb!"

Kneeling beside her, I say, "That's all right. Here's what we're going to do. I'm going to tie one end of the rope around you and use the other end to pull you up. When you reach the log, you'll have to figure out a way to lever yourself on top, then shinny across the log to safety. After you've untied the rope from around your waist, I want you to tie a rock to the end and throw it back down it me. Do you understand?"

"Yes. Please, please, get me out of here!" Tears flood down her cheeks.

"I'm going to do that, but I want you to listen to me. You're dazed and not thinking right. It's almost dark up there. There's an ice hollow filled with sleeping hides and food just to the north. I pulled a big log into the fire before I left, so it should still be burning. You'll be out of the crevasse before I am. Please add more wood to the fire. We'll spend the night in the hollow and head down the glacier tomorrow."

"Y-Yes, I will. Tie the r-rope around me. Haul me out of here!"

"Hand me the lamp first. You'll need both hands to hold on to the rope."

Reluctantly, she hands it to me, and I set it aside. The red gleam grows fainter as I tie one end of the rope around her waist and reach for the other end. Testing her weight, I pull her up until she's just off the floor.

"Keep pullin'. Do it!" she orders. "Get me out of here!"

She's heavier than she looks. Fortunately, the rope has not iced up yet, which is a relief. I keep pulling, until she lets out a soft cry of joy.

"I'm at the log!" she shouts.

I hold tight to the rope and look up. Sunbird is having a hard time trying to get on top of the log. When she finally manages to lever herself up and over, I hold my breath. She's on top of the log, sliding across it.

"You all right?" I call.

No answer. The campfires of the dead have blazed to life in the graying sky.

Wind could be blowing my voice away. It might take some time for her to untie my knot from around her waist, so I lean back against the ice wall and expel a relieved breath.

I did it. Despite all of Arakie's horror stories, I saved her.

Bowing my head, tears press hotly against my eyelids. I close my eyes for just a few moments to let the elation wash through me. I'm so relieved that my heart is racing. Then I hear . . .

Thunk.

A slapping and swishing sound follows.

The realization seems to take an eternity.

Jerking open my eyes, I see the rope lying in a tangle on the floor in front of me. All of the rope. It's no longer draped over the log.

"*Sunbird!*" I scream in terror.

She leans over the crevasse and calls, "I—I dropped the rope, Lynx. S-sorry."

"How could you do that? Now I have no way out of here!"

"I . . . I—I'll go get help." Staggering sideways, she almost falls into the crevasse, before she steadies herself, and vanishes.

"Wait! At least throw down my pack so I'll have something to eat! It's right there beside my spear. Sunbird? *Sunbird!*"

A soul-numbing fear possesses me. The kind of fear that leaves no room for any other emotion. All my grief and guilt, the things that have tormented me for days, vanish. My eyes are wide open, wider than they have ever been in my life. Every shadowed undulation in the walls stands out—maybe a handhold, a toehold.

"Breathe. B-breathe."

The lamp consumes the twig, and the tiny flame gutters out. All around me growls climb through the ice walls and shake the air. I feel as though I'm huddling in the throat of a monster.

"Think. You have to think!"

Trying not to panic, I sit down, draw up my knees, and prop my elbows on them while I consider my dilemma. This time of season darkness falls fast. Soon I won't be able to separate the log from the ominous black blanket pulling across the sky. If I'm going to try to throw the rope up over the log, I have to do it in the next finger of time.

Scrambling across the floor, I kick a rock loose from the ice and tie the end of the rope around it, praying it's big enough to carry the rope to the log. The problem is that braided leather ropes are heavy. I heave it upward with all my strength. As the rock sails up, the drag increases. Soon, too soon, I see the rock falling back toward me and have to leap aside before it knocks me senseless.

I pick it up and draw back my arm again . . . *Where's the log? Is that it?* Desperately, I hurl the rock upward.

A few heartbeats later, the rope batters down around me in a tangled heap.

I run for the rock. Night is settling in earnest over the Ice Giants, and I stare up with my mouth agape. The log is invisible, and the sky . . . the sky is not pale green from the glow of zyme but deep velvet blue. I stare at it for too long. Is this the sky my ancestors saw a thousand summers ago? A dark expanse slashed in two by the Road of Light?

All around me, the crevasse shakes and crackles, as though about to shatter and bury me forever.

When the quake ends, the faint gleam from the campfires of the dead begins to fill up the chamber, and I hear waves licking at some distant shore. The sound is coming from below me. Looking down, I blink. The elders speak about ancient underground lakes of meltwater that collect in pockets inside the bodies of Ice Giants. Is that what I hear? Water sloshing after the quake?

Picking up the rock, I heave it upward with all my strength, aiming at where the log must be.

A few heartbeats later, the rope batters down around me like a giant sky serpent falling to earth. I can't give up! I hurl the rock upward again. And again. For an entire hand of time, I cast the rock up, trying to carry the rope high enough to drape it over the log. But it continues to slam down around me.

When I decide to give up for the night, my arm is aching. I slump to the floor in tears, completely powerless against the cold and darkness. Wind must have picked up outside, for I see snow gusting over the top of the crevasse, blotting out the stars. Snowflakes filter down around me. It isn't another storm, is it?

My heart thunders while I try to figure out what will happen inside the crevasse. Will snow fill it up? Will it smother me?

"S-stop thinking the worst!"

For a few instants, I consider heading for the bottom of the crevasse to see if Sunbird ate all the food I lowered to her. But that's too frightening. Water has been trickling down there all day, freezing in new places, changing the shape of the tunnel. It may not even be large enough now for me to wrench my shoulders through.

"Wait for morning. That's all you can do. When you can see better, you'll figure it out."

Besides, I'm so tired. Maybe if I get some sleep, I'll think better.

Stretching out on my side on the floor, I close my eyes . . .

———

I wake screaming, struggling to free my arm from the ice. My body warmth has melted me into the glacier. Though I manage to tear loose, I suddenly realize the truth. I can't allow myself to lie down. I have to sit up so that when I nod off, I can jerk awake. Panting in terror, I drag myself back against the wall and concentrate on slowing my heartbeat.

Panting, I stammer, "I'm alive. I'm all r-right."

Other sounds emerge.

I can hear more than just the closest Ice Giants. In the background, beneath the loudest roars and shrieks, I'm surrounded by the voices of distant Giants. I hear arguments, and despair, and lovers whispering to each other. Hundreds, maybe thousands, of Giants speak at once. And the reflections! The campfires of the dead pour light into the crevasse. I lean my head back against the wall and watch ancient, long-limbed dancers leaping and twirling in time to music I can only faintly decipher. Hollow horn trumpets and hoof rattles create most of the rhythms, but I can also make out the lilting of bone flutes.

As my eyelids grow heavier, the dancers laugh and spin faster, and tiny tornados of snow bob and weave around me.

I keep nodding off, but every time I start to fall over, I wake with a gasp and straighten back up.

At one point, late at night, I wake screaming when a hand clamps over my mouth.

Creatures tiptoe around me, their feet tapping the ice like falling raindrops.

The crevasse has come to life.

Every shadow and flicker of light breathes.

30

QUILLER

Before I step out of the lodge with my spear, I turn to smile confidentially at the children sitting like dark lumps in the back. They're all trying not to cry, but they are. Crow is licking the tears from Jawbone's face while he pets her.

"Everything is all right," I tell them. "You are safe. Nothing's going to happen to you while I am gone."

Jawbone chokes out the words, "But we don't want you to go."

"It will only be for a short while. I give you my sacred oath. Now climb into your bedding hides. I'll be right back." As a last thought, I add, "Crow, guard the children."

The black dog obediently walks to the door flap and lies down with her nose resting on her paws to keep watch on the world outside.

As I duck through the door flap into the zyme glow, I see the men standing around the fire, facing east, studying something.

At first, I don't see it. Then it moves.

There's a very strange wolf standing at the edge of the trees with one foot lifted. He's only half visible through the dark weave of trunks, but he looks huge, and his head is shaped differently from a dire wolf's. His muzzle is longer and narrower.

By the time I've reached the fire, the men are speaking to one another in whispers, as though afraid the wolf might overhear their conversation.

"Where's his pack?" I look around the circle.

RabbitEar says, "Seems to be a lone wolf. Probably out scouting for his pack, but he's an odd one. He's been slinking through the trees, watching us, cocking his head in such a humanlike manner that Basher thinks he's a spirit wolf."

Basher thrusts a hand toward the wolf. "Well, look at his color! That's not ordinary. When he steps full out of the trees into the firelight his gray coat flashes like the inside of an abalone shell, and the tip of each hair shines like polished copper."

When the animal takes a step forward to sniff the air, I see what he means. In the flickering light, the strange hue seems more illusion than real. The purple shade appears and disappears, sometimes as deep and dark as a bruise, but the tips of his hair shimmer reddish-gold.

"He's beautiful," I say.

The wolf takes another step toward us, and I swear he's looking straight at me. He tilts his head in a wistful way. It's an expression full of longing, but it's not human longing, it's feral and ferocious, hungry in a way that only another wolf could fully understand. Those yellow eyes search mine. He's evaluating me, seeking my weakness.

Gripping my spear, I run straight at the wolf. His gaze never wavers. It's locked with mine.

Mink shouts, "What are you doing?"

"Showing him that he doesn't scare me," I call back.

The wolf lets me get to five paces away before he snarls in protest, and then backs up and leaps away through the forest shadows, disappearing so completely that I don't even glimpse his strange coat as he vanishes through the trees.

Basher calls, "Even spirit wolves are afraid of you, Quiller!"

"They'd better be," I yell, but my eyes are on the darkness out there, trying to find him. I can feel his presence. He's hidden himself for now, but he'll be back.

Turning, I see Mink and Basher laughing and smiling. Rabbit-Ear, however, is frowning at me in concern, as though it worried him that I trotted out to face the wolf alone. And I realize that less than one half-moon ago, he would have been laughing with Mink and Basher. Things have changed between us. I am about to make things worse.

When I reach the fire, Mink claps me on the shoulder. "You have second watch," he says. "I'll take first watch."

"Good. I'll see you at midnight," I say, and turn to Rabbit-Ear. "May I speak with you alone?"

"'Course."

I lead him a short distance away from the fire, out of Basher's and Mink's hearing, and say, "I have a favor to ask of you."

"Anything. What is it?"

"The children are upset that I'm leaving tomorrow. Jawbone asked if you could sleep in our lodge tonight. I think it would ease their worries. If you wouldn't mind?"

A swallow goes down his throat. "Are you sure, Quiller?"

"Yes."

31

LYNX

In the dream . . .

I'm four summers old and tossing and turning beneath the heavy hides that cover me. When I finally manage to roll to my side, facing the door flap, cool wind blows over my fevered face. The wonderful aroma of roasting bison ribs fills the wind. I can't wait to be strong enough to rise and have breakfast with my family. I know people will gather around me and sit rapt as I tell the story of how I walked to the Land of the Dead, and came back. I saw things there last night. Long-dead people and monsters from before the zyme that shook the earth with their gigantic feet. Mother and Father, and my brother Mink, will come to listen to my stories. Quiller will sit beside me and tell me everything is going to be all right.

And maybe the lion will come again. The big lion that stuck its head through the door flap last night, and gave me something sweet to drink. I was so thirsty . . . so grateful . . . but I feel sicker this morning . . .

I heave a sigh and try to roll to my back, but my body won't budge. Strangely, my arms and legs feel as if they're tied down. I try to call out for Mother, but my voice is so soft I can barely hear it. I can't . . .

With a roar of panic, I rear up and begin fighting the ice that sheaths my left arm and leg. When did I fall asleep? I don't even recall closing my eyes! In terror, I slap my belt until I finally manage to find my ax and chop myself free, then I scramble backward to sit against the ice wall, where I sob like a lost child.

Through the shimmer of tears, I see the holes I spent half the night hacking into the ice walls. Hundreds of them. They look like they were chopped out by a madman with no thought or plan. A man possessed of such desperation he was just chopping at anything and everything. Which I was. By midnight, the water that had been sheeting down the walls all day froze and iced over every hole I chopped.

I gaze upward at the log that spans the crevasse. It's later than I thought. Almost dawn. The sky has a faint lavender hue, and the icicles that hang from the bottom of the log have started to melt and drip like rain.

But I'm still alive. *I'm alive!*

On the opposite wall, my rope is little more than a tangled heap mounded with ice. While I was frantically chopping handholds, the leather rope was soaking up water from the floor, growing heavier and heavier, too heavy to lift, and there's no way to dry it out.

Gods, why didn't I listen to Arakie?

Sagging forward, I brace my elbows on my drawn-up knees and try to think. Why am I so warm? Only moments ago, I was freezing. It's comforting, but the warmth also makes me long to sleep. Maybe I can? Just for a couple of hands of time? Besides, it won't be so bad this time. I've noticed that each time I fall asleep my body melts less and less ice. Doesn't make any sense. I sit back against the wall and fold my arms over my chest.

Sl-sleep for a while.

Bizarrely, though I know what I'm saying, the words that come out of my mouth make no sense. They're gibberish. Of course, it doesn't matter. There's no one to hear me—except the ancient Spirits, flickers of light, that twinkle around me, and they don't care if my words make sense or not.

Somewhere in the belly of the glacier, my nonsensical jabbering seems to have caught the attention of one of the Ice Giants. His voice is a faint echo:

. . . *the specimen that I've been epigenetically altering has given me hope for* Denisovan reecur. *I know they are on the verge of extinction, and probably a failed experiment, but I believe if we can give them more time . . . No, no, I'm listening. . . . No, I do not think the mutations in the surviving* Homo erectus reecur *examples are more promising. I find no convincing evidence of adaptation. After all, their numbers have dwindled to barely a handful. How can you . . .*

I topple onto my side and can't rise. Drifting in and out of delirious naps, I listen to the Giant tell a long tale of the terrible war that engulfed the world just after the zyme . . . about death rising out the oceans near Seacouver and flying around the world gobbling up entire continents.

Then the Giant goes quiet. No more stories, no more groans. Am I no longer worth its time? Maybe not. My breathing has gone shallow and quick, as though my lungs can't get enough air, but I don't care. I long to drift forever in the numbing warmth . . .

32

QUILLER

Just before dawn, I blink my eyes open and find myself wrapped warmly in RabbitEar's arms. My forehead presses against his bearded cheek, and he's lightly stroking my bare back. The rough texture of his callused hand soothes me, for I'd forgotten what his lover's touch feels like.

"Almost dawn," he whispers. "Didn't want to wake you, but I know you want to leave early."

Lifting my head, I gaze into his eyes. They shine with a mixture of dread and warmth. The children still sleep around us beneath mounds of hides. The sounds of their soft breathing fill the lodge, and fill me with dreams. I long for it to be a moon from now, when we are far south in warmer country. I dream that I've found Lynx and brought him home alive and well, and everyone in Sky Ice Village is safe. We now live beside a forest bursting with game. I dream all this while gazing into RabbitEar's eyes. He makes me see happy things.

"I need to grab my pack and go."

He squeezes his eyes closed for a moment before he sits up. "Have you told Mink yet?"

"No, after breakfast—"

"I'll break the news to him . . . if you want me to."

"Yes, thanks, that'll give me a little more time with the children."

33

LYNX

Faint footsteps.

But I can't open my eyes. My eyelids are heavier than lead. They won't budge. As I drift back to sleep, the Giants squeal and shake the crevasse with powerful hands, clearly trying hard to wake me, but I ignore them until fingers lightly touch my shoulder.

Wake up, my husband. You have to wake up.

I must have tried to lift my head. I hear the ice that welds my hair to the floor crack loose.

Let me speak with you? I need to speak with you.

"S-Siskin?"

When I drag my eyes open, I see her slowly take shape in the darkness. Around her, firelight shimmers, reflecting from the seashells that cover her red doe-hide wedding dress. Black hair falls over her shoulders and frames her perfect face with its small nose and full lips. In the background, dozens, maybe hundreds, of our ancestors stand watching me.

"Thank you for letting me come back to speak with you."

"I'm sorry, my wife. I was afraid. I didn't want you to tell me that you hate me."

"Oh, Lynx, I could never hate you." Siskin sits down beside me and tenderly places a half-transparent hand against my frozen cheek. "How could you ever think that?"

"You are so beautiful," I weep. "I miss you. I'm sorry I let you die."

"You didn't let me die. Your soul flew away. Your body was a husk when the lions were killing me. It wasn't your fault."

I stare up at her with blurry eyes. "Your brother said that only a coward's soul flies away when someone he loves needs him. He told the council to cast me out."

"Bluejay was heartbroken and not thinking right. Soon and forever, he'll regret that he said that. Forgive him. He just loves too deeply. When you see my brother, please tell him I love him. And tell Bluejay that Grandfather wants him to know how proud he is of the things Bluejay has done to help our people. Grandfather says he is keeping a place of honor by his fire for Bluejay."

For a time, I just lie there looking up at her while she strokes my ice-clotted hair. The feel of her warm hand and the sight of her beautiful face bring me such joy. I have to tear my sleeve loose from the floor so I can lift my hand to touch the claw marks that slash across her throat.

"Take me with you, Siskin. I'm dying. You know I am."

"Our ancestors tell me that you have a destiny. They tell me you must live."

"Me?" I ask dreamily. "But I'm a coward."

"You have never been a coward."

"But I ran in battle, and I froze when you were—"

With tears in her voice, she says, "You are the bravest man I have ever known. Despite all the warnings, you came down here to save the Rust woman. How many men would have done that?"

"Yes, and she left me—"

"She set you on your path. You owe her a great debt of gratitude. Take my hand now. It's time for you to get up." She extends a hand to me.

"Siskin, I can't. Ice has covered my legs, and I'm so weak, I can't break loose."

"Take my hand, my husband. I'll help you."

Behind her shoulders, our ancestors watch to see what I will do. Their voices resemble ice shattering in the distance. Two old men say I will just give up, that my courage is as thin as water.

Siskin reaches down and grabs my hand.

When she pulls me to my feet, I stumble into her arms, and she holds me tightly. Such relief surges through me that I feel light-headed.

"Siskin?" Choking on tears, I whisper, "Siskin, just let me go with you? I don't want to be here any longer. I'm so tired. I want to be with you and my ancestors."

"I know you do. But it won't be too long until you see us again. Sooner than you can imagine. Before that happens, you must walk the path home."

"There's n-no way out. I-I've tried." I hug her hard against me and weep into her long silken hair. Gods, it's comforting to have her here with me. I don't have to face death alone now. She will talk me through it, ease the way for me.

"Listen to me, Lynx," she says to get me to stop crying. "Stand up straight. Listen to me. You must follow me. I'm going to show you the way out."

Siskin is the only thing I ever really wanted in my life. To be able to look into her eyes while we watched our children grow up. That was my perfect dream.

Slowly, tenderly, I run my fingers down her cheek. "Don't leave me again."

"I've always been here, my husband, standing right beside you. Now, try to concentrate." She pulls away and points to the tunnel that leads deeper into the glacier, to the place where Sunbird was trapped. "There. You see? That's the way out."

"Don't even think about going down there! It's so narrow now that you'll never be able to get through."

"Follow me." She walks to the tunnel, gets down on her belly, and slithers through. From the darkness, she calls, "Through here. This is the way, man of the People. I show you the way."

As I weakly drag myself into the tunnel, I realize instantly that's it much more narrow than last time.

"Siskin! Where are you?"

Down here. Follow me. It gets wider down here.

Wrenching my shoulders along the tunnel fills me with mind-numbing fear.

Just keep coming. You're very close.

When I almost topple over the edge of an abyss, I gasp and slither backward. Extending my hand, I find only air in front of me.

"Siskin? This chamber falls away into nothingness. I can't climb out there!"

Stretch your hand out to your right, and follow my voice. There's a shelf. I'm standing right here, just ten hands away from you.

Slapping at darkness, my palm finally touches the shelf, and I slither out of the tunnel onto the narrow ledge and stagger to my feet.

Gods, what is this place?

A vast ocean spreads in front of me—an ocean without zyme. Its endless black surface curves, heading off toward a horizon that seems to be days in the distance, with nothing in between, no islands or waves, just a watery expanse of shining black. I seem to be floating on the surface, wrapped in a faintly blue sea fog. Just floating. Cocooned in rumbling voices speaking an incomprehensible language far older than humans.

Follow me now.

Her hand touches my arm. Light, but there.

"Let me just catch my breath!"

We must hurry, Lynx. Hurry.

Siskin's steps tap along the ice shelf ahead of me.

Feeling with my feet, I determine that the shelf is about four hands wide here. If I keep my shoulder against the wall, and walk slowly, maybe I'll be all right.

I'm just ahead of you. Hurry.

"How do you know this leads to a way out?"

Keep walking. Have faith in me.

"I—I do."

For an unknown amount of time, I stagger along the shelf until a strange pine-scented breeze blows through the cavern. Probably the same breeze that fanned my lamp when I first found Sunbird. Where is it coming from? Gods, Siskin is right. There's a way out!

It isn't far, Lynx. Come this way.

My feet grate on dust or gravel. The footing is better, more secure. I walk faster.

"Where are you?"

I'm standing in the mouth of the cavern waiting for you.

Relief surges through me. "I don't see you." But up ahead there's a patch of lighter darkness.

I stepped outside into the beautiful gleam of the campfires of the dead. I'm waiting for you.

I hurry forward as fast as my wobbling legs will carry me.

As the light grows stronger, I see fantastic shapes buried in the ice. Huge rectangles and pyramids topple over each other, and recede forever into the belly of the Ice Giants. Though frozen and still, their angles reflect the faint light like polished slate mirrors. What are they? Wandering traders often tell winter stories of monstrous crumbling villages, the ancient villages of the Jemen, that go on forever beneath the ice, but I thought they were all myths and legends.

Lynx. You must come. Now.

Forcing myself to turn away . . .

I see the opening to the world beyond the ice.

Run. Run! Get out of here!

I need light and air like a dying man needs food and water. When I'm outside, my strength fails and I fall to the ground on my hands and knees, then scramble through the snow to get as far from the crevasse as I can before I crumple.

"Siskin?" I scream her name. "Where are you?"

My shout trails away in the wind and I crumple to the ice, where I curl up on my side, shaking so hard I can barely breathe.

34

QUILLER

I've finished dressing and readying my weapons belt and pack. Through a gap in the door flap, I see RabbitEar standing beside Basher with his arms crossed and his brow furrowed, as though he doesn't really like what Mink is telling him. Crow lies curled by the fire, the closest place to thick strips of mammoth heart that roast on sticks leaned over the flames.

Basher shakes his head. "Well, it's idiotic."

I turn to the children slumbering around me, and my heart aches. The girls are snuggled together beneath one bison hide, while Jawbone lies rolled up in an elk hide near the door. The boy insisted on sleeping with his spear in his hand, just in case he had to jump up in the middle of the night to help RabbitEar fight off a lion or bear. Though deep asleep, he still clutches it tight.

Steps *shish, shish* in the sand outside.

"What's happening?" I softly call, trying not to wake the children.

RabbitEar answers, "We have strips of mammoth heart roasting over the flames for breakfast. You might want to start getting the children ready." He pauses. "Need my help?"

"No, I can do it. But thanks. We'll be there soon."

"See you then." He reluctantly walks away, and it occurs to me that perhaps he wanted to help the children get dressed.

Jawbone sits up and rubs the sleep from his eyes. "Was that RabbitEar? Is it time for you to go?" Tears strain his voice.

"Right after breakfast. Do you want to help the girls get ready?"

"Yes, Quiller."

Jawbone crawls over to gently shake Little Fawn's shoulder. "You need to wake up now."

Little Fawn yawns. "I'm awake."

Jawbone wakes the other girls by whispering, "Get dressed. Breakfast is cooking."

While Little Fawn dresses herself and Chickadee, Loon shrugs on her coat and walks over to stand beside Jawbone. Without a word, she tucks her small fingers into his palm. Jawbone holds her hand as he waits for me.

Reaching for my coat, I say, "Jawbone, I'm going to adopt all four of you. I made that decision yesterday. Is that all right with you?"

Little Fawn and Loon shout "Yes!" and start leaping around. Chickadee toddles over and climbs into my lap to hug me. "Will you be my mother now?"

"Yes, I will."

Jawbone wipes his eyes on his sleeve. "Will RabbitEar be our father?"

The question stops me cold. For several instants I don't know what to say. The girls stare at me expectantly. RabbitEar slept in the lodge last night. The children, obviously, made assumptions. "You like RabbitEar, don't you?"

All of the children smile and nod.

Lifting Chickadee, I set her on the floor and rise to my feet. As I grip Chickadee's hand and walk for the door flap, the other children fall into line behind me. Just before I step out in the darkness and cold, I say, "We'll discuss it when I come back

from my trip. Why don't you all run to RabbitEar and ask him
if the mammoth heart is ready to eat?"

"All right, Quiller." Jawbone clutches his spear and charges
for the fire with the girls right behind him.

Ducking beneath the lodge flap, I gaze eastward at the Ice
Giants. Pale blue and roaring, they shiver my soul. After this
long, can Lynx possibly still be alive? And he may not even be
out there. He may have made it home days ago, gotten into the
boats with everyone else, and headed south. But none of that
matters. In another hand of time, I'll put the children in a boat
and say goodbye. Every paddle-stroke will take them farther
and farther away from me. I told Lynx I'd find him, and I will
do everything I can to keep that promise.

Squeals of delight ring out.

When the children race up and start eagerly asking Rabbit-
Ear questions, he turns away from Mink and Basher and
crouches down to speak with each child. The girls crawl all
over him, which leaves RabbitEar laughing. While he answers
the girls' questions, Jawbone stands a short distance away with
his new spear propped on the ground in front of him. Such
longing etches the boy's face that it's wrenching for me.

The girls charge off to examine the mammoth heart strips,
then RabbitEar opens his arms and Jawbone runs into them. I
can't hear what he says to the boy, but Jawbone looks up at
RabbitEar with serious eyes.

"Quiller?" Mink calls and walks across the sand toward me.
He's tied his long black hair back with a leather cord, but
strands have blown free and whip around his face.

I wait for him. I suspect this is not going to be pleasant.

Halting in front of me, he says, "Don't do this. If you leave
to go looking for Lynx, you'll lose everything you love. Don't
do this!"

"Have you given up on Lynx?"

"As of this morning . . . yes. Breaks my heart, but it's time to let him go. He's dead."

"I'm sure you're right, but I must try to find him."

Mink's gaze moves to where RabbitEar has his arm around Jawbone. He is examining the boy's new spear, discussing it, apparently. Jawbone is smiling. Mink's eyes tighten as he watches. "RabbitEar loves that little boy, you know."

"I do."

As he kicks at the sand, Mink says, "I need every warrior, Quiller. There's no telling what we will face as we head south trying to find our people. I need you. RabbitEar and the children need you. Think hard about this."

"I've thought it through carefully, Mink. I'll hunt for one half-moon. If I haven't found him by then, I'll run south along the shore until I find you."

"And be hunted by every pack of wolves and pride of lions in the world."

"Probably."

Mink glares at me, then turns away and shakes his head. "I'm wasting my time. There's no talking you out of this insanity, is there?"

"No."

Mink nods and walks away, returning to his conversation with Basher.

Resolutely, I march to RabbitEar, take his arm, and say, "Jawbone, RabbitEar will be right back, all right?"

"Yes, Quiller."

I guide RabbitEar a short distance away and release his arm. His face darkens when he sees my expression.

"What's wrong?"

Propping my hands on my hips, I can't help but spread my

feet, as though I'm readying myself for a fight. RabbitEar scans my face and gives me a questioning look.

"I want to make something perfectly clear to you. While I'm gone, you'll be taking care of the children for us."

"Us?" His eyes narrow in preparation for my response. "You and Lynx?"

"No. You and me."

His embrace crushes the air from my lungs. In my ear, he says, "If you're gone for more than one half-moon, I'll come looking for you, so make sure you're back."

"I'll be back."

35

LYNX

The glittering campfires of the dead have started to fade. Gods, it's cold. Really cold. How long have I been aimlessly wandering around? I have to find my way back to the frozen forest in the ice hollow, where the deepest coals in the fire pit might still be warm.

Inhaling a breath to steady myself, I force myself to think.

"Have to . . . find my pack. Pack and spear."

Standing on the bare promontory in the wind, I feel dazed, not quite here in my freezing body. But I recognize the major landmarks. Walk. Most of the ice has blown clean of snow, which makes the journey easier. One foot in front of the other.

A short time later, I see the hollow shining like a bowl of starlight turned on edge. Inside, the branches of the ancient towering trees are draped with icicles that cast a thousand shivering reflections over the camp inside. The woodpile, fire pit, tripod, and my rolled bedding hide appear to be sheathed with flickering diamonds as fine and clear as quartz crystals, but blue, bluer than any sky I have ever seen. I think it's real . . . maybe not. Could be a vision.

When I stagger forward, the facets of light shoot around, bouncing from diamond to diamond, flashing rainbows, and giving birth to the misshapen shadows of long-dead creatures that crawl over the walls. I wonder when they lived in this world? Before the zyme? Or after the Jemen sailed to the stars?

The trail of seven or eight dire wolves slices the snow in front of the hollow. They were headed downhill at a leisurely trot. It's a measure of my feeble mind that the sight does not bring a rush of fear. Instead, I stumble across their trail and continue toward my refuge.

Down the slope to my left, the crevasse is little more than a black maw in the white. The log still spans it. Tomorrow I will follow Arakie's sled trail home.

"Where's my p-pack? I'll need it."

Turning away from the hollow, I stagger back to search for it, but stop when I realize that by now, even if it's covered with windblown snow, I should see a lump beneath the snow. My pack is not there.

Sunbird must have taken it.

Reeling and lurching on my feet, suddenly I'm not sure where I am. In the far distance, a vast green meadow rolls outward to the horizon. No . . . no, that's zyme. Not a meadow. The ocean.

Home is that direction.

I must walk home.

I slog through the snow headed downhill . . .

A nagging thought keeps trying to surface, to rise into my mind, but I—I . . .

"*The hollow. Get to the hollow.*"

As though my feet know where they're going even if I do not, they turn me around and make me go back to the hollow.

When I enter it, I think I'm dreaming, again. Everything exists in a fractured mirage of blue light. The boiling bag hangs from the tripod at the edge of the dead fire. Wood is piled beside it. My sleeping hide lies rolled in the rear, and my cup rests beside one of the tripod's legs.

If this is a dream, it's the best dream of my life.

On the verge of collapse, I can't sleep yet. Not until I have a fire going and something warm in my stomach. Not if I want to wake up.

Reaching for a branch, I pull it from the woodpile and see a man down the slope. He stands in the middle of a haze of blowing snow, staring straight at me.

"Arakie?" I cry and leap to my feet. *"Arakie!* I'm happy to see you!"

"You saved her," he calls in a voice filled with crackling ice crystals. "Did you save yourself?"

"My . . . myself?"

The image wavers, as though I'm looking at him through a wall of water. Then he vanishes into the white haze, and I'm sobbing like a six-summers-old child.

36

QUILLER

Just after dawn, I help RabbitEar shove both boats into the ocean and stake their tether ropes to the shore, then we finish loading the rolled bedding hides in the large boat and bags of mammoth jerky in the small one.

When we're done, I wipe my sweating forehead on my coat sleeve and gaze out at the water where the whitecaps shimmer green from filaments of zyme. The children have already climbed into the big boat and stretched out on the packs in the middle with Crow between them. As they pet Crow, her tail thumps the packs. Crow loves children. The girls seem to be talking about the seagulls that drift over them. Each time the birds tilt, their wings turn golden in the fires of sunrise, and the girls laugh.

RabbitEar softly asks, "You all right?"

"Sad. That's all. I don't want to leave, but I have to do this."

"I know."

I give him a faint smile. "Should be a good day to paddle south. Sea is calm. Almost no zyme rolling in. Just a few filaments. If all goes well, you'll find the rest of Sky Ice Village by tomorrow or the next day."

RabbitEar doesn't say anything for a time, then he exhales hard. "Will you let me try one more time to—"

"Speak your mind, RabbitEar. I value your opinion. I always have."

"You sure?"

"Yes."

RabbitEar props his hands on his hips. The posture stretches his coat tight across his muscular shoulders. "If I were out there in the wilderness, it would kill me to think you had left four little children to come searching for me. I would not want you out there."

The pastel light glints in the Salmon clan designs on the front of his coat. I take a moment to appreciate how the sea breezes toss his red hair about his face. "I wouldn't go looking for you, RabbitEar."

"Good."

"You can take care of yourself. And I know it."

"That's right. No matter what happens in the future, don't ever forget that. I will expect you to grab the children and run while I fight."

I stare blindly into his eyes, but barely see him, for I heard all the things he did not say, all the hopes that filled his voice, and I'm seeing the future . . . laughing children playing in our lodge, snuggling warmly beneath the hides with RabbitEar's arms around me on long winter nights . . . growing old together surrounded by our grandchildren.

Hesitantly, as though not sure how I will react, RabbitEar reaches out and takes my hand. The bones of his fingers feel large and awkward twined with mine. From the corner of my eye, I see Jawbone smile.

"I need to get started for the Crushing Mountains. Let's go help Mink and Basher pack up the last items from the lodges, then I'll be on my way."

In a low voice, he says, "All right."

37

LYNX

Tap. Tap. Click, slap, slap.

I open my eyes with a gasp and find myself staring up at the translucent roof of the hollow. Dawn has blushed color into the thin ice roof, turning it faintly lavender, but yellow clouds sail beyond the lens. Flames crackle beside me. Off and on throughout the night, I recall feeding the fire. The flames still warm my face. How I long to remain rolled up in this hide and sleep for days, but as my eyelids start to fall closed again . . .

Slap. Slap.

When the sound finally registers, I sit up. "Arakie?"

Just outside the hollow, no more than ten paces away, a giant beaver slaps his tail on the snow. He's eighteen hands long, and if I was standing up, the top of his back would reach to my shoulders. He outweighs me by four or five times. His massive head is cocked slightly to watch me through one black eye. Every time he exhales, white clouds of breath puff from his mouth and drift upward in the windless morning air. Frost covers his face, sparkling from his whiskers, lashes, and the tips of his ears. His big front teeth are long and yellow. Giant beavers are river animals. What's he doing up here? He must have walked up one of the vast rivers that flow out of the Ice Giants down to the sea, hunting for food.

Slowly, so as not to startle him, I rise on shaking legs. In response, the beaver slaps his tail twice and swings around to face me. As I reach for a branch, a makeshift club, I notice he's chewed the trunk of one of the frozen trees. I must have slept through it. He walked right into the hollow and I didn't hear him at all. Thank the Jemen it wasn't a lion or a bear.

"Go away now, beaver." They rarely attack humans, but I am so weak that if he charges and hits me, he could break my legs. I wave the branch at him. "Go away!"

Giant Beaver scuttles backward and bounds down the slope, but he keeps looking back at me and threateningly slapping his tail on the snow.

Squinting against the glare of sunlight, my eyes don't register it at first, then I realize he's wading through a smooth expanse of white. The sled trail is gone. Completely gone. Last night's wind erased it as though it never existed.

All around me, I sense a thunderous invisible presence as old as the earth and as remote and cold-hearted as the frozen wilderness outside. It presses in upon me, judging me and issuing vast unalterable decrees that I am unworthy of the slightest attention.

Adding more wood to the fire, I see my half-full tea cup resting beside the hearthstones. Woodenly, I look at the tea bag suspended from the tripod. I must have warmed it up and drunk at least half a cup. Why am I freezing to death? Doesn't matter. I sit before the flames like a soulless lump, and rock back and forth. I'm too tired to drink the other half cup of tea.

Instead, I topple onto my side and close my eyes. I suspect I'm dying, but I don't have the strength to worry about it.

My last waking thought is to wonder if Giant Beaver was trying to show me the way home.

38

QUILLER

The wolf is after me.

I'm not worried yet, because he's alone, but he is an odd old wolf. He's made no aggressive moves, but he paralleled my course all day like an eerie escort. Since nightfall, he's grown a little bolder, coming in close enough for me to see his eyes flashing as he walks along, matching my steps. The tips of his hair, which appeared coppery in firelight, shimmer frosty silver in Sister Moon's glow, but the rest of him has shaded a deep, dark purple that flashes as he haunts the darkness.

To make matters worse, I have the gut instinct that I'm headed in the wrong direction.

As the crescent of Sister Moon descends toward the ocean, the long shadows cast by the drifts and boulders stretch across the snow like dark fingers, all pointing eastward toward the highest peaks of the Ice Giants.

"Is that what you're trying to tell me, Sister Moon?"

Inside the medicine bag that hangs from the leather cord around my throat, I can feel Sister Moon and Bull Bison breathing, moving.

"Lynx is up there to the east?"

The possibility worries me. I'm following a mammoth trail north into the vast wilderness of the Crushing Mountains. If he's up there in that stunning mosaic of shadow and moonlight to the east, by the time I come back this way, he'll be long gone.

The more I think about it, the more worried I become. Beginning my search far to the north in the Crushing Mountains made sense yesterday, but my conviction is dwindling. If that's where he was abandoned, he would have started running for home the instant he was freed, and his trail was long ago wiped away by the storms. If he's still up there, he's dead. Am I searching for his body, or a living person? I have to be honest with myself. The risk I'm taking is only worth it if he's alive. Which means I should veer off onto the bison trail that winds up the mountainside, heading east.

I lift my spear and prop it on my right shoulder, and the wolf lets out a low growl. He knows spears, which means he's been hunted.

My spirit helpers are telling me to head east. I'm sure of it. Sister Moon is pointing me that direction, and it's a bison trail that will lead me up there into the shining peaks of the Ice Giant Mountains.

Breaking into a steady, distance-eating trot, I veer onto the bison trail and begin climbing the steep slope, heading due east. Huge bull bison tracks mark the trail ahead. The wolf matches my stride. I see him out there, silent as death. Wolves are smart. If he had his pack with him, a dozen wolves could surround me and take turns charging me. The first time I cast a spear, they'd be all over me. I'd still be alive when they ripped out my belly and tore open my throat. Before I died, I'd get to watch them lapping up my blood.

But he's alone. He won't attack until he knows he can kill me.

I admire that. He's a cunning old beast. Being hunted by him is an eerie pleasure. I cast a smile his direction.

"Keep dreaming of the taste of my blood, brother wolf. When you get hungry enough, you'll make a mistake, trot in too close, look away at the wrong instant. That's when I'll kill you and warm my belly with your meat."

At the sound of my voice, the big wolf lopes farther out into the darkness where I can't see him.

"You know a threat when you hear it, don't you?"

I hold straight on up the slope for another hand of time, following the big bull's tracks, cross a flat covered with dead tundra wildflowers, and drop down to a trough where a small stream flows. Glacial meltwater has a uniquely pure fragrance. It's not earthy like the rivers that run down by the shore. Up here it smells eons old and sweet. When I squat to dip up a handful to drink, the furrow of a sled catches my eye. Snow has almost filled it in, but someone towed a sled across the stream here and headed for the copse of pines just to the south. In this angle of moonlight, the trail casts a thin hairline of shadow, and the shadow curves and twists around boulders and cracks in the ice, then disappears in those trees.

Rising to my feet, I feel a vague apprehension. It could be Lynx on his way home. Or twenty Rust warriors who escaped the Great Horned Owl Village slaughter. By now, Wind Mother would have erased the shallower human tracks that would warn me.

When I start walking beside the sled trail, the wolf slinks along like a sparkling ghost two hundred hand-lengths away. Breath crystallizes around his muzzle when he exhales. His ice-coated whiskers shimmer. I can probably hit him from here . . .

The instant I grip my spear, he leaps away.

My gaze moves back and forth, keeping the wolf in sight while I search the landscape. If it is Rust warriors, I don't want a war party sneaking up on me.

Quietly, I place my feet alongside the sled trail, slowly making my way toward the pines.

When I see reflections of firelight dancing through the swaying branches, I stop to study the elderly man moving around the edges of a tumbled heap of underbrush and deadfall, plucking dry sticks and twigs from the depths, carrying them back to his fire. The sled rests beside the flames. The man lying on it is covered with hides. All I can see is his big face and a silver shirt collar around his neck.

My body goes on high alert.

I narrow my eyes at the old man. White hair hangs limply about his sunken cheeks and he has the smallest brow ridge I've ever seen. He's not one of the Rust People. Why is he caring for one? There's a vague familiarity about the old man.

I glance to my left to locate the wolf, who is staring so fixedly at me that his eyes are huge firelit moons.

As the old man carries his armload of wood back to his camp, he calls, "Why don't you come in and share my supper? Squirrel soup is pretty bland, but it's hot. You must be cold out there."

My spine snaps rigid. I haven't made a sound. How could he know I'm here?

When I step out of the shadows into his firelight, the elder's wiry white brows arch. "Ah, Quiller. Hunting for Lynx, I presume. I'm glad to see you."

Momentarily confused, I stare at him, then I stride forward. "You wouldn't know that unless you'd seen Lynx. Where is he?"

The elder dumps his load of firewood and crouches before the flames to warm his cold hands. His lion-hide cape falls around his bony body in fire-lit folds. "Wish I knew. I expected him days ago."

When I get close enough to really see him, I suck in a surprised breath. "I—I saw you. Before. At the wedding—"

"Yes, you did."

Surprise has made me careless. If he has friends, they could have me surrounded by now. While I search the trees, I ask, "Who are you?"

"My name is Arakie. I'm no threat to you. You can lower your spear and sit down."

I'm too anxious to sit, but I do lower my spear. "Where is Lynx?"

The elder pulls a chunk of wood from the pile, tosses it into the flames, and points to the cups that rest on the ground. "Please, dip a cup of soup. It'll warm you up. How long has the spirit wolf been dogging your trail?"

He gestures to the darkness over my right shoulder, but I don't need to look.

"He's not a spirit wolf. He's a real wolf. He's been following me all day and all night. He's like my shadow, always there and silent as death."

"Ah . . ." Arakie sighs. "A spirit helper, then. Yours? Or is he tracking you for someone else?"

"He's not my spirit helper."

"Hmm. Well, I've been listening to a pack of spirit wolves howl all night. They've been out hunting ghost partridges, but they're on their way here. Sit, please. You need to eat something before they arrive."

"Hope it's not actually real wolves."

The elder cocks his head and his eyes narrow as though he is listening to a voice on the night air. After several moments, he says, "Really? What makes you think that?" He pauses to study the wolf. "Well, that would be interesting. I guess we'll see, won't we?"

"Are you talking to me, elder?"

Out in the darkness the wolf bares his teeth. I can see them glinting in the firelight. A low growl carries on the night breeze.

Arakie shouts, "Give her just a few moments! She'll be back to you soon enough."

The wolf lays his ears back and trots down into the trees fifty paces away.

My gaze slides back to the snowy-haired elder. Grudgingly, because I know I'm wasting time, I crouch, grab a cup, and dip it into the steaming bag hanging from the tripod. I am hungry. Just the fragrance makes my empty stomach growl. It tastes good.

"Elder, what happened to you at the wedding camp? Bluejay said you vanished and left only giant lion tracks."

"That's a bit fanciful, isn't it?"

All around me, where glacially smoothed rocks and trees disturb the flow of wind, a sweet symphony of whimpers and whistles fills the air, the music of stone and wood. It contrasts sharply to the deep grating voices of the Ice Giants.

By all rights, I should be polite and ask this old man his clan, people, and all the details of what he's doing out here alone . . . but he's right. I have other concerns. "Where did you last see Lynx?"

"I last saw him hanging his head over a crevasse." He flicks a skeletal hand toward the high jagged peaks to the east, where snow gusts across the high country in sparkling veils. "Talking to a woman buried in the ice at the bottom. That man's sister." He uses his chin to gesture to the Rust man sleeping on the sled on the other side of the fire.

"Why was he doing that?"

"He was going to try to save her. Despite my best efforts to dissuade him, he was willing to sacrifice everything to save one person. And he chose the most vulnerable person." A wistful smile turns his lips. "My people call that altruism. It is our most valued—"

"Well, my people call it dimwitted! He should have gone for help. Where—"

"You should talk, dear. What are you doing out here alone? You could be home nice and snug—"

"Where is Lynx?"

"Well." He exhales the word. "I suspect he's dead, because he lowered himself down into the crevasse and couldn't get out again. I warned him not to, but he did it anyway." Awe touches his voice. "Amazing."

Almost breathlessly, I say, "Are you telling me he's trapped in a crevasse?"

He's grinning when he asks, "Bull Bison led you right to my sled trail, didn't he? All you have to do is follow it to the place where it forks. But you must take the right fork, or you'll run into that pack of spirit wolves."

My heart races. I'm about to ask him how he could possibly know about my spirit helper, but then it occurs to me that there are bull bison tracks all along his sled trail. He probably has no idea my spirit helper is Bull Bison. "Your sled trail may be gone in the higher elevations. I need to know exactly where the crevasse—"

He sternly points a finger at my chest. "Stop looking for shadows on the walls inside your medicine bag. There are none."

"Shadows?" I shake my head, completely baffled, and glance down at my medicine bag.

His voice turns soft and melodic. "Bull Bison has shown you the way. All you have to do is listen. Find the place where my sled trail forks, and go right."

"Are you deaf? I just told you your trail may be gone! Wind Mother has been scouring the slopes up there. I need you to point out the location of the crevasse."

He rubs his cold hands together in front of the leaping flames. When his eyes tighten, he opens his mouth to say something, but doesn't. It takes another five heartbeats before he quietly asks, "Dying for someone you love is the easiest thing in the world, isn't it?"

"I'm not going to die. I'm going to find Lynx, and together we'll head south until we find our people."

He gives me a curious smile. "You have all amazed me. It's such a delight."

There's something unearthly about this old man, wild like the darkness out beyond the firelight, something that unnerves me.

Finishing my soup, I set the cup down and get to my feet. Yellow eyes flash down in the trees. The wolf is pacing, back and forth, in a rush to have me join him again.

"Thank you for the soup, elder. I think I'll be on my way now."

"Be careful, Quiller." Pointedly, he adds, "And be respectful. Tread lightly the halls of the dead."

As I back away from his fire, I pull my spear from my quiver. I have no idea what he's talking about it, but I don't like the sound of it.

When I've backed beyond the halo of firelight, the wolf silently trots forward with his ears pricked. As I run up the sled trail, he parallels my path.

39

LYNX

The next time I open my eyes, it's afternoon, and sunlight penetrates the thin roof of the hollow and slants down across my face. How long did I sleep? The fire has burned down to gray ash and the wood pile is gone. I must have used it up. Dragging myself to a sitting position, I briskly rub my cold face.

Giant Beaver's trail is still there. It's melted into a shining ice trough that winds down the side of the Ice Giants, heading toward the distant sea.

Stumbling to my feet, I almost collapse to the ground before I manage to get my feet under me. I'm too weak to do anything except place one boot in front of the other as I walk out of the hollow and step into the trough.

———

By dusk, I'm staggering and gasping for air. Meltwater cascades down the beaver's trail like a small creek. My boots squish as I trudge along. Down the slope, maybe another one half-hand of time away, a ridge of black stone angles off to the west. It will be a good place to rest.

After I eat a handful of snow, I gander at the ridge. Giant Beaver's trail has been obliterated by hundreds of bison hooves. I can't see his trail continuing down the slope.

I'll find it when I get there. And even if the trail has vanished, if I just keep heading due west, I'll reach the coast by nightfall. The thought buoys my strength.

When I curve around the base of the black cliff, I stop.

An overturned sled rests on its side against the rocks. All around it, the snow has been churned up by a mixture of bison and wolf tracks. I know that sled!

"Arakie?" I cry out and break into a shambling trot. "Arakie? *Where are you?"*

Running through the melting snow is like skating on ice. I can't keep my feet under me. I keep falling, rising, running again.

By the time I reach the sled, I've figured out most of the story. Three dead dire wolves lie partly covered with wind-blown snow. Two have been gored and trampled by bison. One was speared through the heart. There's blood everywhere. From the tracks, there must have been ten or twelve wolves. Is the rest of the pack still close?

Their tracks run off in every direction. They could be hunkered down on their bellies out in the trees, watching me and licking their bloody muzzles.

I trot for the sled. The ropes that tied Taiga to the sled were sawn through with a bone knife. He was probably strapped down, watching as the wolves surrounded them. Arakie must have cut the ropes.

In the heat of the fight, either the wolves or the bison repeatedly flipped over the sled. The impressions dent the snow.

Given the amount of blood, this could not have happened too long ago, or animals would have eaten all the bloody snow. How is that possible? Arakie left three days ago. Or . . . or is it four? Five? I don't know.

One set of bloody wolf tracks leads off to the southwest, down into the trees. Mixed with the tracks are the rounded curves of a man's boot prints.

I cautiously head for the trees.

When I enter the cold shade of the pines, the scent of blood is strong. Piles of deadfall the height of a man clutter the grove, exactly the sort of sheltered place wolves would come to lie down and digest a fresh meal. The blood trail disappears into the depths.

Two more dead wolves lie a short distance away, their throats ripped out. All around them giant lion tracks mark the snow. Unmistakable tracks. Nightbreaker's tracks. They're filled with frozen blood. The lion was injured in the fight.

And far back through the dense weave of trees . . .

The breeze picks up the motion of a cloak, billowing it behind the man who hunches on the log in the deepest shadows.

"Arakie!"

He jerks around, props his walking stick, and unsteadily rises to his feet. "Where have you been? I've been worried sick."

Sprinting forward, I catch Arakie's extended hand in a crushing grip. "Elder, dear gods, I'm so relieved you're all right. Looks like you had quite a fight. Where's Taiga?"

White hair, clotted with blood, straggles around his wrinkled face. He doesn't speak for a moment, as though he finds it difficult. "Taiga is alive, but just barely. When the pack attacked, he dragged himself to his feet to help me fight them off. I was battling two, while another three backed Taiga against a boulder and took turns leaping at him. He was frail to start with. He just didn't have the strength to protect himself. They finally pulled him down."

I let go of Arakie's hand. "Where is he?"

Arakie pauses to wipe his eyes on his lion-hide sleeve, before he gestures with his chin. "Back there by the fire. I bandaged his wounds and wrapped him in an elk hide to keep him warm. There's nothing more I can do for him. I've done the best I can."

Through the wall of flames, I can just make out his hide-wrapped body.

"So you saved the woman in the crevasse."

"Yes, but—"

"Then where is she?" Arakie studies the trail as though expecting to see her.

"It's a long story, elder. I want to hear about you first. Are you hurt? You were limping."

Arakie gestures to his torn pant leg. "I'll be all right. One of the wolves got a piece of my leg. It's a bad bite, but I can walk, slowly. I think we can still make Sky Ice Village by tomorrow. I just need to rest for a while, and eat. There's plenty of meat. Let's make a wolf stew for supper."

When Arakie turns and limps back toward the log, I say, "Elder, wait. Put your arm round me, and I'll help support your weight as we walk."

"Glad you made it out of the crevasse alive."

"And I'm glad you survived the wolves."

As he slides his arm across my shoulders, Arakie smiles, as though unexpectedly proud of me. "I guess your friend Quiller was right. They were real wolves. I thought they were spirit—"

"Quiller?" I say, startled. "What are you talking about?"

"She was here last night. Looking for you, of course. We had a lovely—"

"She . . . she came? She came hunting for me?" I'm at once elated and terrified for her.

"Well, of course she did."

"But that's insane. I told her not to!"

Arakie tightens his arm over my shoulders in a hug. "My friend, insanity and sainthood are two sides of the same buffalo coat. A wise man never knows if he's wearing it hair-in or hair-out. There's the rub."

"What?"

He smiles. "Never mind. Let's go eat."

40

QUILLER

A herd of shaggy bison paw at the snow just below my camp, digging for the grasses buried beneath. Their horns gleam in the light cast by the campfires of the dead, and I hear them breathing and rumbling softly to one another. My people say bison are related to the thunderbirds. I believe it. When you hear a bison calling, it sounds just like thunder in the distance. I followed the herd's trail all day as it wound back and forth across the steepest slopes. I followed it, because it always generally followed the sled trail. Right up until I hit the fork in the trail. Then the bison tracks veered left, and I had to make a decision.

"Up there, Bull Bison? Is that where he is?"

I cradle my tea cup in both hands while I watch my campfire flutter in the night wind. My boiling bag hangs from the tripod to my right. Inside, the last of my rabbit stew steams, scenting the darkness.

I lost my "spirit" wolf escort around sunset, which was a relief. It was a long, hard hike today. He stayed with me until I took the right fork in the sled trail, then the wolf howled at me and loped off, heading for the high country.

I'm probably an idiot for following the right fork, but I needed to make camp anyway. I'll reevaluate my decision at sunup.

The air here smells fresh and crisp. I keep inhaling just to smell it. There is no trace of the pungency of zyme. I've never been this far from the shore in my entire life. It's cold up here. Colder than I ever imagined. Wish I'd packed another pair of boots. But the darkness is mesmerizing. The higher I climb into the heart of the Ice Giants, the darker it becomes. The Road of Light is clearer, stretching across the night sky like a broad slash of white paint filled with the campfires of the dead. If I climb high enough, go deeper inland, will I set foot upon the Road of Light? The possibility fills me with longing.

"Where are you, Lynx?"

Yawning, I finish my tea, and roll up in my sleeping hide with my spear clutched in my hand. Just in case the wolf, or other predators, find me in the night.

Despite my exhaustion, it's difficult to sleep.

Grief has become the center of my journey. I miss my children and RabbitEar. I miss Lynx and my family. I miss the noise and laughter of Sky Ice Village. Probably because I know I may never see any of them again.

I especially miss Crow. Since she was a puppy, we've never been apart for more than a few hands of time. She watched me trot away with sadness in her eyes. I wonder what she must be thinking. The woman she loves went away. She did not return.

A spark of light flashes above me, and I see one of the immortal Jemen soaring across the heavens, leaving a bright, fiery trail. I've never seen that before . . . or seen one of the Jemen going so fast . . . and, strangely, he seems to be coming straight for me. As he tumbles through the sky over my head, I sit up and watch until he disappears just over the curve of the hill to the south, where a thunderous roar erupts. Snow gushes high into the air, and the resulting earthquake throws me around like a seaweed doll. Moments later, I'm showered with ice chips.

"What the . . ."

I leap out of my sleeping hide and brush the chips from my hair and coat.

The bison stampede away, running north across the slope. Breathing hard, I watch them, then turn back to squint at the milky haze where the Jemen came down to earth.

Not that far away from me.

Grabbing my pack and quiver, I run to see.

When I get closer, I start moving like a hunter, slow and patient, easing each step down before taking the next.

The haze of snow filters the moonlight, which turns the mountainside even darker, and the hair on my arms tingles. It's as though I'm out in the open on a mountaintop in a lightning storm and a bolt is just about to crackle out of the sky and strike me down.

My hand has gone clammy. I have to regrip my spear before I can convince myself to take another step.

Am I entering a sacred place where I should not be?

The oldest people in Sky Ice Village tell clan stories about places where ancient creatures walk beneath skies filled with campfires of the dead that went out long ago. Such places are holes in the world. If a person accidentally steps into one, they enter a strange, glittering world from which they can never escape.

The stillness is now so great I can hear mice stirring in the frozen grass.

I stop in mid-step, one foot in the air, when a new sound carries to me. A hissing, it seems to come from all around me, but it has the cadence of language.

Something whispers to me, beckoning me closer.

For a time only my eyes move, searching earth and sky, listening for words. Maybe it's Wind Mother moving through the trees?

Trudging forward through the snow, I crest a rise and look

down upon a huge hole in the ice. Inside the hole, a fiery glow is melting down through the glacier, sinking deeper and deeper into the belly of the Ice Giants. What I thought was a haze of snow is really steam rising.

The Jemen is blazing hot.

As it sinks into their hearts, the Ice Giants let out a terrifying roar that echoes across the icy wilderness.

I slowly edge forward.

But in twenty steps, my mouth drops open.

What is that?

Through the trees, off to my left, there is a faint square of blue light.

Gripping my spear tighter, I veer toward it.

The square is the mouth of a cave. A cave filled with blue light.

"Never seen a perfectly square cave before."

I do the same thing I always do when something really frightens me. I head straight for it. In the gleam pouring from the mouth of the cave, I see the sled tracks. The old man must have hauled the sled inside. For what purpose? Maybe just shelter from the cold and darkness.

When I enter the blue cave, awe expands my chest.

Peculiar drawings cover the walls. Painted in lines with a sharpened stick or a twig, the black curls float in the wavering gleam like hovering ghosts. The lines cover every flat rock face, and recede into the blue glow that gets brighter down the tunnel.

"What are these?"

As I walk deeper, the air smells stale and ancient, like moss that's been growing in darkness for a thousand summers. The cries of the Ice Giants are constant, but beneath them I am aware of other sounds. Shell bells clicking. Indistinct purrs that rise and fall. And, almost below my ability to hear, that strange, haunted whisper.

"Hello!" I call. "Is someone back there?"

If not for that whisper, I would talk myself out of going deeper, but I swear someone is calling for help . . .

I walk deeper through a sea of sapphire radiance.

Black handprints begin to cover the wall paintings, more and more of them, until they almost completely blot out the long, curling lines. Then the handprints become stripes and circles. It isn't until I walk very close to the wall that I realize this isn't paint. The patterns were created by someone trying to wash away the curling symbols with his own blood. Over the summers, the stone absorbed the blood and turned it black.

That whisper again . . .

"Where are you? I'm coming!"

It takes another one hundred heartbeats of walking before I enter a gigantic chamber and find the cages.

My gaze lifts. Broken rectangular boxes are stacked atop one another all the way to the ceiling two hundred hand-lengths above me.

Some of the cages look as though they were demolished with a stone ax. The bars of others were chewed through by whatever was inside.

Ancient stories drift through my head.

Could this be the sacred cave where the Jemen hauled the animals to protect them, so that when they'd killed the Ice Giants they could turn them loose in a new and better world?

As I study the doors hanging from the cages and the broken walls, I feel the death of that dream in the pit of my stomach. Coyotes and bobcats will never again trot along sunlit forest trails. Peregrine falcons will never sail through warm skies. They all died long ago. Did the Jemen hack their cages apart to release them? Or did the enemies of the Jemen find the animals and kill them for food? Some of the animals gnawed their way out, that's for certain. Maybe they lived?

The earth quakes and far back in the cavern I hear splashes, like ice cliffs toppling into a vast underground ocean. I turn to . . .

"*Quiller?*" a panicked voice shouts.

It's a shock to hear my name down this deep.

"Basher?" I call back.

"Yes, come quickly!"

I race back up the incline past the curlicues painted upon the walls. Is it possible that they are stories about the death of the sacred animals? Do they chronicle the lives of the great heroes who tried to save them and failed? Maybe the wash of blood was left by the last Jemen to guard the animals? The man who became the story killer?

The whisper . . . calling for help.

Elder Hoodwink says there are places deep in the cavernous belly of the Ice Giants where voices echo forever. I'm convinced that's what I'm hearing. The last desperate plea of the story killer.

When the square mouth of the cave comes into view, I see Basher standing like a black silhouette with his fists clenched, breathing as though he's run all the way to find me. Clouds of his breath fill the air.

"What's wrong? Did you track me here?"

"Yes. Hurry! Rust People attacked us. I barely escaped with my life."

41

LYNX

While Arakie sips a cup of hot tea, I stir the bag of wolf stew suspended from the tripod, and glance at Taiga. Streaks of moonlight fall through the trees and dapple his body. Bundled in hides, only his pale bloodless face is visible in the weave of branch shadows.

Arakie lowers his cup. "He was doing so much better. Well enough to carry on a conversation. I couldn't believe how valiantly he fought off the wolves."

"Thank the gods you aren't hurt worse than you are."

The elder closes his eyes for several long moments, then he lifts his tea cup and sips. The tea is made from the soft inner bark of birch saplings. Though slightly bitter, the brew heals and cleanses.

"So, how did you save the Rust woman?" I remove the wooden spoon from the bag and dip my cup into the steaming broth.

"I did exactly the opposite of what you told me. I went down into the crevasse, tied all of our ropes together, and lifted her out."

"I see. Then where is she?"

Gesturing helplessly, I say, "After she made it to safety, she dropped the rope back into the crevasse. I was trapped for days."

Arakie blinks solemnly at me. "I'm sure that was enlightening. How did you get out?"

"My wife came back from the Land of the Dead and helped me." Using my fingers, I fish out a chunk of wolf meat and chew it. "She guided me to a hole in the ice that led to the surface. She told me she doesn't hate me."

"Glad to hear that."

The power of the dire wolf is flowing into me, making me stronger. I swallow the bite of his meat, and reach for another. As the forest floor grows colder in the night, ice crystals begin to shimmer on the fallen logs and rocks.

"Arakie, what's *Homo erectus*?"

For several stunned heartbeats, he stares at me. "Where did you hear those words?"

"In the crevasse, one of the Ice Giants told me stories about ancient wars, and long-dead heroes, and death rising out of the oceans near Seacouver. And *Homo erectus reecur.*"

His bushy eyebrows draw together. As his shock slowly fades, he sets his cup down and clenches his fists. In a clipped voice, he orders, "Tell me every word you heard."

"I don't remember a lot of it. Some I didn't understand at all. The giant talked about *Denisovan reecur.* What is that?"

After a deep breath, Arakie sits up straighter. I can see thoughts cascading behind his eyes. "You. Your people. Re-created. That's what 'reecur' stands for. The letters r-e-c-r."

"And *Homo erectus*? Are they people, too?"

He inhales a breath, and exhales the words, "That's debatable. You call them Dog Soldiers."

"Do you also know about the frozen village in the ice? I saw it just before I stepped out into the fresh air."

He sits up straighter. "I do not. Tell me about it."

Memories run through my heart, making it pound. "The ice was clear, almost translucent, and buried in the heart were giant shapes, rectangular lodges hundreds of hands tall, shorter square lodges, and pyramids. Many of the lodges had toppled and lay on top of each other, but most were still standing."

He reaches out to put his hand on mine. "Lynx, you have to take me back and show me the place where you came out of the crevasse. I had no idea all those caverns were connected, or that sound carried so far down there. I need to—"

"May not even be there now. It was melting every instant. The Ice Giants have probably swallowed it by now."

"Maybe," he agrees, but desperation lines his face. "However, if there is any chance that I can find the caverns of the last Jemen . . ." Hope trembles his words. "I have to find them."

A flock of herons sails through the darkness high above, and their melodic voices carry across the night.

After another drink of wolf broth, I prop my cup on my knee. "The caverns of the last Jemen? That's where you think I was? Then maybe it wasn't an Ice Giant I heard. Maybe it was one of the Jemen? Hoodwink says the Earthbound Jemen still walk in the great cavern where they hauled crates filled with magical animals just after the zyme."

Arakie bends forward, props his elbows on his knees, and massages his temples. "Does he?"

In the middle of the Road of Light, as though following it to the Land of the Dead, one of the Jemen flies among the campfires of the dead at a slow, steady pace.

"Do you have the courage to take me to the village frozen in the ice, or do I have to find it myself?"

That darkness still crawls across the walls of my soul.

"No, I—I'll take you. But don't we have to tow Taiga to a healer?"

"Yes, you'll show me after that. It's important, Lynx, more important than I will ever be able to explain to you."

42

QUILLER

When we reach the crest of a hill, I see the green glow of the ocean in the distance and a fire flickering in the moonlit ruins of Sky Ice Village. People walk in front of the fire, making it blink. Occasionally, I see the flash of silver clothing.

"Someone's down there."

Basher nods. "Probably sitting in our lodges and eating our mammoth steaks."

"While we catch our breaths, tell me what happened. In detail. I want to know what we're going to be facing."

Basher pants for a while before he says, "We were still loading the boats when a dozen Rust warriors trotted out of the trees. Three of them tried to chase me down. I headed for the forest with spears landing all around me. Didn't lose them until nightfall. That's when I saw your trail climbing the slope. It was a dark line in the moonlight."

I gird myself for his next answer. "Did they kill Mink and RabbitEar . . . and my children? What happened to my children?" My voice is shaking.

Sympathy lines his face. "I ran straight into the forest, Quiller, trying to lose them amid the trees and shadows. Didn't see anything after that, so I don't know. Sorry."

I start down the trail again. As I veer wide around deadfall in the trail, I say, "Are you sure there were only a dozen?"

"Could have been more. Didn't really have time to count. But that's all I saw."

"All right, let's go sneak up on their camp and find out if our people are dead."

I plunge down the other side of the hill with Basher right beside me. When we enter the trees to the east of Sky Ice Village, they seem to move, shifting, whispering around us, trying to warn us that something is creeping through the darkness out there. A big pack of dire wolves would be the worst thing right now. We'll have to climb to get away from them, and then Rust warriors will just walk right up and spear us in the branches.

Go slow. Move like a big cat. Easy. Smart. Listen for the rhythms of paws on snow or feet snapping twigs.

"Quiller?" Basher calls with hushed urgency. "I hear . . ."

The warriors drift out of the forest like wisps of smoke. A few are barefooted, and here and there a bloody scrap of hide wraps an arm or leg. Clearly, they've been in a fight. Though their faces are invisible, their ragged silver clothing flashes like patches of hoarfrost drenched in moonlight.

"Throw down your weapons!" a man shouts.

I toss my spear down, then slide my quiver from my shoulder and place it on top of my spear.

Basher does the same, and whispers, "I count five."

"Yes. Five."

"Why aren't we already dead?"

"About to find out, I suspect."

They appear too weary to hurry, too weary to care if there might be more Sealion People with us. As they surround us with a ring of spears, they peer neither left nor right, but straight at us.

Basher and I exchange a mystified look, and I whisper, "You think our people gave them those wounds?"

"I'm sure they got in a few good casts before they went down, but they were outnumbered six to one."

As the enemy warriors come to a stop around us, a young man, his spear butt dragging the ground, wavers, and stares at me with a filthy face so dulled by fatigue that he appears to be sleepwalking. Can't have seen more than twelve summers. He's a head shorter than me, with matted dirty-blond hair.

When he simply can't stand any longer, the youth staggers, then his knees buckle and he collapses to the ground. The two men closest to him fall out of the circle and walk over to kneel beside the young warrior. Without a word, one of the men hands his spear to his friend, then slips his arms beneath the youth's body and lifts him. The boy wakes and indignantly cries, "Put me down, Redstart! Let me go!"

"I'm goin' to carry you back to camp and lay you by the fire, OtterTail. You need to get warm and eat somethin'. Then you'll be all right."

"No, let me go, please. These people slaughtered my family in their sleep! I 'ave the right to kill them."

My blood goes cold. Is that why so many of these warriors are barefooted? They leaped straight out of their beds and into a battle? *With Sealion People?*

"Isn't goin' to be a fight," Redstart says. "Now stop thrashin' around."

The youth reluctantly relaxes in Redstart's arms. "I want to fight."

A big man, clearly the War Leader, stalks toward me with his eyes half squinted. "Are you Quiller?"

Suspicious, I answer, "Yes."

"Jawbone tells me that his family is gone, killed by illness and lions. He says that he and the girls are no longer White

Foam clan, but 'ave become Blue Dolphin clan of the Sealion People." He tilts his head in a slightly threatening manner. Death lives in those black eyes. "That true? Did you adopt our children?"

"Yes, I did. They were alone. If I hadn't claimed them, they'd be dead."

He glares at me. "And the warrior named RabbitEar is your husband? He says he is their father."

I don't even hesitate. "He is, yes."

My eyes lock with the War Leader's, each of us evaluating the other.

Finally, he uses his spear to gesture to the dark trail that winds down through the trees. "Start walkin'. You know the way."

43

LYNX

A narrow strip of dark water hugs the coastline in the distance, but beyond it, a solid blanket of glowing zyme stretches into infinity.

Struggling to keep my balance, I tow the sled up a low hill and stop in a grove of spruces on the top. It's not yet morning, but we've been on the trail for two hands of time, and Arakie has fallen far behind. He's struggling, using his walking stick like a crutch, propping it and hopping forward on one foot. His bitten leg must be hurting much worse. It's no wonder. This is broken, rolling country, wretched to travel through, especially just before dawn, when it seems to be colder. To make matters worse, we're both half wet and shivering, perpetually soaked with sweat from our efforts.

Only the sight of Mother Ocean lessens my misery.

Wiping the ice crystals from my eyelashes, I call, "Are you all right, elder?"

"Keep moving, Lynx."

"No, I'm going to wait for you."

The rocks that line the trail are decorated with long icicles. In the gleam cast by the campfires of the dead, they resemble glittering fangs. I search the trees, looking for big cats perched in the branches, but see only an owl blinking.

"Dawn is still a good hand of time away. Why don't we rest?" I call.

Breathing hard, Arakie finally hobbles up beside me. The first thing he does is bend down to place his fingers against the big artery in Taiga's throat. The youth's jaw has gone slack. His mouth hangs open.

Arakie straightens and winces. "His heartbeat is very weak. You must go on without me, Lynx. Taiga needs a healer badly. You have to get him to your village as quickly as you can."

"I'm not leaving you, elder. Not again."

"Surely you've noticed that Taiga has not regained consciousness. That's a very bad sign. He could be bleeding to death inside. At the very least, his wounds are pouring infection into his bloodstream. He's dying."

"And if I leave you, you'll be killed by wolves or lions or—"

"I've fought them off many times. I'll do it again if I'm attacked." The elder's voice is stern and confident. His sharp eyes dare me to contradict him.

"Get started." Arakie wobbles on his walking stick. "It'll be morning soon."

"Let me help you sit down first. You need to rest. Are you hungry? I could get a fire going—"

"I was starting fires long before you were born. Way long before. I don't need you. But Taiga does. Now go."

I hesitate. "If I leave and you die, I will never forgive myself, elder."

"And if Taiga dies because you stayed with me, I will never forgive you, so you're doomed either way. Move! You're running out of time." Arakie keeps glancing down the hill toward the glowing coast as though desperately worried.

For a long time, I examine Taiga's sunken cheeks. In the pale light, his skin looks greenish gray. The hide over his chest moves with shallow, quick breaths. When I gander at Taiga, images of old battles flash behind my eyes, and I see screaming children running, women falling to their knees and shielding their babies with their bodies while they plead for their children's lives—battles where Rust People murdered my family and friends. It wasn't so hard with Sunbird. After all, she wasn't a warrior. Not that I know of. But Taiga must be, and that means he's almost certainly killed someone I loved.

If I must choose one man to save . . .

Taking the sled's reins in my hands, I turn to face Arakie. The elder is staring at me with curious eyes, as though fascinated by my choice.

"If I come back and find you torn to shreds, I'm going to kick the bloody pieces around—"

"Yeah, yeah, I get the general idea." Arakie lifts a hand and waves me down the hill. "Get going. I'll be in Sky Ice Village by noon."

Reluctantly, I tow the sled down the hill.

As I get farther away, I hear Arakie talking to himself . . . or maybe he's conversing with Sister Sky, or even just the spirits he sees moving through the air around him.

44

QUILLER

The big Rust warrior, Redstart, shoves me down between RabbitEar and Mink, where they sit before the central fire, but my gaze is on my children. War Leader Cedar has gathered them at his feet and is quietly questioning them. I can't hear his words, but Jawbone and Little Fawn keep glancing worriedly at me.

RabbitEar leans sideways to press his shoulder against mine and whisper, "Wish you were far up in the Crushing Mountains facing down a pride of lions. You'd have better odds of surviving."

"I can see that," I say as I scan the abandoned village, silently counting warriors. Fourteen. And a woman with long blond hair standing at the edge of the trees talking with two more men. Seventeen Rust People.

"Any sign of Lynx?"

"Never got that far."

My gaze returns to my son. Jawbone says something to Cedar, then nervously licks his lips and looks at me and RabbitEar. Jawbone's smart. He knows his answers matter, for he can feel the deadly heaviness in the air.

Cedar gently pats Jawbone's shoulder before he walks over to stand beside Mink. As he props the butt of his spear on the ground, firelight coats his heavy brow ridge and shadows his eyes, turning them into black holes in his face. "Were you in the battle? I don't recall seein' any of you."

Mink shakes his head. "Which battle? There have been so many, I—"

"Two days ago your people attacked one of our smallest villages to the south of here. It was unprovoked! We saw your village sitting here on the shore three days ago, and we passed by. Why did you attack us?"

I exchange a glance with RabbitEar. We both know what must have happened. With Mink out of the way, the other warriors had voted to make Hushy the new temporary War Leader. That's why Sky Ice Village had hurriedly packed up and left. They'd seen the rusty boats passing by, and Hushy had talked the council into authorizing an attack against their enemy. While the rest of the village climbed into the boats, he'd probably led his warriors on a War Walk down the coast, keeping track of the Rust People until they'd made landfall, then he'd ambushed the smallest village while it slept.

The blonde woman walks across the sand with the two men flanking her, and silently stops beside Cedar. Her big head seems gigantic on her starved body. She looks like she hasn't eaten in weeks.

Mink says, "None of us were involved in the attack. We were on a scouting mission to the north. That's how we came upon Great Horned Owl Village, and found these children. We—"

"War Leader Cedar," Jawbone interrupts, and ducks his head in apology. "I beg for the lives of these people. These warriors saved us."

Cedar places a comforting hand on Jawbone's shoulder. "I hear your words. Now please take the girls and get in the boat. That way I will know you are safe."

"Yes, War Leader."

Jawbone collects the girls, and together they trot across the beach to climb into the largest boat. The girls sit on the packs, but Jawbone remains standing, his legs braced against the waves that rock the boat. Standing backlit by the zyme, he is a small, dark figure, his face barely visible.

I don't know where Crow is. I've been searching for her since we arrived. Did she try to protect the people she loves? If she leapt for the throat of a Rust warrior . . . she's probably lying dead in the forest.

Cedar nods respectfully to the Rust woman. "Matron Sunbird, the decision is yours."

She takes two steps forward and fixes hard blue eyes on Mink. "Then you know nothin' of the battle, is that right?"

"That's right. By the time we arrived, Sky Ice Village had already been abandoned. We had no idea where our relatives had gone. We were planning to paddle down the coast to find them."

"Won't be necessary." Emotion narrows Matron Sunbird's eyes. "Most of your relatives are dead."

"You killed them?"

Sunbird lifts her eyes to watch the children in the boat, as though she finds it difficult to finish the story. "Your people killed twelve men, women, and children. Many were sick. They could barely get out of their bedding hides. We sent out four war parties to hunt down the cowards who attacked them."

Cedar adds, "With the fresh snow on the ground, their trails were easy to follow."

Mink's face is expressionless, just listening.

Sunbird pauses and seems to be waiting for some kind of response from Mink.

My belly knots up. Mink must be wondering if Gray Dove and his two sons are among the dead, but his face shows no emotion at all.

Sunbird shifts her slung arm to a more comfortable position, as though it hurts. Was she injured in the battle? "When the lions attacked Great Horned Owl Village, my brother and I ran into the mountains, tryin' to escape, and we got caught in the big snowstorm. I slipped and fell into a crevasse. A Sealion man saved me. I owe him a debt."

A Sealion man . . .

Mink asks, "A Sealion man who had escaped the battle?"

"No. A man who had been abandoned in the wilderness at the order of your foolish elders. A good man."

My heart thunders. I see Mink swallow hard.

"Where is he? Is he alive?"

After a long hesitation, she says, "He died in the crevasse after he climbed down to save me. I promised him I would bring help, but—but I was freezin' and dazed. Not thinkin' right. Just kept staggerin' downhill. When I saw our boats in the ocean, I followed them to where our people had camped. Your attack came that same night."

"And, afterward, you no longer wished to save him," Mink finishes the sentence for her.

Tears fill her eyes.

Cedar slaps Mink in the face with the butt of his spear. "We destroyed the war party that attacked us, but we do not know where your village is camped. Where are they?"

Wind blowing in from the ocean carries the scent of dead bodies across the abandoned village. The strips of painted hides around the scaffolds have come loose and flap in the wind, snapping out flashes of red, blue, and yellow. Set against the background of waves, they seem so beautiful.

Mink gives the big War Leader a sidelong gander. "I just told you I don't know where my relatives went."

With lightning quickness, Cedar twirls his spear in one hand and stabs Mink in the shoulder. When he withdraws the iron spearhead, Mink grunts softly in pain. Blood soaks his coat and runs down his back. "Did you plan to meet somewhere?"

Just before he says it, I can see thoughts moving behind Mink's eyes. "You're standing here wasting time with me . . . while the rest of our warriors are slaughtering another of your villages."

"You have no more warriors, and I know it."

"The War Leader that attacked you is simple-minded but effective. He attacked your smallest village to draw your warriors away so the bulk of his forces could concentrate on more rewarding targets. While you squandered time tracking a handful of our warriors through the snow, he hit your main village."

RabbitEar gives me a warning glance. That's exactly the sort of thing Hushy would do. Pick the most isolated village, then create a diversion to draw off as many of the warriors as he could. Once they were gone, he'd send in his main force to destroy another village. But why would Mink tell Cedar?

At some level, Cedar must believe Mink, for a hint of panic tightens his eyes. "Then you are right. I'm wastin' my time here. I should just kill all of you and hurry home."

Jawbone must have heard. He starts crying in the boat.

45

LYNX

As Father Sun crests the ice peaks to the east, a wave of light spreads across the forests, painting the top of every tree yellow and turning the ice a deep gold. The morning air carries the pungency of zyme.

When I step onto the well-trodden mammoth trail that leads home I'm so happy tears blur my eyes.

" . . . almost there."

It hasn't occurred to me until now, but the first thing the council will ask is if I accomplished the task they gave me.

" . . . *we must not ignore the possibility that Lynx is alive because an old spirit-filled lion saw something inside him that none of us do. Something powerful. Something important. Maybe something critical to the survival of the Sealion People. The simple fact is that either Nightbreaker decided not to kill him, or he could not kill him. The council has discussed this, and all believe Lynx has been chosen by the Jemen. We must know why . . . which means Lynx must find Nightbreaker and ask him.*"

In the eyes of the elders, I have failed.

Once, what seems eons ago, I considered making up a story. But it seems foolish now. I will just tell them the truth and accept the consequences. If the council exiles me permanently, I will ask Arakie if I can live with him, at least for a time. If not, I will venture out into the wilderness to find my fate alone.

After ten summers of living by myself in the heart of the Ice Giants, who will I be? I have no idea. But I'm no longer afraid to find out.

"We'll be there soon," I tell Taiga over my shoulder. "Our holy man will save you. I give you my oath."

His jaw is slack, his face too pale to be that of a living man. I consider dropping the reins and walking back to see if he's breathing, but either he is or he isn't. Hoodwink is Taiga's only hope. The faster I get him there, the better.

Gripping the reins tightly, I tow the rocking sled over the frozen mammoth tracks that gouge the mud.

Sunlight slants through the pines and gleams on smoke-colored trunks, dead-fallen logs, and standing dead grasses. Out in the trees, something whimpers. I tilt my head to listen . . .

Crow lopes out of the shadows with her tail tucked between her legs and her tongue lolling from her mouth. When she hits the trail ten paces ahead of me, her long body stretches out as she runs as hard as she can to reach me.

"Crow!" I crouch down, catch her in my arms, and hug her. "What are you doing out here alone? Where's Quiller?"

Crow frantically licks my face, then wrenches free of my arms and charges down the trail toward the village.

Frowning, I rise. When I'm not following her fast enough, Crow whirls and charges back to leap on me. Her big paws striking the middle of my chest almost topple me.

"Crow, what's wrong? Where's Quiller?"

The black dog shoots down the trail toward the village again.

Which makes me go still and quiet.

The hair on the nape of my neck prickles as I search the trees and the trail ahead. Something is wrong. Really wrong.

I pull my spear from my quiver. The shaft is very cold in my grip.

Can I risk leaving Taiga here for one finger of time while I make my way through the trees to a place where I can see the village? Strapped to the sled, he is completely vulnerable to any predator that wants him.

When Crow races back, whining, I lay the reins down and step off the trail into the forest shadows. Crow falls into line behind me. She knows I'm on the hunt and moves so silently her paws barely stir the dry pine needles.

I hear faint voices.

And see sunlight glinting from bone and ivory spearheads. The warriors are almost invisible where they crouch behind tree trunks.

Not breathing now, I slip behind a boulder, and whisper to Crow, "Lie down. Don't move."

Crow lies down and goes so still she might be a stuffed dog-skin.

One man uses hand signals to tell his warriors where to move in the trees. Soundlessly, they obey.

"Kinglet, are your men ready?" a voice softly calls.

Bluejay!

For several moments, I am stunned. Why are they surrounding their own village? When the truth begins to dawn, I grip my spear so tightly my knuckles go white.

I don't dare shout or trot down to join them. That distraction could get them all killed. Helplessly, I watch Bluejay's war party move through the trees like prowling wolves.

Maybe, if I can veer around to the north, I can . . .

A lion growl echoes through the trees, and my spine goes rigid.

Taiga.

Lions have found Taiga.

46

QUILLER

My ears strain, trying to hear what War Leader Cedar and Matron Sunbird are saying five paces away, but they're keeping their voices too low.

"Be ready," RabbitEar hisses to me, and seems to be massaging a cramp in his leg.

Redstart watches him suspiciously at first, then apparently dismisses the action, for he turns back to watch Sunbird and Cedar.

It's an amazing sleight of hand. RabbitEar pulls a deer-bone stiletto from his boot and tucks it up his sleeve. "Do you have any weapons?"

"No, but OtterTail has a war club and a meteorite knife tied to his belt."

Since I arrived, I've located and memorized every weapon on every belt.

"Easy to untie?"

My head dips in a barely discernible nod. OtterTail sleeps two paces away, and his war club is tied to his belt with a simple slipknot. In less than four heartbeats, that can be in my fist.

RabbitEar gives me a smile, the kind of smile that only warriors about to die can give one another. It's a silent promise that neither will die alone.

Almost too low to make out the words, he orders, "When the time comes, run for the boat. Shove out to sea. Head south. I'll guard you for as long as I can."

I nod. We both know the stakes. Our children stand side by side on top of the packs, watching. Occasionally, Little Fawn speaks to Jawbone, but the boy's gaze never leaves the two of us.

"Where will I meet you?"

RabbitEar laughs softly at my optimism. When he turns, there's so much love in his eyes, my throat goes tight. "Find a beautiful place, Quiller. Build a lodge. I'll join you soon."

We both know it's a lie. But it's a good lie.

"Don't take too long. I'll be waiting for you."

He's staring straight into my eyes, smiling, when he says, "I won't."

As Father Sun rises higher into the morning sky, a swath of luminous gold paints the water and stretches across the beach. Every grain of sand glimmers and twinkles.

Cedar props his spear over his shoulder and spreads his feet in front of Matron Sunbird. She nods at something he says.

Cedar calls, "Let's kill these Sealion vermin and go home. Ready your spears."

Men trot forward with their spears.

When Cedar aims his spear at Mink's heart, Mink doesn't even flinch, just takes a deep breath and peers out at the ocean as though enjoying the mosaic of shadows that paints the zyme. Three more warriors gather around Basher, RabbitEar, and me. The rest of the Rust warriors stand off to the side, appearing bored, apparently just waiting for it to be over.

Cedar draws back his arm . . . and war cries erupt from the trees to the east.

Bluejay charges across the beach with a dozen Sealion warriors behind him, which gives Mink the opportunity to lunge for Cedar's spear.

While Basher and RabbitEar leap on the warriors closest to them, I dive for the war club tied to OtterTail's belt, pull the slipknot, and run for the boat with the club in my fist. Heavy feet pound after me.

Don't stop. Don't stop. Get to the boat.

At a dead run, I pull the stake that tethers the boat to the sand and splash into the ocean, where I slam my shoulder into the side of the boat and shove it out to sea.

Just as I heave my body up and swing one leg into the boat, a Rust warrior grabs me around the waist and drags me backward into the ocean. I'm looking up through a wall of water when I see RabbitEar leap upon the man and repeatedly plunge his deer-bone stiletto into the Rust warrior's back. Blood turns the ocean around me red.

"Fight me, you coward!" RabbitEar shouts.

"Filthy savage!" The dazed Rust warrior releases me, spins around, and attacks RabbitEar.

While RabbitEar struggles against the dying man's desperate grip, he yells, "Go, Quiller! Get in the boat!"

I scramble back into the boat, grab a paddle, and madly head out into the water.

When I turn to look back, Sealion and Rust warriors are careening across the village, throwing spears, diving for cover, rolling, and coming up with knives or clubs in their fists. Basher lies near the fire with a spear through the heart.

Bluejay and Mink are engaged in a standoff with Redstart and Cedar. Bluejay holds Matron Sunbird in front of him like a shield, a long bone knife pressed against her throat.

"No!" Cedar cries. "Don't kill her!"

Mink shouts, "Tell your warriors to drop their weapons!"

As the boat gets farther and farther from shore, Jawbone cries, *"RabbitEar! RabbitEar! Come on!"*

RabbitEar staggers away from the dead Rust warrior with the waves dragging at his legs, then turns and slogs for the village to get back into the fight.

47

RABBITEAR

When my feet hit the sand, I hear a strange quaver eddying across the battle.

It starts low, barely audible, then slowly transforms into a cacophony of deep-throated growls that seem to be coming from everywhere. As they grow louder, clashing warriors back away from their opponents to call panicked questions back and forth.

"Where are the lions?"

"Do you see them?"

In the amber gleam of morning, their tan bodies seem to melt with the deepest forest shadows, leaving their pale faces to float amongst the pine trunks like disembodied heads.

"Blessed Jemen, they're everywhere," Kinglet calls from my right.

Each warrior, Rust or Sealion, turns to aim his spear at the trees.

Nightbreaker stalks out of the shadows and stands in the middle of the mammoth trail with his chin up, eyeing the humans on the beach in a superior manner. The huge old animal is covered with blood.

"Mink?" Kinglet calls. "What should we do?"

Mink turns to give Cedar a hard gander. "I count around

twenty lions. Either we fight together, War Leader, or we all die here."

Cedar swallows hard. Without taking his gaze from the lions, he says to Sunbird, "Matron?"

Bluejay relaxes his arm across her throat long enough for Sunbird to say, "Fight the lions! We can kill each other tomorrow. If any of us are left alive."

The rest of Nightbreaker's pride, little more than bobbing shapes, are faintly luminescent as they emerge from the pines and encircle the warriors on the beach.

Nightbreaker's nostrils flare as he scents the air, and his gaze picks out each person, resting on each man's face for a few heartbeats, before he trots down the trail toward the lion trap.

I stand frozen, waiting for Mink to give the order to cast.

But Mink has his head tilted, watching the regal old lion as he walks into the trap and trots to the rear where the pile of lion bones are heaped. Nightbreaker starts panting as though he ran all the way to get here. The other lions stay just beyond casting range.

"Hold your casts!" Mink calls.

Nightbreaker paws at the bones, then slowly moves along the length of the trap, licking at each place where the log bars were gnawed. When he sees the bison carcass, his nostrils flare again. He walks straight to it, looks at the rope that holds the trapdoor up, and sinks his teeth into the carcass and tugs it hard. When the trapdoor falls closed with a thunderous bang, locking him inside, the old lion jumps. But there is no enraged roaring or frantic leaping at the bars. Instead, Nightbreaker flops down beside the bison and rests his head upon his paws, his wide eyes fixed upon the mammoth trail as though he knows someone's coming.

I suck a breath into my starving lungs and glance at the other warriors. No one has moved. Nor have the lions that create a great semicircle around us. If the animals attack, there's nowhere to run except into the ocean. Then all the lions have to do is wait us out. I've seen it happen. The lions wade through the waves, forcing their human prey into the depths where they have to swim. Then they just follow the swimmers down the shore. Finally, exhaustion and desperation take over. Drowning people try to make it back to land.

"Who is that?" a Rust warrior calls.

The man appears on a deeply shadowed portion of the mammoth trail, a black shape with hair blowing about his face in the sea breeze. There's a grating sound like something being dragged over rocks.

Mink takes a step forward, but stops when the lions shift positions. *"Lynx! Go back!"* he shouts.

Sunbird sucks in a breath. "Lynx!"

I'm confused. From his position on the mammoth trail, Lynx must see the lions. Why doesn't he break and run for the trees? Instead, his sled bangs and clatters, as he continues dragging it down the trail toward the village.

Sunbird cries, "Lynx, stop! There are lions!" She sprints for him, but Cedar catches her arm and drags her back.

"Let me go, you fool! That's Lynx, and he's towin' Taiga!"

Cedar keeps his hand clamped on her arm. "Matron, if they are alive in one hundred heartbeats, I will release you."

Now and then, I see things in the forest depths. Faintly iridescent faces hover far back in the trees. Probably more lions moving in. They seem to approach, then glide through the screen of trunks before slowly withdrawing into the shadows again. Some have a bluish tint, like the glaciers. For a moment, I wonder if the Ice Giants have taken human form and walked down to join the fight.

When Lynx drags the banging sled down past the lion trap, he stops to speak with the old lion inside. Nightbreaker must be panting again, for his breath clouds in front of his muzzle.

"Lynx!" Sunbird struggles against her War Leader's restraining hand. *"Lynx, run. What's the matter with you? Wake up!"*

Lynx goes rigid. He seems to have turned to stone.

"Oh, gods," Mink whispers.

As though each step takes monumental effort, Lynx drags the sled between two lions. I can't believe he isn't already dead, but maybe the animals are as stunned as everyone else.

When Lynx gets to within five paces, Cedar releases her and Sunbird charges out to meet Lynx, hugging him so hard, he staggers.

The lions stalk forward, positioning themselves where it will only take a single leap to kill both Lynx and Sunbird.

Warriors hiss questions and brace themselves to cast.

Nightbreaker lets out a low roar and, in utter silence, the lions trot away, vanishing into the trees as though they've been spirit animals all along.

48

LYNX

Everyone gathers around the fire, watching sparks whirl upward into the sky, while they listen to my stories. As dusk settles over the beach, the sweet fragrance of burning pine fills the air.

Sitting cross-legged between Mink and RabbitEar, I clutch my cup of hot tea in both hands. Crow lies half asleep beside me, gazing out at the ocean, as though she saw Quiller vanish there and is waiting for her beloved friend to return for her.

I reach down and gently pet her. Her fire-warmed back feels good after the long days of bitter cold.

"I don't believe it," Bluejay says. "My sister came to you when you were dying? By then she would have been in the Land of the Dead. Why would she return?" The pink scars on the lower half of his face reflect the firelight.

My gaze drifts over OtterTail and Taiga where they rest beneath heaps of hides on the north side of the fire. Both seem better, sleeping soundly. Sunbird spent two hands of time treating and wrapping both their wounds—using herbs I found for her in Hoodwink's lodge.

Out in the lion trap, Nightbreaker watches me with sleepy, half-lidded eyes, as though wondering what's taking me so long.

I expel a deep breath, and answer, "She gave me a message for you."

Bluejay stiffens. "Message?"

"Yes, she said, 'When you see my brother, please tell him I love him. And tell Bluejay that Grandfather wants him to know how proud he is of the things Bluejay has done to help our people. Grandfather says he is keeping a place of honor by his fire for Bluejay.'"

Tears shine in Bluejay's eyes before he wipes them away. "That sounds like something he would have said."

I take a drink of tea and close my eyes. I wish Quiller was here. Just to see her, to be with her. "Then I saw the giant lodges of our ancestors."

Murmurs eddy around the circle as warriors exchange glances.

Mink frowned. "You had a vision?"

"My wife led me through a narrow crack in the bottom of the crevasse to a hole in the ice that led outside. It was absolutely black inside the crevasse, but just before I stepped out, light from the campfires of the dead streamed into the ice cavern, and I found myself gandering out upon an unbelievable vista of giant lodges, hundreds of hands tall, frozen in the depths of the ice."

One of the Rust warriors makes a deep-throated sound of disgust. "Hundreds of hands tall? I don't believe it. How could anyone build a lodge that tall? There are no trees that tall in the entire world. What were they made of?"

"Pounded meteorites, I think. I could see rust on some of the beams, just as we find on your iron weapons. I—"

"Ridiculous!"

Sunbird sits so still, she doesn't seem to be breathing. "No. Lynx is telling the truth. I saw them. Sometimes lights flashed in the cavern below me . . . like . . . like oil lamps being carried through the ruins by people. I didn't think they were real. I saw so many strange things. But Lynx is right. It looks like a vast village of giant lodges buried behind a wall of ice."

Rust warriors turn in unison to stare at her.

Cedar says, "You saw many strange things?"

Her gaze remains on me when she answers, "People long-dead came to me. I saw my great-grandmother and her mother. They told me that my mother was dead, and I was now the Matron of the White Foam clan. They said I would be a good leader if I listened well to those around me. Then they told me they'd sent a Sealion man to save me."

Cedar says, "Our ancestors sent a *Sealion* man to save you? Why?"

"I don't understand the ways of spirits, War Leader. Maybe just because he was at hand."

From the lion trap, a barely audible, deep-throated growl rumbles.

No one else glances at the old lion trapped in the cage, but Nightbreaker is now all I see. The hair on his white muzzle flickers with firelight. His eyes have become my whole world.

I'm coming. Very soon.

Mink puts a hand on my shoulder. "Hoodwink said that if you returned from your spirit quest, you would become one of the greatest shamans our people have ever known."

High up in the Ice Giant Mountains, dire wolves howl. The beautiful lilting song echoes across the distances.

"That's probably why Matron Sunbird's great-grandmother came to tell her about Lynx. She knew he had great power," Cedar says, and blinks at me. "It seems strange to me that the ghosts of the White Foam clan agree with your holy man, Hoodwink."

"Forgive me, Lynx," Sunbird says hoarsely. "I shouldn't 'ave left you in the crevasse—"

"Yes, you should have. I needed my dead wife to save me. We had so much to say to one another."

Bluejay bows his head and stares at the ground for several moments, then he rises to his feet with his spear clutched in his hand. "Don't know about the rest of you, but I believe the visions I have heard tonight. Going to find my bedding hides and dream about giant lodges buried deep in the ice."

When Bluejay walks away, several Sealion warriors follow him to find their own beds.

Mink gets up and stretches his back muscles. "Deputy Kinglet, please select four warriors to take first watch."

"Yes, Mink."

War Leader Cedar counters, "I, also, will select four warriors. Just in case your people try to slit our throats in the night."

"We won't," Mink says, "but I'd fear the same thing if I were you."

The War Leaders nod warily to one another.

I notice that RabbitEar keeps giving me sidelong glances, as though he has something to tell me, but not until we are alone. It's about Quiller, though. All night long, each time he says her name, a soft warmth enters his voice.

Mink gestures to the lion trap. "Before we all find our bedding hides, someone should kill that lion."

Kinglet said, "I'll be glad to—"

"No." I rise. "He's my responsibility. Mine alone."

"You?" Kinglet says as though surprised that I would volunteer to kill anything. But as he studies my face, he shrugs. "Very well. He's yours. If you need help, I will be standing at the south end of the trees. Just call out."

"I won't need help."

Kinglet gives me a doubtful glare, and walks away to tap

men on the shoulders. Kinglet and the other warriors disappear into the darkness to take up their guard positions, and Cedar begins moving through the Rust People, assigning guard duty.

As people drift away from the fire, Sunbird comes to me.

I reach out to gently touch her broken arm. "How's your arm?"

She smiles. "Hurts, but it's healin'."

"I'm glad."

We stand gazing at each other until Sunbird says, "You saved Taiga's life, and my life. I won't forget."

"I'm glad I was there to help."

She squeezes my arm. "Good night."

I watch her walk away through the fire-lit ruins of my village.

RabbitEar stands up beside me with his head bowed and his jaw clenched. He waits until I turn to face him before he says, "I'm glad you're safe, Lynx. But there are some things that must be said between us."

"RabbitEar, I've known for a long time that you love Quiller."

As though mildly surprised, he looks me over carefully. "I do. And I won't give her up to you or anyone else. We have four children now, Rust children that we adopted. Do you understand? They need me."

My pulse drops to a slow, sad drumbeat. I've lost her. I always thought that if I ever got lonely . . .

"I'm glad. You will be a much better father than I could ever be."

"You won't interfere? Try to—"

"No. Never again. I give you my sacred oath."

RabbitEar nods once, as though here in the firelight, we've sealed a bargain.

"You've changed, Lynx. Grown up."

"Have I?"

RabbitEar smiles and walks away across the village toward Quiller's lodge, where he crawls inside. I wonder if he's used to sleeping there. Then I let it go . . .

And I turn toward Nightbreaker.

49

LYNX

As I trudge through the darkness with my spear in my hand, cold air blowing down from the Ice Giant Mountains buffets my hood. The brittle scent of snow rides the wind. By midnight, I suspect the world will turn blindingly white.

As I walk farther from the firelight, the beach grows colder and darker, but I've started to sweat. Each time the wind shifts, I feel certain it's been blocked by someone—or something—a presence that has, for an instant, stopped in front of me to delay me. Once, it sniffed at me, scenting me, as though identifying me before allowing me to pass.

Nightbreaker waits with an ancient patience. The closer I get to the trap, the more widely the giant lion opens his eyes, and a low, eerie growl reverberates through the air.

Gripping my spear, I imagine myself thrusting the spear into the caged lion's heart. He can't get away. Can't fight back. He's completely vulnerable.

When I'm five paces away, Nightbreaker rises to his feet and bravely faces me with his head held high. He must know what's coming.

It's late and dark, and I'm alone. My breathing has gone so shallow I'm light-headed.

When I stand beside the cage, the air starts to glitter. Everything about the lion assaults my senses, his wild smell, his yellow eyes and massive head.

"Came here to kill you."

The old lion's panting frosts the air.

All I can see now are his shining eyes, staring at me expectantly. As though Nightbreaker has already made peace with his fate, he's just waiting for me to thrust my spear between the bars and have it over. He steps closer to the bars, as if making it easier for me.

Far back in my mind, I hear screams and the sound of arms and legs striking tree trunks. *Lynx, a lion has got me. He's dragging me. Help me.*

Our faces are barely four hands apart. I can smell the blood on his coat and his meat breath. He was probably hungry and ate some of the bison carcass.

"Why didn't you kill me that night? I should have been the one to die, not . . . not everyone else. You were standing right over me. I saw you. Why did you let me live?"

Nightbreaker softly paws at the bars, his claws raking the wood, urging me to get on with it.

"Are you really Arakie?"

As though by now the answer should be perfectly obvious even to a dull-witted imbecile like me, Nightbreaker blinks lazily.

For just a brief instant, I find myself inside the old lion, gazing out upon the human camp through his eyes, at the fire-lit lodges and skeletal lodge frames, the burial scaffolds on the beach. The colors change, going from dim to brilliant. Where moments before the lodges on the far edges of the village were shrouded in darkness, now they are quartz clear, all their details intricate. The way the shredded lodge covers dance in the wind is fascinating, and brings me the distinct scents of the humans inside, the herbs, the dried meats . . .

A sublime otherworldly wonder swells my heart and filters outward through my arms and legs—and I suddenly understand that this old white-faced lion has *ventured so far into the emptiness for another's sake that surrendering to the darkness has become the path of salvation.*

Nightbreaker licks his muzzle. Waiting.

I walk to the door of the cage.

"I'll see you soon," I say, as I pull the rope to lift the door of the trap.

Nightbreaker is eye to eye with me when he walks out of the trap, staring at me, growling softly.

I turn my back to him and plod toward the fire.

The almost soundless tapping of his paws on sand seems timed to my heartbeat.

Shouts and screams go up from the guards when they see Nightbreaker loping away into the darkness.

50

LYNX

We're almost ready to leave," Mink says as he walks up beside me, where I stand staring out at the endless zyme that stretches into infinity.

I take a deep breath and hold it in my lungs for a time. In the distance, Crow trots along the coastline, flushing birds, wagging her tail. The familiar fragrance of the zyme is like a balm on my tired soul.

"Have people calmed down yet?"

"'Course not. Nobody likes you very much today."

"Nobody ever liked me much."

"I liked you. For the life of me, I can't understand why you did it. Nightbreaker is a killer."

All morning long, people have been casting strange glances at me, grumbling about the release of Nightbreaker—the old lion everyone hates. Behind me, I hear voices, and wood being chopped, and smell mammoth steaks cooking over fires.

"It's not going to be an easy boat ride for you, sitting beside people who are angry—"

"Not going with you, Mink."

Mink frowns. "What are you talking about?"

"I'm staying here."

"Are you insane? Why?"

"I have to find my friend, Arakie."

Mink grabs my shoulder and swings me around so fast I stumble.

"Stop being a fool. He's probably dead. You can't stay here alone." Wind whips Mink's long black hair around his face. "There's a chance that we can meld the Sealion and Rust Peoples together and stop killing each other. Matron Sunbird has decided that she will speak for us before the Rust People Council. Because you saved her, she wants to make peace. She believes in you. Don't you understand that you could become a great and powerful holy man, a legendary leader? Just as Hoodwink said you would."

"Don't want to be a legend."

As though confused, Mink shakes his head. "Then what *do* you want, my brother?"

"I just . . ." Seagulls squeal and flap out over the water, their wings glimmering with sunlight. "I want to find Arakie. He was hurt. He needs me."

Mink shoves me hard. "My crazy brother! What's the matter with you? I wish Quiller was here. She'd talk sense to you."

I give him a faint smile. Now that I know I've lost her, I miss Quiller more than I would have ever thought possible. "Mink, could you tell me what happened between Quiller and Rabbit-Ear?"

The air seems to go out of Mink's lungs. He takes a new grip on his spear. "Didn't RabbitEar tell you?"

"He just told me he loved her and they had adopted four children together."

Mink, never one to spare my feelings, says, "They're married. Or will be."

It's a shock—but not entirely. She needs a man she can depend upon. I am not that man. At some point during my spirit quest, she must have realized that.

"Good. That's good."

Mink's angry expression softens. "She loved you with all her heart, you know?"

"She'll be happy now, Mink. She wouldn't have been happy with me. I would have let her down."

Mink stabs the butt of his spear into the sand and leans against it as he frowns at a small crab that crawls across the beach just beyond the reach of the waves. Crow is following behind it, sniffing at it. "What are you going to do out here alone?"

"Don't know yet. Guess I'll figure it out." I turn and hug my brother hard. "I'll miss you."

Mink pounds my back with a fist. "You will always be welcome in my lodge. Someday, come home."

———

One hand of time later, I stand in the middle of the abandoned lodges and watch the boats buck the waves as they are paddled out to sea. They had to empty most of the dried meat from the smaller boat to make room for all of the Sealion and Rust Peoples, but it means I have enough food for a moon. Hide bags heap the shore.

Crow perches on top of the packs in the big boat, watching me, as though worried about leaving me behind. Mink will make sure Crow gets back to Quiller.

As I listen to their voices growing fainter, I realize these may be the last human voices I ever hear. What if I never find Arakie? I keep my eyes on Mink for as long as I can, until the boat passes beyond the curve in the shoreline and disappears, then I clench my fists and take a deep breath.

"Now what?" I whisper. "Where should I look for Arakie? Maybe I should wait here for him a little longer."

It's comforting to think that I can just sleep in the old lodges for a while. Until I work up the courage to trudge back up into the Ice Giant Mountains to look for him. He didn't try to find the cavern with the giant lodges by himself, did he?

Silently, I amble through the village, petting the bare lodge poles, remembering the people I loved, saying good-bye to the life I have always known, before I walk out to the beach and solemnly weave between the burial scaffolds with their fluttering ribbons.

For a long time, I stand in front of Siskin's scaffold. I saw her. I touched her wounds with my own hands. She isn't dead. She just walked over the next hill to wait for me. That hill . . .

As I gaze up at the magnificent, shining glaciers, I see a herd of helmeted muskoxen moving slowly down a trail near the crevasse. Their big bodies appear puny and insignificant, but everything does when cast against the desolation and booming voices of the Ice Giants.

I try not to stare too long, because I know what will happen. They will open their invisible eyes and stare back. Already, I feel their presences seeping through my skin and ribs, crushing my lungs.

I stride for the mammoth trail that leads high into the mountains. While fear tingles across my chest, there is also comfort in the aloneness. No one expects anything of me now. Not my brother, or Quiller, or my clan, or my people.

When I pass the open lion trap, I instinctively follow Nightbreaker's huge paw prints. The old lion broke into a run here. As he stretched out, his tracks grew farther and farther apart, as though he was loping toward something. I walk for another finger of time before I find the other lion tracks coming in from all directions, surrounding Nightbreaker. Some were leaping. Several ran circles around the old lion, as if joyously greeting a long-lost friend who had mysteriously vanished and just returned to them.

With each step I take, I become more certain that everything in my life, everything that's gone before, was a distraction. This moment of walking straight out into the wasteland of ice is the only thing that has ever really mattered.

When I break out of the trees and gander up the steep slope ahead . . .

I see him. On the next hilltop. His hand is in the air, waving to me. Arakie may have called out, but if so, the wind blew his voice in the opposite direction.

Relieved to see him alive, I sprint up the trail, following lion tracks the whole way . . . because they lead straight to him.

"Sick Lynx, what are you doing here? You should be heading south with your people."

Slumping down on the rock beside the old man, I say, "I decided to stay."

"Yeah? Why?"

For the first time, I feel truly awake. Wide awake. Everything around me has a shimmering, faintly blue halo.

"I had to find you. To make sure you were all right. I guess I wanted to commit an act of love that looks like madness."

I smile at him, but Arakie does not return my smile. He stares hard into my eyes, probing the depths of my soul.

At last, he slides off the rock, grabs his walking stick, and says, "Come. There's something I need to show you before we head to the crevasse."

"You still want to go find the caverns of the last Jemen?"

He hesitates for a long time. "I need to know what happened to them. I may not find the answer there, but I have to search for it."

51

QUILLER

Little Fawn, who naps on the sand to my right, yawns and says, "Do you see him yet?"

"Not yet."

I take a deep breath and slowly let it out. Where I stand guard on shore, I can see the sunlit blanket of zyme rolling all the way to the western horizon. The tallest humps flash golden, and cast curious reflections through the decomposing skeletons of long-dead monsters that rest on the shore. I have no notion what they are. No one does. Were they pure white birds? Giant birds? Their insides were hollowed out long ago, leaving long tubes, but they have birdlike wings on their tails. As the tide comes in, waves explode against the massive hulks and spray shoots high into the air.

I have been exploring them for days. They have very thin skins that glitter in the sunlight, and zyme will not grow on them, which means they have no iron in them. The gaping wounds in their bodies—the longest, cleanest cuts I have ever seen—were caused by something else. Knives wielded by giants that walked the earth before the zyme? Yesterday, I spent the entire morning inside the belly of the largest bird, studying the curlicue images that coat every spot of skin—the same kind of images I found in the blue cave, I think. I'm convinced it is a story. No one would go to such effort unless he or she was desperate to tell the story of what happened to the strange creatures.

Heaving a breath, I resettle my feet. I feel as though I've been facing northward my whole life, waiting for RabbitEar . . . or Lynx . . . or any of my lost people to appear, either in the water or on the sand.

Three days ago, I found the pitiful remnant of the once great People of the Sealion camped here on this dry tundra that extends southward along the edges of the Ice Giants. In total, thirty-two People of the Sealion survive, fourteen of them children. My entire family is dead, my parents, sister and brothers . . . all gone. All killed in the battles with the Rust People. Grief pervades every moment of my life. And the lives of all the survivors.

I think we know the truth. We aren't going to make it. Soon, too soon, the Sealion People will be dead and gone.

Six little girls chase each other around the lodges. Loon is in the lead, but several of the older girls are right on her heels. The youngest children, including Chickadee, jump up and down on the sidelines, laughing, oblivious to the depths of the sorrow around them. Jawbone stands a few paces away with his feet braced and his spear in his hands. Standing guard over the girls.

I finally understand what RabbitEar meant.

We spend all of our lives searching for someone who will let us stand guard over them. Someone who will let us protect them . . .

It's the silent promise we give to those we love.

My new home stands on the south side of the tiny ring of lodges. The freshly tanned mastodon hide that covers the ribbone frame shines golden in the fading rays of sunset. Salmon and blue dolphins decorate the lodge cover, painted by my children. By our children.

"Quiller?" Jawbone calls, and suddenly lurches forward three steps, then lets out a small cry, and breaks into a dead run.

I turn around.

The bull boats are packed with people, but RabbitEar stands on the packs in the middle of the lead boat, waving.

Jawbone races toward him, waving back, calling *RabbitEar! RabbitEar!* The entire village erupts in cheers. As people begin rushing for the beach, I don't move. Relief has made my knees weak, and I just want to savor this moment. I know it will be a moment I return to again and again over the long winters ahead when we are lying in our lodge with our arms around each other, remembering.

Forcing a few calming breaths into my lungs, I finally sprint up the beach, smiling and waving.

52

LYNX

These are Quiller's tracks," I say in surprise, and kneel to hold my torch closer to them. Yellow light flickers over her boot prints. "I would know them anywhere."

From the trail behind me, Arakie calls, "I guess so. You followed in her footsteps most of your life, didn't you?"

"Yes, I did."

Smiling, I turn around to watch him carefully making his way through the pines that grow at the base of the cliff. Limp white hair hangs around his wrinkled face. He looks tired and gray in the evening light. "What was she doing here?"

Lifting his walking stick, he points to the giant crater just down the hill from us. All around it, trees lie snapped off and tossed around as though destroyed by an explosion of wind. "I imagine she came to explore that. Come on, let's go look at it."

Walking to the rim of the huge hole in the ice, I wait for him. A twisted pile of metal fills the belly of the hole, and the ice around it is smooth and polished, as though it's been melted.

When Arakie climbs to the rim beside me, I say, "One of the Meteor People?"

The rumbles, whistles, and grating shrieks of the Ice Giants ride the wind that sweeps across the mountains.

Arakie leans on his walking stick as he looks down. Quietly, he replies, "No, just another bit of flotsam that tumbled from the sky. It is a testament to the magical designers that it stayed up for as long as it did."

"Designers? Then it was made by the Sky Jemen?"

"Yes, a very long time ago." Arakie looks sad when he turns and uses his walking stick to point. "See that cave cut into the base of the cliff? That's where we'll camp for the night."

When I turn to look, my mouth drops open in surprise. "That's a cave? Why is it blue?"

"You'll see. Follow me."

Long before I get there, I hear singing. The melody is very soft, but the notes are so pure and sweet and filled with yearning that it's terrifying in its beauty.

"Do you hear that?"

He stops to listen. "Of course."

The melody fades to a whisper.

At the mouth of the cave, windblown snow has partially filled Quiller's boot prints, but it's clear that she went into the cave. Kneeling, I touch the tracks, and love for her fills me. It's a good thing Arakie told me she'd tried to find me, to rescue me, for neither Mink nor RabbitEar had mentioned it. With everything else that was going on, it was a minor point, I suppose.

Rising to my feet, I lift my torch higher, examining her trail. "She went into the cave."

"Yes, she's a brave one. That's another thing I did not expect, though I hoped for it."

Arakie hobbles to the mouth of the cave and rests a hand against the entry to gently pat the stone. "It is easy to go down into Hell . . . but to climb back again, to retrace one's steps to the upper air—there's the rub."

"The rub? That's the second time you've said that word. What does it mean?"

His elderly brow furrows. "It's an old saying. The Jemen said it a lot toward the end. From the start, they should have been concentrating on creating creatures that would flourish in Hell. Your people, for example, thrived during the last ice age. Instead, the Jemen stumbled along, retracing their steps, trying to find the way back to the upper air, until they almost missed their chance to save humanity."

Arakie looks me up and down, as though scrutinizing my physical structure—the way my arms and legs are attached to my stocky body. There's a hint of pride in his eyes.

"What's Hell?"

He laughs softly and looks away. "Life, Lynx. . . . Now."

Patting the stone one last time, he lowers his hand and walks into the glowing blue cave.

I remain outside for several moments, studying Quiller's tracks. She was alone and running when she arrived. She stood for a while, looking off in the direction of the crater, and it occurs to me that perhaps she saw the "bit of flotsam" come down?

When I walk to the cave and enter, I find Arakie staring at the walls with a loving expression.

My gaze flits over the strange symbols that cover every flat rock. In the torchlight, they seem to be dancing upon the stone. The painter must have been rushed, drawing as fast as he or she could, for the black images run together in long strings that are all nonsense. I think I can make out the shape of a tree, or maybe a spiral, but if that's what they are, they were drawn in a state of madness. And there are thousands of them.

Arakie plods to stand beneath one large rock face and his eyes move across the images from left to right, then he cocks his head as though listening to a voice.

"Can you hear the voice of your spirit helper in here? Sister Sky speaks to you even under the earth?"

"No." Reverence sculpts his face. "It's my ancestors who speak to me at this panel."

"You understand these rock paintings?"

Stroking the stone, he answers, "I do."

Carrying my torch to paintings across the tunnel, I try to understand the pictures, but I can find no shapes that represent things in my world. There are no bison, or wolves, or mammoths. "What does this one mean? Looks like two snakes coiled around each other, mating."

A smile turns his lips. "It's a double helix."

"Is it a wisdom teaching? From your ancestors?"

"Yes. In fact, most of these scribbles are mathematical formulas people considered precious. Some are love letters, or just the names of loved ones. A few are prayers to gods that died centuries ago."

I'm not going to ask about the word "mathematical," because I have the feeling his answer won't make sense to me anyway. "Will you explain more of the paintings as we walk?"

"Maybe. If I can bear it." Extending his hand, he orders, "Give me the torch. I'll lead the way down."

When we enter the cave of the broken cages, Arakie's pace picks up, trying to get through it quickly . . . but my feet root to the floor. Torchlight flutters across bars that look like they were chopped apart with an ax. Others were clearly chewed through by the animals that had been imprisoned inside.

"Is this . . . Arakie! Is this the place where the Earthbound Jemen took the cages of animals?"

"One of them."

Awe-stricken, my voice comes out hushed. "There were other caverns filled with animals?"

"All over the world."

Arakie walks to a perfectly round hole in the stone just tall enough for a man to walk upright, then he shoves the torch through and looks around, as though searching for malevolent creatures that might have taken refuge there, before he walks down the tunnel.

"Be careful up here, Lynx. There's a drop."

I've followed him no more than ten paces when the singing begins again, and I sense a presence hovering around me, touching me with butterfly-like wings, barely there. When pictures start cascading behind my eyes, I shake my head, trying to stop them, but they won't go away. I see exploding suns that have never known darkness, and spiraling campfires of the dead flying outward across black emptiness . . . images I cannot comprehend, but they are overwhelming.

"Hey, stop dreaming. Come down here."

At the sound of his voice, the singing stops, and the images vanish.

Arakie slips over the drop and disappears, leaving the tunnel ahead of me open, so that I can see into the next cavern.

Awestruck, I just stand and stare. No one could ever imagine a place like this.

The greatest shamans tell stories of ancient oceans that wash upon shores far beneath the Ice Giants, but this is no story. Motionless, too still to be real, an endless expanse of water spreads out in a gigantic half-moon. I try to chart the shoreline to judge the size, but can't.

Sitting down, I dangle my feet over the edge of the drop and quietly let my gaze drift over this strange world beneath the ice.

The gleam of Arakie's torch sends reflections fluttering over a ceiling hundreds of hands above me, but the far horizon stretches way beyond the torch's puny ability to illuminate.

"I'm going to grind out the torch now, Lynx."

"What? Why?"

Arakie extinguishes the torch in the sand, and tosses it aside.

When the yellow light dies, I stare at the pinpricks of blue that sprinkle the shoreline like fallen turquoise stars.

This is the source of the blue light.

"Watch this." Arakie picks up a rock and throws it. Where the stone skips, brilliant blue patches of phosphorescence blaze. "If you drink enough of this, you'll piss sparkles."

"Where are we?" I lightly drop over the edge and land on my feet beside him.

"The ocean before the zyme." Longing touches the old man's voice. "The blue is bioluminescent algae. Same family as the zyme, but zyme spreads a thousand times faster. It had to if we were going to cool the hot-house earth we lived in."

"I saw this, or . . . or part of it, I think. In the crevasse. At least I don't think I imagined it."

"Probably not. This paleo-ocean surfaces in a number of caverns beneath the ice. I once walked for days along this shore, trying to get a feel for the size, but it twisted around through hundreds of caves and caverns. I finally got hungry and turned around. You can't carry enough food with you, and there's nothing to eat down here in the darkness."

"Do you think this cavern might connect with the crevasse?"

"It must, or you wouldn't have heard my voice talking about Denisovans and *Homo erectus*."

"That was you?" I say in surprise. "Why didn't you tell me—"

"Come on." Arakie waves his hand. "I'll show you. It isn't far now."

We skirt the edge of the slight waves. As our steps fill with water, shining blue footprints appear behind us. I keep turning around to look at them, fascinated.

The deeper we go, the stranger it becomes. A vast web of heavy black beams crisscrosses the air above us. Many have collapsed into the water. Others hang like gigantic spears ready to plunge down at any instant. Did the ancient Jemen shore up the roof here, to protect this cavern? Tilting my head far back, I try to glean some sense of how the beams were connected, but find none.

"We're almost there."

Arakie ducks into a square tunnel, clotted with rubble, and pauses to search the smaller tunnels that branch off in all directions. Turning right, he braces a hand against the wall, and continues for another twenty paces. The ancient hinges wail when he shoves open a door.

We pass through into a chamber that is roofed, floored—even the walls are covered—with strange rectangular crystals. They are smooth and as translucent as panes of ice, but clearer than any ice I've ever seen. One of the panes winks. Three long red flashes. Three short green flashes. Three long red flashes. A pause, then it starts over. It keeps repeating.

The upper portion of the chamber crumbled long ago, leaving holes in the wall. The blue gleam from outside penetrates, creeps across the room, and seems to be spawning in the darkest corners. Curious tools line a long shelf . . . clear tubes, metallic creations with no rust, blocks with crumbling leather bindings. All are neatly arranged in a row. The spines of the blocks are covered with the same curious images that cover the walls of the cave.

"What is this place?"

Arakie props his walking stick and his eyes slowly move across the room. "When they stopped coming, I no longer had the things I needed to repair her." His voice constricts. "Quancee's dying. I can't stop it. I've tried."

"Dying? You mean it's alive? The . . . the room is alive?" I spin all the way around to see it.

When Arakie tenderly strokes the blinking pane, it blurs suddenly, like an eye filling with tears. "Does she think and love and feel despair? I think so. But alive? I've never known the answer to that question." He lets his hand fall.

Invisible tendrils of emotion reach out and touch me. Feather light. "Arakie, I feel—"

"It's all right. She won't hurt you. She doesn't know how to do that."

Her eerie, timeless presence tiptoes around inside me, and I feel a strength born of patterns understood across unfathomable chasms of time. Barely above a whisper, I hear a woman singing.

Frightened, I say, "Why did you bring me here?"

All the strength seems to go out of Arakie, leaving him just an old man in a lion-hide cape with eyes the color of the sky. "When something so immensely beautiful dies, someone needs to bear witness."

"You mean . . . she's dying right now? This instant?"

"Maybe not this instant, but very soon. Quancee and I have done the best we can to prepare you for the future. The rest is up to you. If I teach you what little I know about her, will you care for her until the end? Will you tell her story? Her story is important."

"Yes, of course. But I'm sure you can tell it far better than I." *They prepared me? How?*

As his fingers trail down the shimmering panel, squiggly golden lines appear. "I'm not going to be around for much longer, Lynx. And I'm glad of it. I've been ready to go for a long time. I've just been waiting for you."

When the enormity of Arakie's words sink in, I turn away and walk back into the cavern, where I can breathe. Standing on the shore of the luminous paleo-ocean is like being in a dream. Blue light flickers through the air and across the water.

Arakie remains with Quancee for some time. Finally, I hear his agonizingly slow steps coming.

I can't bear to turn and look at him. My gaze clings to the vast open water that seems to go on forever.

When he gets close enough, I say, "Why didn't you tell me you were dying?"

"Because it was none of your business. Until now."

"But I was hoping you would be my teacher."

"Right up until the very end, I will. After that, for as long as she's alive, Quancee will teach you."

"She is a teacher?"

"She's your true spirit helper, Lynx. Just as she has been mine since long before the Ice Giants were born." He taps my shoulder with his walking stick. "Now, cheer up. This is going to be more interesting than you ever imagined. We'll camp here tonight. Tomorrow, we'll head to the crevasse. I need to search it before my duties here are done."

53

LYNX

With Arakie's bad leg, it takes us three nights and a day to reach the place where I climbed out of the crevasse.

As I hike toward it, the golden light of evening slants across the Ice Giant Mountains, turning the vast, broken country into a jumble of light and shadow. It's so beautiful. From the mouth of every crack and crevasse, moans rise, but they are soft, muted, as though the Giants have decided to rest for a time.

"Are you all right?" Arakie calls from lower on the slope.

"Yes," I answer, but I'm not.

Five paces ahead, the black hole in the ice is dead-still and drowned in darkness. Soon, I know, the gleam of the campfires of the dead will flow into the lightless labyrinth we are about to enter, but for now dread fills me. I suspect I'll be afraid of the dark for the rest of my life.

"Are you sure this is it?"

I turn to look at him.

On the trail below me, he is little more than a shuffling figure cloaked in deep shadows, but his white hair catches the last rays of sunlight. He keeps glancing at the wolf that climbs the slope to his left. The strange animal has followed us, loyal as a camp dog, for two days. Last night, while we ate supper, the wolf sat on his haunches no more than ten paces away, pointed his nose at Sister Moon, and howled long and hard until a chorus of other voices joined him from all across the glaciers. Arakie says he's another of my spirit helpers. I don't know what to think.

"The hole has melted out more, so it's bigger than when I last saw it. But, yes, this is it."

How strange that in the great quietness of dusk, I smell Siskin's scent all around me, flowery, like the tundra wildflowers she wore in her hair on our wedding day.

Kneeling down, I remove my pack and pull out the stone bowl of hot coals and bundle of twigs I saved from our last fire. As I slowly place twigs atop the coals, I blow on them until a single flame crackles to life.

Arakie shuffles up behind me, carrying a quiver stuffed with three birch-bark torches. "Wasn't sure I was going to make it over that last rise."

"This is a bad idea, Arakie. We should wait until morning to do this."

"No, let's do it now. I want to know if this is where they went." He pulls one torch from the quiver slung over his left arm and hands it to me.

Made of shredded birch bark, dipped in pine pitch, it should burn for at least a finger of time.

I hold the torch in the tiny flame until it catches, and rise to my feet. The big wolf, long and lean, advances cautiously, whining.

While Arakie tries to catch his breath, he pants, "Wonder what he wants?"

"I'm sure he's trying to tell us we should wait until morning."

"Trying to tell you, maybe. He's your spirit helper, not mine. Listen to him if you think you should. But I'm going in."

Arakie steps forward, takes the torch from my hand, and hobbles to the rounded mouth of the cavern, where he places a hand against the ice and peers inside for a time. Finally, he walks into the maw and vanishes from sight.

The wolf slinks closer to me, growling. He's an old animal, wary, with a mottled gray coat that shines faintly lavender in the gleam of dusk. My gaze traces the battle scars that crisscross his hide. Fangs and claws have taught him that only the strong survive in this glacial wilderness. He's probably a pack leader, but I haven't seen his pack.

As the darkness intensifies, pale moonlight fills the air and Sister Sky begins to dance over our heads, her whirling skirt flashing green and purple across the heavens.

"I'll be back," I tell the wolf.

He barks at me.

"I'm going to do it, no matter what you say. But it won't take long, I promise."

When I enter the mouth of the cavern, I see Arakie thirty paces ahead, methodically making his way along the edges of the paleo-ocean, and I wonder if this is the same body of water that appears in Quancee's cavern. The gleam of his torch skims over the black expanse of water.

I trot to catch up with him.

"How much farther to the frozen village?" he asks.

"Don't know. I was dazed and freezing when I was here. I thought it was just inside the mouth of the cavern."

Arakie lifts his torch higher, trying to see ahead, but the darkness swallows the light. There is no ceiling. Instead, a blanket of phosphorescent sea fog hovers above us, eddying just out of reach. As we walk deeper, the rumbles and shrieks of the Ice Giants echo with hollowness, as though there's too much space, too many caverns to carry their cries, so that by the time they reach us they have the empty, forlorn ring of ceremonial bells struck in the Land of the Dead.

Arakie stumbles, and I grab for his arm to steady him.

"Are you all right, elder?"

"Yes, it's just that . . ." He waves the torch about, trying to see more of the cavern. "I think I've been here before."

"You've been in this cavern before?"

Arakie shakes his head and gazes out across the underworld ocean. It is motionless, the black surface as smooth as freshly knapped obsidian. Our torchlight bounces off it and flashes through the fog crawling over our heads like lightning through storm clouds.

"No, I've never been in this cavern before, but my cabin overlooked Boundary Bay. I used to watch the boats come in, and there's something about this place . . ."

"Familiar?"

He exhales hard and lifts his torch higher. "I'm probably imagining things. Let's keep searching for the village in the ice."

As we walk deeper, the fog begins to shred and dissipate, leaving the gigantic cavern naked to our torchlight. The ceiling must arch three hundred hands over our heads, and smaller caverns branch off from this one, receding in every direction, like a honeycomb born in the belly of the Ice Giants. Our torchlight briefly flares in these smaller caverns, then we pass on, continuing along the edge of the vast, quiet ocean.

"It seems impossible that I could have been this deep when I saw the frozen village. I swear, it was right beside—"

"Time is different when you're freezing. You could have been walking for days, Lynx."

I don't like that possibility. Arakie only has two more torches in his quiver. If we have to . . .

Half buried in the pewter-colored gravel in front of me, something glitters.

I bend down and pick it up.

It's flat, silver, and made of a metal I've never seen before. There's a hole in the top of the square, as though it was worn as a pendant. Rubbing it off on my coat sleeve to remove the rime of ice and dirt, I see a string of pictures drawn in the center. Pictures like those on the walls of Quancee's cave. This would be worth a fortune among my people. I could trade it for a moon's worth of dried meat or fish.

"This is beautiful. What is it?" I hold it up.

Arakie squints at it at first, then his face slackens with wonder. He takes it from my fingers and turns it over and over in his palm. "Dog tag."

"What?"

"It's a . . ." He pauses, considering. "It's a warrior's pendant. At the end, everyone was military."

When he hands it back and lifts his torch higher, I see more dog tags twinkling in the far darkness, scattered along the edges of the black water.

"Lots more up there."

"I see them." Arakie walks forward with the torch extended in front of him.

I don't follow right away. I'm filled with questions. Did the people from the frozen village gather handfuls of dog tags and toss them at the water like wishes or prayers? Sealion People cast shell pendants into sacred springs to appease water spirits. Maybe they were trying to appease the ghosts that walk the shores of this underground ocean? I have seen those ghosts. I know they're here.

Afraid that I have interfered with some ancient Jemen magic, I crouch down to gently place the dog tag in exactly the place I found it, half buried among the gravel.

"Forgive me for disturbing this prayer. I did not mean—"

"Come here, Lynx."

Arakie is twenty paces away, but I haven't taken more than five steps before I see the gigantic village frozen in the ice. "It is real. I wasn't sure."

"It's real."

Arakie's torchlight dances among the lodges, turning them into pale blue prisms that flash the colors of the rainbow. It's even more magnificent than I remember. When he shifts his torch, the gleam flares upon the faces of the tallest lodges, and I gape at the flickers of light that leap like spirits from roof to roof. Buried in the ice high above, the pointed tops seem to be holding up the roof of the cavern. Some of the lodges toppled long ago and crushed the shorter lodges, but many are still standing towers, and they continue back into the ice for as far as our feeble torchlight can touch.

Stunned, I'm afraid that if I move, this astonishing dream will evaporate like mist in sunlight.

I do not see the bodies until I walk up beside Arakie and find him staring at them with tears in his eyes.

Arranged in a long row, some sit upright, others curl on their sides. Over the centuries, their skins freeze-dried and shrank tight over their skeletons, then they were covered with ice. Hundreds of details clamor for my attention. I must memorize everything to tell my people, but such awe fills me, it's difficult to concentrate. These are the dead gods of my people's legends. Heroes from before the zyme. I so desperately want them to live again that it's a physical pain in my chest.

Reverently, I whisper, "I didn't see these . . . last time I was here."

"You probably didn't come down far enough."

The people who sit upright have one hand resting upon a dead animal that stretches across his or her lap, as though they petted them until the very end. The people who lie curled on their sides have their arms around animals, clutching them to their hearts.

Every mouth, human and animal, holds a dog tag that shimmers in the torchlight.

Each sleeve bears the blue ball filled with the campfires of the dead and the red bird wing. Arakie's clan. These are his people. Which I would have known anyway. They have the same small brow ridge and oval face that he has.

He is one of the Jemen.

"Why did they place the dog tags in their mouths?"

He shifts his weight, and a wave of alabaster brilliance flashes from the frozen faces of the dead. "Maybe to tell wayfarers who they were . . . or maybe they are obols."

"Obols?"

"Payment." Arakie bends over and holds the torch close to one man, as though trying to recognize that shrunken gray face. "To the ferryman who would take them across the river that divides the world of the living from the world of the dead. They probably hoped the tags would be enough to grant them passage. The ferryman valued duty. And honor."

My gaze strays to the other dog tags at the edge of the ocean. Did some people simply walk into the water, never to return? And their dog tags washed up later? Or were they paying the gods of the underworld to let them pass?

"What are the strange animals they hold?"

He stares for a long time before he straightens up and begins pointing them out. "A mule deer fawn, a Cymric cat, a black-footed ferret. That's a mountain lion cub. That's a bald eagle." He sounds heartbroken. "That's a coyote. They used to serenade the night with their beautiful yips and howls."

"But what happened? Did the Jemen kill the animals?"

He lets his hand fall limply to his side.

For a long time, he stares into the depths of the frozen village where torch shadows compete with rainbow flashes, then his gaze lifts to the ceiling, and he seems to be seeing beyond it to the Road of Light routinely traveled by the Sky Jemen.

"When they knew there was no one left . . . I'm sure the futility got to them. They couldn't bear to watch. They brought the animals up here, to a place they loved, to die with them."

I try to imagine what they saw when they sat down here for the last time. It must have been beautiful or they would not have chosen this spot. Was the ocean still blue? Could they see boats coming in?

Bowing his head, Arakie turns away from me. "Let's go, Lynx."

"But don't you want to walk farther down? What if some of your clan walked deeper into the caverns to live? We have two more torches. We could—"

"No, I don't."

When we walk out of the cavern, the glacier is a cold nude pearl, enameled with moonlight. The battle-scarred wolf lies a short distance away with his chin on his forepaws. At the sight of us, he sits up and cocks his head.

Arakie walks a few paces, then slumps down on the ice and drops his white head into his hands.

I continue standing in the mouth of the cavern.

The Ice Giants have gone silent. In the dazzling quiet of autumn, the only cadence is the underworld ocean behind me, licking its own wounds, patiently washing away the ruins of dark gods.

Slowly, I wander to where Arakie slumps, and sit down beside him.

Offhandedly, Arakie gestures to the wolf. "*Xenocyon texanus reecur.* Late—"

"Reecur . . . re-created."

"Correct. Late Pliocene hypercarnivore. Notice that while

he's as big as a dire wolf, his skull is longer and leaner, and he only has four toes on his forepaws, whereas dire wolves have five. That's because *Xenocyon texanus* is much, much older. His people trotted around the world two million summers before dire wolves were born." Arakie pauses. "I could be wrong, but I think he's the last of his kind."

"Like you?"

Arakie looks at me sadly for a moment, then he returns his gaze to the wolf, and to the glittering vastness of the Ice Giants beyond, where a haze of falling snow obscures the highest peaks. "Yes."

I try to feel the word, before I say, "Xenocy . . . ?"

"For now, just call him Xeno. The words will come easier as you learn more."

As I study the strange wolf, I wonder if Xeno's people fell victim to a more ferocious killer, one that should never have existed, an unholy creation . . . no, *re-creation* . . . of the Jemen. A killer that is gone now never to return.

"I hope teaching me will not be useless. I'm not very smart."

Lowering his hands, he lets out a sigh. "Or brave, as I recall. Lynx, if all you ever do is keep limping along, bandaged by dreams of a future where you and your people are still alive, my hopes for this world will not be dead."

Wind blowing down the glaciers carries the sweet tang of pines. I draw it into my lungs and hold it for a time.

"I think I can do that."

Xeno pushes to his feet and bares his fangs in a snarl. As he lightly pads forward with his head low and his ears laid back, fear tightens my belly. He has his gleaming, feral eyes fixed on me. He stops less than two paces away, close enough that in one bound he could have me by the throat.

Arakie says, "I don't think your spirit helper likes you very much."

While I gaze into the ancient wolf's eyes, eyes filtered through the varnish of moonlight, I have the feeling I've just set foot on a path that should not be trodden. But having seen the dead gods, I could more easily give up my own life than this path.

"That's all right. Nobody has ever liked me much."